WITSEC BOOK ONE

FIND ME

ASHLEY N. ROSTEK

FIND ME

Edited by Alexandra Fresch of To the Letter Services

Cover design by The Dirty Tease

Formatting by Savannah Richey of Peachy Keen Author Services

BOOKS BY ASHLEY N. ROSTEK

1

My feet felt cemented to the floor as I stood frozen by fear.

"Shi, run!" Shayla cried out just before Mr. X slid his knife across her throat, silencing her forever.

Blood poured like a crimson waterfall from her neck. Her gray eyes were wide, filled with terror as they bored into mine.

I couldn't move.

I couldn't look away.

With each passing second, I had to watch the spark of life within her eyes dim.

Mr. X unhooked his strong arm from around Shayla's middle and shoved her forward. Without resistance she fell, crumpling to the floor in the hallway right in front of my bedroom. Blood pooled around her, seeping into the beige carpet, and staining the ends of her cotton candy pink hair a bright red.

My heart raced at a painful rate, booming in my ears with a rapid **thump! thump! thump!**

Internally, I begged myself, **Move! Run! Do something because he's coming!**

My gaze tore away from Shayla—my sister, my twin—to Mr. X. His booted foot took an ominous, slow step over her body while his monstrous coal eyes held mine. There was blood splattered across his face, clashing against his alabaster skin. An evil smile pulled at the corners of his mouth as he took another step, then another, closing the distance between us.

*"**Shiloh**," he sung my name. His voice was light yet haunting and made my entire body tremble. I'd never forget his voice, no matter how much I'd wish I could.*

*My soul screamed, **Run! Run! Run!***

But my body wouldn't listen.

Mr. X finished his walk down the long hall to stand before me. As if stuck in a trance, I watched him lift his bloody knife.

Closing my eyes, I screamed.

"Shiloh!" Firm hands grasped me by my upper arms and shook me. "Shiloh, wake up!"

My uncle Logan's gruff voice broke through my chains of fear. Forcing my eyes open, the first thing I saw was his face. I sat up panting, drenched in sweat. If it hadn't been for Logan sitting next to me, I would have panicked because I didn't immediately recognize my surroundings. Blinking away the fog that still lingered from sleep, I took in the dark, bare room, from the few boxes stacked in the corner to the very uncomfortable air mattress I was lying on. Slowly, my memories came back to me. This was my new house. It was our first night sleeping here. I was safe. Mr. X didn't know where I was.

"Christ, Shi," Logan cursed, running his tattooed fingers through his coffee-brown hair. "It's been a while since you've had a dream like that. I'd be surprised if you didn't wake the neighbors."

I clenched my jaw. How did I respond to that? *I'm sorry?* Why? I couldn't control what I dreamt or how messed up my past was.

Logan sighed. He was kneeling on the floor next to my air

mattress, looking tired, in nothing but black boxer briefs. The rest of his body, from his shoulders to his toes, was covered in colorful and beautiful tattoos. The ex-Navy SEAL turned U.S. Marshal was an ink addict. I had no idea how he got away with being so heavily tattooed working for the feds. But what did I know? I just wished he'd invest in some PJs.

"What time is it?" I asked, my voice sounding coarse. I pushed a strand of sweaty lilac hair away from my face. Seeing the bright color still took me by surprise. I'd dyed it the wild shade for my eighteenth birthday a few days ago as a way to honor my sister, Shayla. She'd dyed her light brown hair all kinds of crazy colors to set herself apart from me—her identical twin. She'd been the lively and edgy twin, who gave our parents hell, where I was the shy and obedient daughter who was too timid to disappoint anyone. I wished I'd been more like Shayla. Maybe she would still be alive today.

Logan stared at me for a moment, like he was debating how he should answer. Not that it'd do him any good. "A little before five." He got to his feet. "Wear your tracker," he ordered over his shoulder as he stalked out of my room.

I crawled off my air mattress and went inside my closet. Flipping on the light, I opened one of the boxes on the floor full of my clothes that needed to be hung. I dug around until I found a pair of leggings and matching tank.

Even though it was summer, and we were now living in the desert, I still put on an athletic zip-up jacket with thumb holes in the cuffs. I had scars on my arms. They were hard to look at and I hated the attention they drew. I pulled my hair up in a messy bun, grabbed my tennis shoes, and put on my GPS anklet tracker before making my way toward the front door of my new house I'd received the keys for yesterday.

I'd bought this three-bedroom Craftsman without even seeing it first. I had been relieved and happy it had looked just like the pictures the realtor had sent me. Because Logan and I had been hidden away in the Alaskan mountains for the past year, I'd had to do the entire house-buying process online and through email. *Why?* Well, because of WITSEC—a.k.a. the witness security program or witness protection.

My life in WITSEC had started the summer before my senior year. Because I'd been weeks away from turning seventeen at the time and Logan was my only living relative, he had been assigned to watch over me, thus resulting in him taking a break from his job. Logan's position as a U.S. Marshal and my guardian had given him a little pull in deciding where we would be sequestered. Alaska had been beautiful but cold and isolated. The nearest neighbor had been miles away and it had been an hour drive to town, which had a population of no more than five hundred people. It was the perfect place to hide, temporarily. I'd needed time to recover, rehabilitate, and get a crash course in intense survival skills from Logan. Just in case. The past year had been the hardest of my life both emotionally and physically. But now that I was eighteen, Logan wanted to return to work and I needed to move on and finish high school.

Sitting on the wood floor by the front door, I was slipping on my shoes when Logan came back out of his room. He was dressed in jeans this time. My eyes were grateful. He held a small handgun in a shoulder holster. "Put this under your jacket. It's small and lightweight."

I unzipped my jacket and slipped it off, revealing the long scar on my inner right arm. It started at the crease of my elbow and ended at my wrist. Even a year later, I could feel the phantom sensation of Mr. X's blade tearing open my skin.

Around both of my wrists and ankles were inch-wide scars. I supposed I'd given those to myself. For hours, I'd rubbed my skin raw and bloody in order to escape from the tight rope bindings Mr. X had put me in.

Just by looking at my wrists, one could guess how I had gotten them. They always guessed wrong, though. Back in

Alaska, each time we'd driven to the closest town for supplies, I would receive lewd stares from men, and one time in line at the grocery store, an old lady had called me a sexual deviant. Everyone around us, even the cashier, had frozen and glued their gazes on me. Mortified, I'd dropped my basket of groceries and practically ran out of the store. I regretted how cowardly I had acted. I wished I could have been more like Shayla in that moment. She would have flicked her colorful hair, looked that old lady in the eye, grinned, and said, "Jealous?" But I wasn't as strong as my sister had been. At least not yet. I was working on it. Until I found that strength, I refused to leave the house without wearing clothes that covered my scars, no matter the temperature outside. Just thinking about the heat, I started to second guess my move to Arizona. Only a tiny bit, though. It was beautiful here, with its breathtaking mountain views and vast deserts.

I dropped my jacket on the ground and took the leather gun holster from my uncle before slipping my arms through the holes. The straps rested over my shoulders and across my back, allowing the small holstered gun to hide between my left arm and ribs. Logan glanced down to make sure my slim black GPS anklet tracker was around my right ankle, then back up to the holster before I covered it with my jacket. I caught him taking me in from head to toe. I twirled around for him because I knew he was memorizing my appearance and exactly what I was wearing in case I didn't come back.

"Don't forget your phone," he said.

I opened my mouth to argue, then snapped it closed. *Crap!* I'd left it in my room. I would've noticed I didn't have it eventually. It was my source of music and who ran without music? I dashed back into my room to grab it and my Bluetooth earbuds. When I walked back into the living room, Logan wasn't there. I didn't search him out to say goodbye. Instead, I walked out the front door, put my earbuds in, selected my running playlist, and stuffed my phone into the snug side pocket of my leggings.

It was gray out. Standing on the front lawn, I could see the rays from the sun shining from behind the mountains as I did a few stretches. After I was warmed up, I headed north through the neighborhood.

∼

Three and a half hours later, I slowed to a jog on my way back to the house. I was soaked with sweat and my breathing was labored and raspy. Logan was sitting on the top step of the porch waiting for me while texting on his phone and sipping coffee from a Styrofoam cup.

Note to self, pick up coffee mugs today.

He looked up at me as I paced the front lawn with my hands on my hips, trying to cool down. He shook his head. "If you quit smoking you wouldn't sound like shit."

"I'm down to one cigarette a day," I wheezed before bending over with my hands on my knees. "I think I'm going to puke."

Three and half hours was a new record for me. I knew all the ins and outs of my new neighborhood now. It was a big one and my new house was smack dab in the middle. I had ventured down all the streets, passing my house a few times, and when I'd started to feel like I was going to throw up I'd known it was time to stop.

"You pushed yourself too far," my uncle admonished.

I didn't argue. I did, however, ignore the disapproving look he was giving me as I focused on breathing. He didn't approve of my "therapeutic methods" but wasn't the type to dissuade me either.

"Your furniture should be here in a few hours," he added.

Apart from a few boxes already here that held personal things like clothes, toiletries, and memorabilia from before I went into WITSEC, I'd had to order furniture to fill the rest of the house. It was scheduled to arrive later this morning.

I'd been able to purchase all of it and this house with some of the life insurance money I had received from both of my parents and my sister after they'd been killed. It wasn't the only money that had been left to me, but I liked to pretend that money didn't exist. It was blood money to me, and I didn't like having it. I didn't like having the life insurance money either, but Logan had convinced me to use it. He explained that my family had gotten life insurance for a reason and that was to make sure I was taken care of. So I compromised. I'd live off the life insurance money until I finished college and got a job. If I budgeted properly it'd last me until then and I could continue on pretending the rest of my family's money didn't exist.

"Why don't you go shower and then we'll get breakfast?" Logan suggested. "Yesterday, you said you were craving crepes. Want to go somewhere that makes them?"

I frowned. Logan was a bona fide drill sergeant. If he wasn't ordering me about, something was up. Acting apprehensive was his tell. "If you got something to say, just say it."

His eyes locked with mine and I instantly became nervous. I knew whatever he had to tell me wasn't good.

"Ian called." Ian was his superior and the only other soul who knew my whereabouts. "They got a lead. Highway patrol pulled a man over matching X's description in North Carolina a few days ago. The cop radioed in for backup, but they didn't get there in time. X fled. The cop was DOA. Ian's calling me in to help."

DOA meant *dead on arrival.* My stomach churned, making the urge to throw up even stronger. North Carolina was on the other side of the country, yet it still felt like I was within his reach. As long as he was out there, I didn't think anywhere in the world would feel safe.

I tried to appear calm. On the inside I was freaking out. "When do you leave?"

He stared at me intently, as if he could see past my fake bravado to my terrified soul. "Friday."

That was four days from now. The following Monday was my

first day at my new school. I was going to complete my senior year and if everything went as planned, I was going to try and get into a university nearby. Even though my life had been forever changed and my parents were gone, I was still determined to complete my goals and make them proud.

"I know Friday is a lot sooner than we planned, but we prepared for this," he said.

I couldn't tell if he was trying to reassure me or himself.

2

My furniture delivery was late. The truck didn't get here until noon and it took them a few hours to unload everything. Logan shook his head at the purple couch I'd ordered as it was carried inside. The color reminded me of the suit the Joker wore in Batman. I might have been a closeted superhero nerd and the Joker was my favorite villain, but that was beside the point. The couch had been a bold choice—for me. I'd lived my whole life in bland colors and played it safe because I'd been too afraid to stand out. Look at what it had gotten me.

WITSEC had given me a new life. I couldn't take it for granted. It was time to move forward and I was going to do that bravely and adventurously. Like Shayla. So if I wanted a purple couch, then I'd get the purple couch and the bright yellow armchair to go with it.

For the dining room, I might have gone a little overboard and splurged on a six-seater, turquoise-painted wood table. My mom had used to say the kitchen table was the heart of the home. Some of my best memories from growing up were of dinner time, with my parents and sister sitting around the table laughing while talking about anything and everything. Staring at my new table with its six empty chairs made my chest tighten. My mom had been wrong. It wasn't the table that was the heart. It was the people who sat at it.

The rest of what I'd ordered filled my bedroom and the spare bedroom that Logan was using. I hadn't ordered anything for the third bedroom. Logan was converting it into a panic room of sorts, with a rolling metal shutter on the window and a steel-reinforced door. It wouldn't be a completely impenetrable panic room, but it would hopefully hold up until the police arrived. He was also setting up an impressive security system with panic buttons and cameras, which he was currently drilling into the walls outside the house. To anyone else, a panic room, cameras, and security system might have been excessive. After what I'd been through, it still didn't feel like enough. Not with Mr. X still out there looking for me.

Now that my furniture was here, I needed to go shopping for everything else I would need, like linens and coffee mugs. Not to mention there wasn't any food in the house.

Dressed in ripped, light blue jeans, a long-sleeved white shirt, and boots that had a knife tucked into the left one, I grabbed my purse and headed toward the front door. The delivery men were about to leave, and I was following them out. I had my long lilac hair pulled up into a high ponytail because it was hotter than Hades out. Sweat was already sliding down the back of my neck.

Outside, I could smell grills cooking, hear cicadas buzzing and rock music playing from my neighbor's house to the right. I glanced in that direction. A few cars were parked in the street in front of their house and a group of guys were working on an old classic car in the driveway. I briefly scanned over them, counting six, some just standing around drinking beer and talking while a few actually hovered over the engine of the old car. They all appeared to be friends hanging out, carefree and having fun. *Must be nice.*

"Miss Pierce, I need you to sign here, confirming that everything was delivered." One of the delivery guys held out a clipboard and pen.

Hearing my new last name instead of my real last name, McConnell, was going to take some getting used to. Standing in the middle of my lawn on the stone pathway leading to my car in the driveway, I read over the receipt, verifying I had indeed received everything I'd ordered. After I signed, I was handed a copy of the receipt and the delivery guys drove their truck away from my curb.

The sound of a drill made me glance back at the house. Logan was standing on a ladder in front of my bedroom window, drilling holes to install a camera.

"Logan, I'm running to the store!" I shouted as I made my way over to my car. The group of guys hanging out at my neighbor's stopped talking and I got that feeling of being watched. My car and a short wall made up of oleander bushes that separated their property from mine was all that was standing between us.

Logan stopped drilling and looked over at me. "What'd you say, Shi?"

"I'm going to the store," I said, opening my car door.

"Do you have your phone and…everything?" His gaze flicked to my neighbors behind me before pointedly looking back at me. He'd noticed we had an audience and didn't want to ask if I was armed in front of them.

"Yup. Do you want me to pick anything up for you?"

He glanced at his watch on his wrist, taking note of the time. "No, I'm good. Check in every hour," he ordered and returned to his drilling. I rolled my eyes as I climbed behind the wheel. How was he going to handle leaving me here to fly to North Carolina if he couldn't handle me going to flipping Target ten minutes away?

I put my black Toyota 4Runner in reverse and when I went to look out the rearview window to back out, I caught two of the guys next door watching me. They both had the same shade of pale golden blond hair. One of them had it styled in a faux hawk where the other had that messy, I-just-rolled-out-of-bed style. Their eyes were the same color of light blue or aquamarine. I couldn't tell from how far away I was.

They were both really attractive. If my life wasn't messed up, I'd be crushing hard. But my life was an actual nightmare and that was why I didn't just see two gorgeous guys when I stared at them. I only saw twins.

I looked away with a clenched jaw and backed out of the driveway.

By the time I returned home it was dark outside. Whoever said retail therapy could make you feel better was a liar. After hours of shopping and filling my car to the max, I still felt a heavy sense of dread. Friday would be here before I knew it and then I'd be alone.

Turning off the car, I sat in the darkness, staring at my new house. This wasn't where I was supposed to be. I should have been moving into a tiny dorm room and scrambling to find my classes on a big college campus. A tear escaped my eye and I quickly wiped it away.

"So much for being brave, Shi," I grumbled to myself. Who was I kidding? Buying brightly colored furniture didn't make me brave. At the end of the day, I was still me.

I sighed heavily. I needed to stop beating myself up. Change and moving on took time.

But how did I move on when *he* was still out there?

I opened one of the bags I had on the passenger's seat and pulled out a new pack of cigarettes and a bottle of Jack. I'd been using Shayla's fake ID to buy booze to drown my sorrows. It was a perk of being a twin that I'd been definitely taking advantage of over the past year.

I stared at the bottle of Jack as temptation to open it gnawed at me. Sitting there, I thought back to a time I'd used to look down my nose at Shayla when she'd first told me that one of her bad-influence friends had made her the ID. She'd laugh at me now if she could see the hypocrite I'd become with how I had smoked like a chimney and drunk like a fish this past year.

I made no excuses for how I'd chosen to cope. I knew it had been bad. At the time I hadn't cared. Therapy hadn't been working as fast as I'd wanted it to, and I'd been desperate to numb the pain. At first Logan hadn't said anything when he'd caught me smoking or smelled liquor on my breath. As long as I'd continued my therapy and hadn't slacked off in self-defense training, he'd turned a blind eye. That was, until he'd found fourteen empty liquor bottles hidden under my bed. Logan had dished out some tough love then. He'd told me that my vices were just a band-aid and if I ever wanted to move on, I needed to do it the right way. He was right. I was working on quitting smoking and it'd been a while since I'd had a drink. Running helped the urge. It was a healthier outlet when things become too much to handle. Nicotine, however, was a tough drug to kick. I was slowly winning the battle, though. I was down to one cigarette a day.

I was very proud at how far I had come since I'd lost my family. But then days like today happened. With the news of Logan leaving in less than a week…I was struggling.

I broke my unblinking gaze from the bottle of Jack and set it on the passenger's seat. It wasn't that I had an addiction. I just needed to stop using it as a crutch.

Pulling my lighter from my purse, I got out of the car. In a lazy attempt to hide from Logan, I walked around to the back of my 4Runner and perched my butt on the bumper. I put a cigarette between my lips, set the new pack on the bumper next to me, and cupped my hand around the end of my white cancer stick as I lit it. That first drag of nicotine had me closing my eyes, dropping my head back against the rear window of my vehicle before blowing it out slowly through my lips. Without opening my eyes, I took another drag, basking in the euphoric feeling.

"Smoking kills, you know," a masculine voice said, startling me. My eyes snapped open and I whipped my head in the direction of the source. Standing on the other side of the oleander bush was one of the twins I'd seen earlier today— the one with the messy bed-head hairstyle. I watched as his eyes roamed over me from my lilac ponytail to my boots.

"So can sneaking up on a girl at night," I said.

His lips curled up on one side. He looked right around my age or maybe a little older. He had nice skin. It was smooth and tan, proof he lived in the desert. I probably looked like a ghost and stood out like a sore thumb here with how pale I was.

He stuffed his hands into the pockets of his dark jeans. His t-shirt was black and form fitting, which showed off how lean and fit he was. "I wasn't exactly quiet when I approached. Then again, you seemed lost in your head for a moment there."

I smirked. "You're saying it's my fault you startled me?"

He rubbed the back of his head with a shy smile. "Wow, this friendly introduction isn't as easy as I thought it was going to be."

I decided to cut him some slack and held out my hand over the oleander bush. "I'm Shiloh Pierce. Are you one of my neighbors?"

He stared down at my hand before engulfing it with his larger one. "Colt Stone. And yeah, I live here with my brothers." It took a lot of effort not to react when he said brothers.

"Shi, you out here?" I heard Logan call out from the front porch. I gave Colt a small smile before stepping back to look over at Logan.

I purposely took another drag to show him I was smoking. "Yeah. I'll be inside in a minute." Logan noticed Colt standing behind me and crossed his arms over his chest. When I saw the evil glint spark to life in his eyes, I inwardly groaned.

"You're not peer pressuring one of the neighbor boys into smoking, are you?" he drawled as if really serious.

"Well, you know me. My life of debauchery wouldn't be as satisfying if I didn't add the corruption of others," I said, my tone sounding caustic.

Logan's eyes went vacant for a moment before his expression turned sad. I knew that look. He got that way when I did something that reminded him of my mom. "Yeah, that sounds about right. Carry on," he replied in a deflated tone, then turned to go back into the house.

I stared at where he'd retreated into the house for a moment, biting my bottom lip with worry until I remembered Colt standing behind me. I turned back around on my heels and found him staring at my house with a puzzled frown.

"Sorry about that," I said, bending down to put out my cigarette on the ground and walking over to the trash bins sitting by the curb to throw out the butt. "My uncle thinks it's funny when he tries to embarrass me."

"Your uncle?" he said, tone riddled with surprise.

He wasn't the first to assume that Logan wasn't my uncle. In fact, it had happened all the time back in that small town in Alaska. Logan and I were only sixteen years apart in age and because he took extremely good care of himself, he looked a lot younger than he actually was. Everyone had mistaken him for my boyfriend and rumors had spread like wildfire because that was what happened in a small town. I'd overheard two girls whisper behind me once that Logan and I were into BDSM and that was how I'd gotten my scars, which was freaking disgusting. "Yeah, he's my mom's baby brother."

Colt opened his mouth to say something but was cut off when someone yelled, "Colt!" A guy stepped out the front door of Colt's house and glanced around. When his eyes landed on us, a look of intrigue took over his face and he walked over. "What's going on?"

As he got closer, I got the feeling this was one of the plural brothers Colt had mentioned. They looked very similar, but he was clearly older and taller than Colt by a few inches and his eyes were brown. They had the same pale golden hair. His was shaved on the sides and styled messily on top.

"I was just introducing myself to our new neighbor. This is Shiloh. Shiloh, this is my brother Keelan."

I reached over the oleander bush again. Keelan gave me a charming smile in return before he shook my hand. "Shiloh, huh? That's a pretty name." His voice was smooth and oozed flirtation.

A year ago, I would have swooned. Now, all I felt was caution. It was astonishing how something traumatic could leave you changed to certain things and boys were one of them. "Thank you."

"Colt! Keelan! The movie is about to start!" a really deep and growly voice shouted from inside their house.

I took that as my cue to leave. "I better get inside. It was nice meeting you."

"We better go too before Knox hunts us down," Colt said to Keelan and took a step back. "See you around, Shiloh."

They both gave me gorgeous parting smiles before walking back into their house. I scooped up my pack of cigarettes from the bumper and opened my trunk to start unloading my purchases.

3

Friday got here faster than I wanted. The rest of the week had been crazy busy with Logan finishing up on the panic room and fortifying the rest of the house. He'd even strategically hidden guns in multiple places throughout the house. Under the coffee table, behind the TV, inside the fridge. I wished I was kidding about the fridge. He'd tucked a small pistol between a carton of eggs and the sidewall. I'd positioned a gallon of milk in front of it so I wouldn't have to see it every time I opened the fridge. Those were just a few examples of where Logan had gotten *creative*. If you counted the rifles in the gun safe in the panic room, there were ten guns in my house. Again, it might have seemed excessive, but if Logan thought it was necessary, then it was necessary.

While he'd been busy with all that, I'd finished unpacking and getting the house put together. I'd also joined a gym and I'd finished registering for school. I was officially a senior at Copper Mountain High School. My classes were pretty standard, apart from the two AP classes I was taking. The only class I was nervous about was gym class. I wasn't afraid of the class itself. It was the changing in front of others. High school girls were the worst. My sister had been popular and downright awful. As her sister I'd gotten a free pass despite being quiet and nerdy, which had been who her group of *friends* would bully. I wouldn't have her as a buffer at this new school. I had more than just the scars on my arm, wrists, and ankles. I had two really bad ones on my stomach and one on my back shoulder. The ones on my stomach were from stab wounds that had almost killed me. If gym class hadn't been a requirement to graduate, I would've tried to drop it in exchange for another class.

"I could have driven you," I said as I followed Logan out to the curb where a car service was waiting to drive him to the airport.

Rolling his suitcases behind him, he said, "It's easier this way. Airports are a nightmare."

I chewed on my bottom lip nervously as the driver of the car got out and helped Logan load his bags into the trunk. This was it. I was going to be on my own for who knew how long. Logan hadn't left my side since I'd woken up in the hospital a little over a year ago. He'd helped me heal, stood with me through my pain, and held my hand after I'd had nightmares. He'd helped me become stronger, a fighter, a survivor. I told myself I wasn't going to cry, but my eyes were beginning to burn.

Once his last bag was loaded, he turned to face me. His shoulders slumped. "Shi." He sighed and pulled me into his arms for a hug. "I'm going to catch him."

My tears fell and my body shook with silent sobs. What if he did find him and Mr. X killed him? What if Mr. X found me and Logan wasn't here?

I squeezed my arms tightly around Logan's back, trying to absorb his strength because no matter how much I wanted him to stay, he had to go.

His hand stroked my hair. "You are to check in by text two times a day on the burner phone. Never try to reach me on your regular phone. It's too easy to track the signal back to here. Make sure you find a range to practice your shooting and keep practicing your escape drills in the house. You can do this, Shi. You are the strongest person I know."

I took in a deep, shaky breath before stepping back. With the sleeves of my shirt, I wiped away the tear tracks and nodded. "Okay. I've got this."

"I'll try calling you Monday night after you're out of school."

I gave him a forced parting smile, then watched him climb into the car and be driven away. After he was long gone, I turned to look back at my house and tried to remind myself that this was the plan. This was where I needed to be. I had my goals to achieve and my new life to start. Everything was going to be okay. I could do this.

Feeling a little more determined, I went back inside. It was just after seven in the morning and I had the whole day to do... absolutely nothing. For my sanity, I had to keep busy. Silence and boredom were a recipe for flashbacks and panic attacks. Speaking of recipes, I guessed I could bake something. I'd used to love baking. Maybe I could run by the store, but after I went to the gym first. It was the perfect plan to stay busy.

Desert Stone Fitness was a highly reviewed gym in town. It had all the bells and whistles. An indoor pool and an indoor track on the second floor. It even had a boxing ring smack dab in the center of the large room with all the workout equipment surrounding it. It also provided many classes such as yoga, spin, self-defense, karate, boxing, judo, jiu-jitsu, Pilates, and Zumba. The gym literally had everything. And because of that, it was crazy busy.

With my gym bag hanging off my shoulder, I made my way to

the women's locker room to lock up my stuff. I'd chosen to wear long purple athletic leggings and a matching racerback top covered by a black, slim fit, zip-up athletic jacket with thumb holes. I pulled my hair up into a high ponytail, put my earbuds in, grabbed my water bottle and phone, then headed out. There was a designated area for stretching on the first floor by the boxing ring. I got stretched and warmed up there first, then went upstairs to the track. It was a mile-long oval track that circled and overlooked the gym below.

I set my water bottle in one of the cubbies for personal items on the wall next to the stairs, selected my running playlist on my phone, and picked a lane on the track.

I'd started running four months ago, slowly building up my endurance. I had read somewhere once that exercise in general was therapeutic for the mind. It either gave your mind a break from the stress or allowed you time to really work through it. The former was true for me most of the time.

Running allowed me to free myself of the pain my memories caused. Nothing else existed as I pushed forward, my muscles burning, lungs expanding, endorphins soaring. If I were to have an addiction, it would be running, and it was one I was guilty of pushing past my limits with. Because some days were worse than others and an hour or two of freedom just wasn't enough.

I ran for three hours before I cooled down by walking the last quarter mile back to my water bottle. My workout clothes were drenched with sweat and there was nothing more I wanted than to take my jacket off. I was seriously considering shedding it for a minute. Then I looked around at all the people and my insecurities won. I settled for just unzipping it.

After the gym, I stopped by the grocery store to pick up ingredients. I might have gone a little overboard with how much

I bought. But I convinced myself that it was okay. I did have the whole weekend of nothing to do.

As soon as I got home, I put my perishable ingredients away and took a long shower. I decided to put on a pair of jean shorts. I had no plans of leaving the house for the rest of the day. I chose to pair it with a black tank, then made my way to the kitchen, where I spent a good chunk of the afternoon.

My kitchen turned into a war zone, or at least it looked like a flour bomb had gone off. Patches of flour and sugar were scattered on the counters. Some had even sprinkled on the tile floor. Mixing bowls, whisks, measuring cups, cookie sheets, and pans filled my sink. Every surface of my kitchen was filled with cooling baked goodies. I'd made two dozen cookies, a pan of gooey brownies, a dozen blueberry muffins, lemon bars, and key lime bars. It looked like I was ready to have a bake sale.

What had I been thinking?

I hadn't. That was the point. With a heavy sigh, I started cleaning up.

I was washing the last dirty dish when my doorbell rang. My heart immediately started racing with fear. I quickly dried my hands with a dish towel as I exited the kitchen into the living room. Barefoot, I padded my way to the front door and peered through the peephole to find Colt, my neighbor, standing outside.

"One second!" I shouted and quickly grabbed a zip-up hoodie from the pile of laundry I'd placed on the couch. I had planned on folding it after dinner tonight while I settled down to watch TV.

Once my hoodie was on, I looked down at my ankles and cringed. I didn't have time to cover them up with pants. Praying that he wouldn't notice, I unlocked my front door. "Hey," I greeted him with a smile and saw that he was holding a stack of mail.

"Hi." He smiled back. I watched as his smile grew the longer he stared at me. "Were you baking?"

I narrowed my eyes at him. "How did you know?"

He chuckled. "You have flour on your face."

Heat scorched my cheeks. Using my sleeve, I wiped at my face. "Did I get it?"

He shook his head, and I could tell he was trying not to laugh at me, which made me flush even more. "Your forehead," he mumbled. I wiped there too, and he nodded.

"Thank you. What's up?"

"We got some of your mail," he said, holding it out to me. "Are you going to Copper Mountain?"

I took the mail from him and before I could question how he would know that, my eyes fell on the top envelope. It was from Copper Mountain High School addressed to Shiloh Pierce. "Yeah. I registered there for my senior year."

"My brother Creed and I go there," he said.

"Oh."

"If you want, I can show you around before class starts Monday morning."

That was sweet of him to offer. It would be the first time I'd be starting a new school without knowing anyone and without Shayla by my side. "I might take you up on that."

At my response he smiled brightly and my heartbeat picked up a beat. "So what were you baking?"

It took me a second to comprehend what he was asking. "Oh, uh." I felt my cheeks getting hot again. As I stared at Colt sheepishly, I got an idea. "Do you and your brothers like cookies, brownies, and such? Because I may have made enough to fill a bakery and there's no way I could eat it all."

His eyebrows rose. "We're growing boys. Of course we do."

I smiled and opened the front door wider. "You're welcome to come in while I pack up a container for you to take home."

He stepped inside.

"If you'll follow me," I said over my shoulder, catching him looking around as we walked through the living room. His eyes went wide when we entered the kitchen. At least it wasn't a mess anymore. "Yeah. One of my many faults is I sometimes get lost in what I'm doing. I've been known to go above and beyond. Especially if I'm having a bad day," I explained as I pulled out a bin filled to the brim with new Tupperware I'd bought the other day.

"You had a bad day?"

I looked away from him. "Yes and no." I didn't elaborate and he thankfully didn't push. "Are you or your brothers allergic to anything? I don't want someone going into anaphylactic shock because I put peanuts in some of the brownies."

He shook his head. "No known food allergies. Can I try one of these?" he asked, pointing to one of the peanut butter cookies.

"Help yourself." I smiled and began filling a plastic container with an assortment of goodies.

Colt took a bite of the cookie and groaned. "Wow, these are good."

I chuckled. "You sound surprised."

With his cheeks puffed out around the cookie, he shook his head. "There you go again. You're kind of a ball buster, you know that?"

I'd been called worse. Stuck up, snob, whore. Not that what he'd said was an insult. In fact, it sounded like he enjoyed that I gave him a hard time.

"I'm glad you like the cookie, but wait until you try the key lime bars. They're my mom's recipe." The moment the words left my mouth I regretted them. I turned away to hide the pain I was undoubtedly showing and busied myself with packing up two-thirds of everything I'd made. Once I had my face schooled and my emotions at bay, I turned back around and stacked two large plastic containers in front of him. "Okay, here you go."

"Are you trying to make me fat?" he teased, taking the containers from me.

"Aren't guys supposed to be bottomless pits? Besides, there's what, three of you—?"

"Four," he corrected.

"There are four of you and only one of me. I still won't be able to finish what I have left but it's nice to know most of everything I made won't go to waste. You taking all this off my hands is doing me a favor, really."

He tilted his head slightly, seeming confused. "What about your uncle?"

Oops.

"He left today," I replied honestly and tucked some of my lilac hair behind my ear. "He was only here to help me get situated."

Colt went quiet as he stared at me. I felt the urge to squirm or palm-smack my face, so I busied myself with packing up the rest of the baked goodies in my own container.

"Don't take this question the wrong way, but do you live here alone?" he asked.

I tensed up. It wasn't wise to advertise that you lived alone to a stranger. Logan would kick my butt if he knew. I forced myself to relax. I'd seen what a monster's eyes looked like. Colt's eyes didn't have a speck of evil in them and my gut told me he was a nice guy.

"Yes." I could tell he had more questions. They were dancing behind his aquamarine eyes.

"I should get back," he said, scooping up the containers off the counter. "Thank you for these."

Relief washed over me, and I followed him back to the front door. When he stepped out onto my porch, he turned back to look at me. "If you ever need anything you can come next door and get me."

I smiled at the kind offer. "Thank you, Colt. That's very sweet of you."

He nodded and took a step back. "I'll see you around."

I gave him a little wave and went to shut the door.

"Wait!" he said, and I paused. He balanced the containers in one hand and reached into his back pocket. "We should exchange numbers," he said as he pulled out his cell phone.

I hesitated.

"You know…for Monday," he quickly added.

"Okay," I said and gave him my number.

After Colt left, Monday didn't seem so nerve wracking.

4

My first night alone was awful. Every time I heard the slightest noise I'd panic. So sleep never happened. The moment the sun was starting to peek over the mountains surrounding the city, I threw on my workout clothes and went for a run. I needed to burn myself out to the point of not caring. Which entailed me running to the point of throwing up. At least I was home when it happened. I just wasn't inside. I tried to make it. I was almost to the steps leading up to my porch when my stomach heaved and up came everything I'd eaten the night before.

For a moment I thought I was going to pass out. I needed to breathe like my life depended on it, which it did. *Duh.* But who could breathe while throwing up at the same time? I heaved twice before I could rein myself in and focus on the delicious air flowing into my lungs. "Crap," I growled, wiping my mouth with the back of my hand.

"Are you alright, Shiloh?" I heard someone say.

With extremely labored breaths and hands on my hips, I turned. Keelan and who I assumed was another one of Colt's brothers were standing in their driveway watching me. Like the twins and Keelan, the fourth brother had pale blond hair. It was buzzed short, military style, and he had golden brown eyes that matched Keelan's. You could tell this guy was the oldest of the four Stone brothers and the bulkiest. The dude had some serious muscles.

They were both dressed in athletic wear with gym bags hanging on their shoulders. Maybe they were heading to work out. Their bodies definitely showed that they went to the gym religiously.

At the moment, I was so worn out I didn't have it in me to feel embarrassed that my neighbors had gotten a front row seat to me barfing my brains out. Not to mention, I was probably red as a tomato and completely soaked with sweat. "Yeah, sorry you had to see that," I breathed. "I pushed myself too hard this morning."

"How long did you run for?" asked the brother whose name I didn't know.

I pulled my phone out to look at the time. "A little over four hours."

Keelan whistled. "Are you training for a marathon?"

I shook my head. "I just like to run."

The older brother frowned a little as he studied me.

"Well, make sure you drink water and take it easy," Keelan said and waved. They both climbed into the old classic car I'd seen them working on the day after I moved in.

Before heading in, I grabbed the hose from the side of the house to clean up my vomit. Exhaustion set in once I got inside and I didn't make it past my couch. My legs felt like spaghetti and putting one foot in front of the other required way more work than I had the energy for. Instead of dragging myself to the bathroom to take a shower that I desperately needed, I plopped down on the couch and let myself drift off to sleep.

"Shi, have you seen my rose gold cuff?" Shayla asked as she dug through her jewelry box on her dresser.

I leaned against her bedroom door frame with a scowl. I couldn't believe she was going to another party. She'd already lost her driving privileges from the last party she'd gotten caught at last weekend. "Mom and Dad are going to kill you if you come home drunk again," I warned.

"Ah! Here it is. What the hell was it doing in my sock drawer? Oh well," she mused out loud.

My sister could be a ditz and that scared me sometimes. "You know, if you stay home, we can binge watch Netflix and gorge on popcorn."

"Or you could come with me and let loose for once," she countered as she slipped on her cuff. She'd gotten it for Christmas from our parents last year. The cuff was designed with two feathers overlapping each other, forming a beautiful bracelet. It was unique and beautiful. Just like her.

I scoffed. "You know that will never happen."

"Lame," she groaned.

"You know why I can't go."

She rolled her eyes and stomped over to her full-length mirror next to her closet. "You haven't heard from Mr. X in over a month. He's probably moved on to better things than sending love letters to a teenaged girl." She fluffed her blue hair. "I'm thinking of changing my hair to pink."

It was my turn to roll my eyes because I swore, she had the attention span of a gnat.

Her eyes locked with mine through the mirror. "Come on, Shi. Maybe you'll meet a guy and finally get past first base."

I scrunched my nose.

"We're going to be seventeen and all you've done is make out with that nerdy transfer student you dated for like a week."

"He broke up with me after a week because I wasn't ready to do more than kiss him. Nerd or jock, guys at our school are major jerks." I sighed. "I'm not going to go, but if you won't stay home with me, please be safe. I didn't absorb you in Mom's womb for a reason. Don't get *behind a wheel drunk or let some asshole spike your drink and ruin my master plans."*

She gave me a warm smile. "I love you, too."

My eyes opened to darkness and shadows dancing on my bedroom ceiling. They flooded immediately as I remembered my dream-slash-memory. I let the tears fall and a pain-filled sob ripped from me. The pathetic sound pierced the silence and echoed off the walls. I winced, then remembered that it didn't matter if I was loud. I was alone. I lay there crying until I didn't have any more tears left. I missed her. I missed them, with every fiber of my being.

Rolling over, I picked up my phone from my nightstand to look at the time. It was almost five in the morning and today was my first day of school. I didn't have time for a run, even though I was desperate for one. Running would have to wait until after school. I did, however, have time for a smoke. I was down to one every other day. Opening my nightstand drawer, I grabbed my pack of cigarettes and lighter.

Because I was wearing very short Spider-Man sleep shorts and a white tank that I was pretty sure was see-through, I scooped up a zip-up hoodie on my way out the front door. Stepping out onto the porch and taking a seat on the top step, I slipped into my hoodie. The sun was slowly peeking over the mountains and it was already getting hot, making me wish I had pulled my long and heavy hair up. I settle with tucking it behind my ears before putting a cigarette between my lips and lighting it. I tossed both the pack of cigarettes and the lighter next to me on the step. That first drag was terribly divine.

"No running this morning?" a deep familiar voice asked. I looked toward Colt's house. His oldest brother was standing there looking like he was heading to the gym again. Like his brothers, he was gorgeous. Very broody and standoffish, which I found totally hot. The Stone brothers had definitely won the sexy gene lottery.

I blew out a puff of smoke. "No time. At least not enough time for my type of run."

"You have enough time to run for half of the amount of time you usually run before you have to get ready for school."

I guessed Colt had told him that I would be attending the same school. "Once I start running, it's kind of hard for me to stop," I said and took another drag.

He eyed my cigarette and judgment hardened his frown. "Where are your parents?" he asked.

My immediate reaction was to be defensive. I forced it down. Mustering the patience I knew I had buried deep, I put out my cigarette and got to my feet. Stuffing my hands in the pockets of my sweater to hide my clenching fists, I leveled my gaze with his. "They're dead."

He grimaced.

Without another word, I turned on my heel and went back inside to get ready for school.

I took my time getting ready by curling my long lilac hair and doing my makeup. I wasn't a makeup expert or anything. I just knew what Shayla had taught me. It had been her dream to become a celebrity makeup artist and because of that I had always been her guinea pig for new looks. I went with light, shimmering colors to enhance my gray eyes and cheekbones. My face was a little heart-shaped and I had pouty lips with a defined Cupid's bow.

Standing in my closet, going through my clothes, I tried to find something cute to wear. I had gone shopping last week for clothes that would cover my scars but also wouldn't cause me to overheat. Wearing jackets and sweatshirts was getting old.

I decided on a cream-colored dress that billowed around my thighs and had long trumpet sleeves. I paired the dress with black thigh-high stockings and black ankle boots. Because the sleeves were gaping at the ends, I would need to be careful not to reveal my wrists. Remembering my dream, I walked over to my jewelry box on my new dresser and pulled out Shayla's rose gold feather cuff. I slipped it on my wrist, and it did a good job at hiding one of my many nasty scars. My fingers brushed over the beautiful bracelet as I stared down at it. At least I'd have a piece of her with me today.

I finished getting ready by sending one of my two check-in texts for the day to Logan on the bare-bones burner flip phone, then stuffed it, along with my regular cell phone, in my backpack. After grabbing my car keys, I was ready to start my first day of school.

5

Copper Mountain was a regular public high school. That was new for me. My old high school had been a private school for entitled rich kids. Copper Mountain sort of had the same feel as my old school, and I had no doubt the students would be the same, too, with their cliques and crap.

I should have been attending college right now—been done with all the drama high school entailed. However, the universe had chosen a different road for me to take. A longer, harder road, where most days I found it paved with broken glass and I was forced to walk it without shoes.

I pulled into the student parking lot. I was a little early, so the lot was pretty empty. Right away, I noticed Colt standing by his navy blue Dodge Charger. Last night, he had texted me that he'd be waiting for me by it. He gave me a little wave and I parked a few spots over from him. Grabbing my backpack, I hopped out. Colt walked over and his eyes widened as I came out from between the cars.

"Uh… hi," I said shyly. Did my outfit look terrible?

"You're really beautiful," he blurted and rubbed the back of his neck as if embarrassed.

My cheeks flushed. No one other than my parents and my sister had said that to me before. I didn't know how to handle it. My first instinct was to shy away by looking down. I resisted the urge. *Be cool. Compliments are supposed to be flattering, not make you uncomfortable.*

"Thank you," I murmured.

His expression became pensive, like I'd done something he found interesting or strange. The side of his mouth began to twitch but he quickly covered it up by clearing his throat. "Are you ready for the tour?" he asked, stuffing his hands in his pockets of his ripped jeans.

I tried not to stare at how nicely his dark blue T-shirt hugged his broad chest and muscled arms. I wondered if he played sports to be that fit. It took effort but I was able to avert my gaze before I got caught and gave the wrong impression. Colt was being a nice neighbor by showing me around and I was only looking for friendship. I nodded, then dug through my bag for my schedule and held it out to him. "Can you show me where my classes are, please?"

He took my schedule to look it over and we made our way out of the parking lot toward the school's entrance. "We have a few classes together. AP English, calculus, and gym. Creed shares a few classes with us too and he's in your art class."

"I'm guessing Creed is your walking, talking carbon copy?"

That made him chuckle. "Yeah, he's my twin."

Hearing him say the word *twin* had me reaching for Shayla's cuff. One day, when I came across moments like this that reminded me of her, it wouldn't hurt so much. I hoped that day came soon. Until then I needed to keep moving forward.

Colt showed me where all my classes were and where my locker was. The halls were quickly filling up with other students. Walking through them, I noticed quite a bit of students staring. A lot of girls smiled at Colt. Not that I could blame them. And I received a few curious glances.

"Colt!" someone yelled, catching our attention. Colt and I paused in the hall and turned. A guy with raven, slicked-back hair and light green eyes was heading toward us. The guy had *football player* written all over him and it wasn't just the letterman's jacket that gave him away. This guy was tall and definitely drank the Kool-Aid at the gym. "There you are. What's up, man?" he said to Colt. They greeted each other by doing that handshake hug thing guys do. "I saw Creed outside. He said you ditched him for some chi—" He stopped talking when his stare moved to me and his green eyes did a slow perusal from my head to my toes before he plastered on a charming smile I was sure he used on all the girls. "Well, hello, gorgeous. You must be new?"

Oh, jeez.

I tilted my head slightly and smirked. "What was your first clue?"

The jock's brows shot up in surprise and Colt laughed. "Shiloh's immune to your charm, dude. Just be nice and introduce yourself or she'll chew you up and spit you out before you even know what's happening."

I folded my arms under my breasts. "I'm not that bad," I mumbled, making Colt laugh some more.

The jock looked back and forth between us before he plastered on that charming smile again. "I'm Ethan. Football god, who not only scores touchdowns on the field but also in the bedroom," he said, wiggling his eyebrows.

Colt groaned, shaking his head at his friend's antics.

At first all I could do was blink at Ethan. Then my head fell back, laughing. He was too much. "Nice to meet you, Football God. I'm Shiloh."

After our unforgettable introduction, the three of us fell into friendly conversation, which mostly consisted of them asking me questions. I told them I was from Alaska, even though I was really from Maryland. They asked me why I had moved here, and I came up with a lame excuse that I wanted to escape the cold when really, I'd closed my eyes and pointed at a map of the U.S. and my finger had just happened to land on Arizona.

"Do you like football?" Ethan asked.

As I was about to answer, a group of students approached, made up of a few of Ethan's fellow letterman jacket-wearing jocks, a couple of pretty girls clinging to their arms, and Colt's twin, Creed. My eyes immediately locked with Creed's. Him and Colt were mirror images of each other apart from a few subtle differences. Creed's pale blond hair was shorter than Colt's and styled into a faux hawk. Creed's demeanor was guarded, stone-like, where Colt seemed softer, friendly. I looked back and forth between the two of them and began to feel that overwhelming sadness again.

Shayla.

I wondered if they had the same connection she and I'd had? Like a part of your soul walking this earth alongside you. I had always been able to feel when she had been close or if she had been upset.

Locking eyes with Creed again, I fought internally to push back my turmoil. His eyes intensely bored into mine as if he could see right through me and see my pain. Feeling exposed, I looked away. I thought I heard someone say something, but the bell rang, and everyone dispersed toward their classes except for Creed, Colt, and me. They both stood there watching me.

"Shiloh?"

I glanced up at Colt. He was at least a foot taller than my five-foot, four-inch height. "Huh?"

He got that pensive look again.

"Sorry. I got lost in my thoughts. What did you say?" I asked.

"It's alright. This is my brother, Creed," Colt introduced.

I forced myself to look back at Creed with a smile. "It's nice to meet you, Creed. I'm Shiloh, your new neighbor."

Creed's stare hardened. "I know. Your bedroom window is

next to mine. You've woken me up every night since you moved in with your screaming."

For a moment, I forgot how to breathe. Logan had said he would've been surprised if my screaming hadn't woken the neighbors. I hadn't known I was screaming from my nightmares every night, though.

"I..." How did I respond to that?

Colt bristled. "Really, Creed?"

"I'll do my best not to disturb your sleep anymore," I said and walked away, eyes glued to the checkered laminate floor.

AP English was my first class of the day. I stepped into the classroom with a minute to spare and took a seat at an empty desk. Colt and Creed drifted in just before the final bell rang. Colt scanned the room until he spotted me and headed over, claiming the desk next to mine to my right. He gave me a small smile, which I returned with my own.

Creed slowly moved through the room, looking around for an empty desk. There was only one desk left unclaimed and it was the one directly behind mine. With a bored look, he walked past Colt and me and sat down behind me. Sitting ramrod straight, I battled the temptation to glance over my shoulder.

Our teacher started handing out stacks of papers with the class syllabus on them to everyone in the front row. I took one and turned in my seat to hand the rest to Creed. His fingers brushed mine as he went to take them, making my eyes jump to his. He was already staring at me. His gaze didn't waver from mine as he took a syllabus and held the rest over his shoulder. Unable to look away, I felt like a fly caught in a spider's web.

Saving me from making a fool of myself, the teacher pulled our attention by asking the class, "Who would like to read the first paragraph of the syllabus?"

With burning cheeks, I turned forward in my seat. Staring down at my syllabus, I read along without comprehending a single word. I felt strange. My heart was racing, and I was anxious but in an exciting way. I couldn't tell if I liked it.

I took a deep breath, an attempt to calm myself.

Colt leaned close. "You okay?" he whispered.

I nodded. My nerves had settled a little and I did my best to focus on the rest of class. I was hyper-aware of Creed sitting behind me and Colt sitting next to me, too. Suffice to say, my body was incredibly stiff by the end of class. When the bell rang, I bolted to my feet and almost groaned at the pleasure of being able to move.

The twins followed me out of class. Once out in the hall, Creed went to the left and Colt and I went right. Colt was sweet enough to walk with me to my next class before heading to his own. Ethan the Football God was in my next class, biology, and insisted I sit by him. I did and for most of the class he talked to me any chance he got. Despite being an unapologetic flirt, he was actually a nice guy. He made me laugh, which was something I hadn't done in a long time.

Lunch time rolled around, and I looked for Colt in the cafeteria. In calculus, he'd asked me to sit with him and his friends. I scanned the huge cafeteria. Students were already congregating at the tables and getting in line for food. I usually brought my own lunch. I'd been so nervous this morning, I'd completely forgotten it in my fridge.

I pulled my phone out from the pocket of my dress, getting ready to text Colt. A hand came down on my shoulder. Startled, I jumped, then turned, finding Colt and Creed standing behind me.

Colt gave me a sheepish smile. "I didn't mean to scare you."

I stuffed my phone back in my pocket. "It's alright. I was getting ready to text you."

He pointed his thumb at Creed. "This one likes to take his time."

Creed rolled his eyes and walked away toward the lunch line.

We followed him. "Ignore him," Colt said, tilting his head at his brother. "He's an asshole to everyone until he deems them worthy. He takes after our brother Knox in that regard, except Knox never finds anyone worthy."

"I can hear you," Creed said over his shoulder.

Colt looked at his brother. "And?"

Creed didn't respond.

"Knox is your oldest brother, right?" I asked.

Colt nodded.

"I've met him. He didn't seem as bad as..." I snapped my mouth shut before I could say more.

Colt snorted and Creed turned around with an ominous smirk. "Bad as what? Me?"

Getting a little tired of his attitude, I squared my shoulders. "Yes."

He appeared surprised yet delighted by my honesty. "How long did you interact with Knox?"

"Briefly," I answered. "And during those brief interactions it didn't escape my notice that he had a prickly personality. But at least he wasn't an outright jerk."

"Ah, you think I don't like you," Creed said with a look of understanding. "Why, because I said you keep me up at night?" He moved up in the line where the trays to collect your lunch were. He grabbed one and held it out to me. "I don't know you enough to dislike you, but I don't know you well enough to like you either. As for this morning, I was tired and I'm not nice to anyone when I'm tired."

Half of me felt guilty and the other half wanted to snap at him for making assumptions about me. At odds over what to do, I said nothing, and I took the tray from him.

He looked at Colt, who had been quiet during mine and

Creed's exchange. "Happy? I made up with our hot screaming neighbor."

Colt sighed as Creed turned to grab a tray for himself. "I was until you ruined it by putting your foot back into your mouth."

I snorted. They were polar opposites. Like Shayla and me. The thought sobered me, and I chastised myself for constantly comparing us to them. I had to stop doing that. Colt was sort of becoming my friend. I wouldn't be able to be his friend if every time I looked at him and Creed, I became overwhelmed with sadness. So no more.

The food here was set up kind of like a buffet. I pointed at what I wanted from the different selections laid out under the glass cover and the cafeteria lady piled it onto a plate. I chose a pre-made sandwich, a bag of carrots, and a water bottle.

"Thank you so much for sticking with me today," I said to Colt. "I've never had to start somewhere new and alone before."

"No problem. How are you liking it so far?" Colt asked.

"So far it's been alright." *I'm not looking forward to gym.*

"Why? Don't you go running every morning?" Colt asked, making me realize I had said my thoughts out loud.

I bit my bottom lip nervously. I didn't want to lie but I didn't want to tell him the truth either. "Uh… stupid reasons."

Thankfully, he let it go. We paid for our food and I followed them over to a table Ethan and a few others were already sitting at.

"Shiloh!" Ethan shouted my name when he saw me walking toward their table.

Startled, I jumped, almost flinging everything on my tray in the air. My cheeks burned. Pretty much everyone in the entire cafeteria looked my way. I had the urge to hide and I inadvertently ducked partly behind Creed, who happened to be closest. He peered over his shoulder at me as I fixated on the sleeve of his black T-shirt while trying to reel in my embarrassment. I didn't like having this much attention. Shayla had been a magnet for it. I'd always liked to fly under the radar.

"Ethan, cool it, man," Colt said.

Ethan looked from Colt to me. He took in my flushed appearance and chuckled.

I was determined to put myself out there a little more to make friendships. In order to do that, I'd need to get past my insecurities. I exhaled before squaring my shoulders and walking out from behind Creed to set my tray down on the table across from where Ethan sat.

"You don't like to be the center of attention, do you, Shiloh?" he teased as I sat down. Colt took a seat on my left and surprisingly, Creed sat in the seat on my right.

"No," I answered honestly.

"I think I need to move to Alaska," Ethan said.

One of his jock friends snorted and asked him why.

"Because I think that's where the rest of the girls as adorable as Shiloh are hiding."

"Not everyone likes to be the center of attention," I said as I opened my sandwich.

All of them either snorted or snickered while shaking their heads.

"You clearly haven't met any of the girls here," Creed grumbled next to me before he took a bite of his own sandwich.

"Nothing but a bunch of shallow, self-absorbed bitches, but at least they're hot," said one of Ethan's jock buddies.

"You better not be talking about us."

Everyone's attention snapped to a girl standing at the end of the table with two other girls flanking her. It only took a quick glance to know which clique these girls belonged to. It was the aura they gave off and the fact that they were pretty, confident, and instantly looking down their noses at me. They of course dressed to look sexy with their midriffs showing, low cut shirts, and shorts so short they should have been sent to the principal's office for dress code violations.

Even though they weren't giving me friendly looks, I tried to remind myself not to judge. Kill with kindness. It would be nice to have a friend who was a girl.

"Why? Were your ears ringing, Cassy?" Creed asked, his voice sounding cold.

The brunette, Queen B front and center, who I assumed was Cassy, glared at Creed. "You didn't think that way when we were together this summer. Why the change of heart?" she asked. Her eyes shifted to me. "Who's your little friend, Creed? She's not exactly your type, or yours for that matter, Colt. A little too innocent looking for the Stone brothers."

"Shut up, Cassy," Colt snapped, sounding beyond annoyed.

"She's not my friend," Creed corrected in a bored tone that drew everyone's attention. He scooped up his bottle of water and without even bothering to look in Cassy's direction he said, "As for my type, an easy lay over the summer isn't either," and then took a drink.

Ethan whistled. "Ouch."

Cassy's face molded into a scowl before she stormed away.

Creed's aquamarine's eyes met mine. "That's what it looks like when I don't like someone."

"Noted," I said.

6

I WALKED INTO MY ART CLASS AND PICKED AN EMPTY TABLE TO SIT at. There were two chairs per table. I was digging through my bag for my notebook when the other chair at my table was pulled out and someone took a seat. I looked up with a smile, getting ready to greet whoever it was, and saw Creed.

Colt had said he was in my art class.

My smile dimmed a little. "Hi."

He studied my face with a frown. "Disappointed that I'm not Colt?"

I tucked some hair behind my ear. "No. Surprised. As someone who feels indifferent about me, I didn't expect that you'd want to sit by me."

"Colt asked me to look after you."

"Oh." I was strangely disappointed by that.

The corner of his mouth lifted. "Besides, how can I decide if I like you or not if I don't spend time with you?"

I leaned back in my chair and crossed my left leg over the right, revealing a little bit of thigh between the end of my dress and the top of my black thigh highs. The movement drew his attention there. I watched as his eyes slowly made their way back up to mine.

I cleared my throat. "What if I've already determined how I feel about you?"

The cocksure smirk that adorned his face made my heart race. "I'd call your bluff."

I smiled despite myself. I didn't know if it was because we were alone, but he seemed different. Not any less intense. His demeanor was more relaxed, and he let other parts of his personality surface. He still made me nervous and I still couldn't determine whether I liked that or not.

Physical education, or gym as they called it, had planted a seed of dread in my stomach that had been growing with each passing hour.

It wasn't that I didn't like to get physical...uh, I meant exercise. That came out wrong. I was still a virgin and I foresaw being one for a long time. I was the type who wanted to love and trust the person before giving up that piece of myself. Seeing how I was in no way seeking to date, it was looking like I was going to be the next forty-year-old virgin. It was okay, though. There was no rush.

As I walked into the girls' locker room, my stomach was a knotted mess of anxiety. I was wearing a white under-shirt beneath my dress. At least some of my nastiest scars would be covered. The gym uniforms were black basketball shorts and short-sleeved gray T-shirts with dark blue lettering on them. My ankles and wrists, not to mention the long scar on my inner right arm, were going to be on display. I did have a dark blue zip-up hoodie in my bag. With it being one hundred degrees out, people were going to notice. I guessed it was better to be the freak wearing a sweatshirt in the summer than the freak with the scars.

I picked a locker in an area that didn't already have a bunch of girls changing and began stripping as fast as I could. A few girls showed up just before the final bell rang and snagged a few lockers near mine. I gave them my back as I finished changing. There was nothing I could do to hide the scars on my ankles because my ankle socks and tennis shoes didn't cover them, and I wasn't going to wear my thigh highs. I drew the line there. Leaving my hoodie unzipped over my uniform, I pulled my hair into a messy bun as I made my way into the gym. A few girls but mostly guys were already seated on the indoor gymnasium's wooden bleachers.

A waving hand caught my attention. Sitting at the top were Colt, Creed, Ethan, and a few of their other friends. I made my way up. Once at the top, Colt stood so I could sit between him and Creed. They both eyed my hoodie. Colt politely didn't comment on it. Creed, on the other hand, was a different story.

"You know it's a hundred degrees out, right?"

"Believe me, I noticed," I mumbled.

"You're going to get heatstroke if you keep that on when the coaches send us outside," he argued, drawing the attention of the others.

Why did he care?

"Creed," Colt said with a tone.

"Aren't you her friend or something? It should be you telling her this, not me," Creed grumbled.

Anxiously, I chewed on my bottom lip. Ethan and the student sitting in front of me turned to look at us. I shifted on the bench to face Creed and leaned in close. His masculine scent filled my nose. Like citrus and smoky cedar. It was a heady combination. *Focus, Shi.* "If I promise to explain my legitimate reason for wearing a sweatshirt later, will you please let it go?"

I didn't know if it was the desperation in my voice or the pleading in my eyes, but he nodded.

More students continued to trickle in from the locker rooms.

Cassy and her squad were the last to join the rest of the class as they walked from the locker room arm in arm.

Ethan turned to get the twins' attention. "When's your first swim meet?"

"Next week," Colt answered.

"You're on the swim team?" I asked.

Ethan snickered. "Because of these fools, our swim team has gone to state for the past three years. Our school's swim team is almost as big of a deal as our football team. Almost."

Colt and Creed rolled their eyes at their friend.

"What about you?" Ethan asked me. "Are you going to try out for a sport or were you on a team at your old school?"

I shook my head. "No. I'm the nerd in the family. Sports was my sister's domain. She was a cheerleader and did gymnastics." I grimaced, looking down. *Why did I just say that?*

"You have a sister? Does she go here too?" Ethan asked. I could feel the twins' eyes on me. "No," I replied simply.

"Darn, that just ruined my fantasy of seeing a Pierce sister dressed like a cheerleader," Ethan teased.

"What about going out for track? Don't you like to run?" Colt asked. In that moment, I could have hugged him for changing the subject. "Running is more of an escape for me. I don't want to turn it into a sport."

"You should still show your team spirit and come cheer for us from the stands. I have a home game next week, too," Ethan said.

"Sure. I'll come dressed in a skimpy cheerleader outfit and hold up a glittery poster board that says, 'Go Team Go!'"

I'd been teasing, but Ethan took it even further. "Now we're talking. Make sure the skimpy uniform is in our school colors and instead of 'Go Team Go!' I'd write out 'Football God.' Just a suggestion, though."

I caught a gleam of mirth in his eye and I fought not to smile. "I think I'll wear my hair in pigtails."

"Add high heels and glasses and you've completed the ensemble," he added.

Attempting not to laugh, I snorted. "I think you're envisioning a naughty schoolgirl, not a cheerleader."

Ethan shrugged. "Cheer me on as either."

I shook my head at him. "You know I'll be going in sweats now, right?"

He playfully pouted. "I figured as much."

With a big smile on my face, I glanced at Colt and Creed and saw that they were staring at me. "What?"

Ethan smiled at his friends. "I think we painted a sexy picture in their heads."

My cheeks turned hot and I looked away. The sound of Ethan grunting drew my eyes back to them. He was hugging his stomach while both Colt and Creed glared at him.

"Ignore him," Colt said.

The coaches came into the gym and called everyone's attention. Attendance was taken before exceptions, rules, yada yada were gone over. Then, we were all ushered outside to run the track for the remainder of class.

The guys stretched next to me. "Shall we make this interesting?" Creed grinned at Colt and Ethan, who looked at him with intrigue.

"What did you have in mind?" Colt asked him.

Creed turned to me and I cocked a brow at him. I guessed I was expected to join in on whatever he had in mind. "First one to complete twenty laps—"

"We're going to be worn out for swim practice," Colt interrupted his brother.

"Pussy," Ethan teased and then he caught me frowning at him. "Sorry."

"It's just practice," Creed said.

"And what do I win when I beat you three?" I asked. Zipping

up my jacket, I bent over to stretch. "I don't think any of you have anything I want."

Colt tilted his head toward Creed. "You could force him to be nice."

That was tempting. I glanced at Creed, who was wearing a scowl. "If I win, you're to be at my beck and call for the semester. If I need a favor, you have to drop what you're doing. Within reason, of course. If I want someone to go shopping with, you have to come. If I want a gym buddy or want to go get mani-pedis, you're who I'm calling to come with me."

Creed didn't hide his irritation. "You want a boyfriend."

I scrunched my nose and shook my head at him. "No." I stood up straight from stretching. "I want you to actually feel the sting of losing." I turned to Colt. "That pretty blue Charger is yours, right?"

He became apprehensive. "Yeah."

"We swap cars for two weeks."

"A man's car is his baby," Colt said, looking nervous.

I put my hands on my hips. "Yeah, and my 4Runner's mine. It has all the bells and whistles. Not to mention the interior is all custom. But before I decided to buy it, I was torn between a candy apple red Charger or my 4Runner. Practicality won. An SUV can provide more. I want to enjoy what I'm missing. Even if it's just for a short time."

"Okay," Colt agreed.

I turned an evil smile on Ethan. "You have to go a whole month without flirting."

He put his hands on his hips with a serious expression. "I don't know if that's possible. It's kind of woven into my DNA."

"I think you can do it," I insisted.

His brows rose. "Fine. If I win, I want you to come to their meets and my games dressed as a cheerleader."

Both Creed and Colt smiled and exchanged a look that was unsettling.

My evil smile dropped. "I'm not wearing a cheerleading outfit or high heels."

Ethan thought about it for a moment. "You'll have to wear school colors, accessorize showing team spirit, and wear pigtails."

"Fine," I grumbled and looked to the twins.

Creed went first. "If I win, I get ten questions of anything I want to know about you answered honestly." My heart rate picked up. I didn't know what he wanted to know, but there were some things I couldn't answer. For one, it was for my safety and two, depending on what he asked, I didn't know if I could emotionally handle it. "Three questions," I countered.

"You want me to be your bitch for an entire semester. That's not worth three questions. Five questions."

I shuffled from one foot to the other. Was I confident I could beat him? Maybe. "Alright. Five questions."

Everyone looked to Colt.

"I want the same," he said.

I had to take a calming breath. If they both beat me, I could owe ten questions total. I suddenly didn't feel as confident as I had a minute ago. I nodded, reluctantly. The twins bet chores at home if they beat each other and when it came to the stakes with Ethan, losers had to be the designated driver at the next few parties.

The four of us lined up, counted down, and took off. I paced myself as I knocked out one lap after another and to my surprise the guys did the same. As we passed other students, it seemed we were the only ones who were actually taking running the track seriously. Pretty much everyone else was walking.

The four of us were evenly matched. As the last couple of laps came upon us, I picked up my speed. Creed and I battled back and forth over first place. With the finish line in view, I pushed my muscles until they burned. Breathing heavily, sweating profusely, I ran with all my might. To both mine and Creed's surprise, Ethan zoomed past us, then Colt. Ethan took first place,

Colt following in second. Creed and I...well, we tied in last place. The upside to that was at least our bets to each other were voided.

"Crap," I puffed with my hands on my hips. I was pacing back and forth, trying to cool down. Colt and Ethan were lying in the grass off to the side of the track. Creed was breathing heavily while bent over with his hands on his knees. "It's so freaking hot," I growled as I unzipped my sweatshirt and fanned it open and closed.

"You need to take off your stupid sweatshirt before you pass out," Creed snapped.

My eyes traveled around us. The rest of the students were heading back to the locker rooms, leaving the four of us behind.

Creed watched me and clearly picked up on my nervous behavior. "It's the end of class. Everyone is heading in if that's the reason you won't take it off."

I debated for a moment. It was unbearably hot out. I didn't think they'd tease me about my scars. That didn't mean they wouldn't ask about them. I didn't have to answer Creed or Ethan if they asked. However, if Colt decided to use one of his questions... *Maybe I could be vague.*

With my mind set, I shrugged off my sweatshirt and tied it around my waist. I held my arms out wrists up so Creed could look his fill. It was better to get it out of the way now versus them sneaking glances. "This is why I'm wearing a sweatshirt."

Creed stared down at my scars, without saying anything. Colt and Ethan sat up, squinted at my arms, then got to their feet. As they approached, I dropped my eyes to the ground. I was past the point of no return now. I hoped I wouldn't regret it.

Colt took hold of my arm that had the long, jagged scar. Very delicately he flipped my hand over, seeing that the scar around my wrist went full circle. "Your wrists match your ankles," he murmured as his thumb lightly brushed over my inner wrist, right along my scar. Creed and Ethan stepped back to look down at my ankles. "You look like you were tied up," Ethan blurted, and Colt glared at him. Ethan winced. "Sorry."

I didn't confirm or deny. Instead, I worried my lip. When I couldn't take their stares any longer, I pulled my arms away to cross them over my chest.

"Please, don't make fun of me because of this. People, especially girls, can be mean, and I could really do without the teasing and assumptions," I said, pleadingly.

For the first time since I'd met him, Colt's eyes turned cold and angry. "Why would we make fun of you? If anyone did, that just shows their shitty character, not because anything is wrong with you. Everyone has scars."

Not like these, I wanted to say.

"This is why you were nervous about gym? You were worried about changing in front of the other girls?" Creed stuffed his hands into his black basketball shorts' pockets as he stared down at me for confirmation. I guessed he'd been listening to Colt and me talk in the lunch line.

I nodded. Looking at the three of them, I could see the question they were itching to ask. *How? How did I get these scars?* I thought for sure Colt would use one of his questions to ask, but the question never came.

"We better head inside and change. School is about to end, and we have to get to practice," Creed said to Colt. The four of us started in the direction of the locker rooms.

"I forgot when I had registered, they'd mentioned there was a pool on campus. It's in that building, right?" I asked, pointing to the square building with a bunch of windows next to the gym.

Colt looked in the direction I was pointing. "Yup. You haven't been in there yet?"

I shook my head.

"You should come watch us practice."

"Can I come another time? I have a few errands to run right after school. I also didn't go for a real run this morning and planned on going to the gym, too." A run in the air conditioning sounded a lot better than running in this heat.

"What gym are you a member of?" Creed asked.

I looked from Colt to him. "Desert Stone Fitness."

Ethan snorted and Creed and Colt glanced at each other.

"What?" I asked, looking at the three of them. "Should I not go there? It had a lot of good reviews online and it's really nice inside."

The three of them just stared at me. Colt gave me that pensive look again, while Creed narrowed his eyes at me, which honestly was the same look as his brother, just a little harsher and could be mistaken for a glare. Ethan looked like he was about to combust with laughter.

"You don't know, do you?" Creed asked.

"If it's a shady place, please tell me and I'll go somewhere else," I snapped. What the heck was going on? I kind of loved Desert Stone. It was perfect with its air-conditioned track and I was thinking about signing up for a self-defense class. I wondered how I'd fare from what Logan had taught me.

Colt looked to Creed again before his pretty aqua eyes returned to me. "No. It's a very good gym. We work there. We just haven't seen you around."

Ethan glanced at the twins with what looked like surprise elevating his brows.

"Oh, I signed up last week and I've only been there twice. Then again, I wasn't looking at anyone. I just beelined for the track upstairs."

"Of course you did," Creed muttered, then shoved his brother toward the boys' locker room. "Let's go get changed."

7

"I'm home," I said as I walked through the front door. *Going to the movies tonight with my friend Liz had really uplifted my spirits and I was glad my mom had talked me into going.*

Right after shutting the door behind me, I felt something was wrong. It could have been because all the hair on the back of my neck rose or because every light was off in the house. It was also quiet. Too quiet.

"Mom! Dad!" I yelled.

There wasn't an answer.

I looked in the living room and spotted my dad lying on the couch. He seemed to be sleeping, but the large dark stain on his white shirt drew me closer. I flicked on the lamp and a scream ripped its way up my throat. I had to clamp my hand over my mouth to keep from screaming out. Tears filled my eyes as I took in my dad's butchered, prone body. His eyes were open, vacant depths. His arm was hanging off the side of the couch, fingers lying limp on the carpet. His entire stomach had been ripped open and his insides were pulled out.

I backed away, praying what I was seeing wasn't real.

This wasn't happening.

This wasn't happening.

Someone grabbed my shoulder and my scream escaped, releasing my terror at a piercing volume.

~

My eyes shot open as I was mid-scream and I sat up quickly. Breathing heavily, I looked around, realizing that I had been dreaming again.

Tears dripped off my chin. I let out a pitiful sob as my hands fisted my blankets.

I wished Logan was here.

The sound of my doorbell ringing almost caused my soul to leave my body. I grabbed my phone from my nightstand to look at the time. It was almost six in the morning. Holding on to my phone, I climbed out of bed and got the gun I had hidden in my nightstand drawer.

The sun was already rising, so I didn't need to flick on any lights as I made my way through the house toward the front door. I peeked through the peephole and saw that a very tired Creed was standing on my porch. I quickly hid my gun behind one of the couch pillows and unlocked the door.

"You're killing me, Shiloh," he grumbled as I opened the door. The scowl he held showed he was ready to erupt on me, but he paused when his eyes met mine.

It was then that a breeze hit my face, reminding me that it was wet. I wiped at my cheeks, sniffling. "I'm sorry I woke you, Creed."

"Are you okay?" he asked, his voice sounding a little tight. I couldn't tell if it was due to him being angry or tired. He looked like he had literally rolled out of bed and stormed over here. His hair was mussed, and he was wearing a white undershirt that showed off the toned muscles in his arms and black athletic shorts.

I shook my head. "I will be." I crossed my arms over my chest.

"I have really bad nightmares. I thought they had stopped but since I moved here, they've started up again."

He frowned. "I can hang out for a while if you want."

My brows tried to reach my hairline. "Oh, that's okay. I know you don't—"

"I wouldn't have offered," he snapped.

The thought of hanging out with Creed, my neighbor who may or may not have liked me, sounded slightly more appealing than being alone right now. I took a step back, opening the door wider for him to come in.

He stepped inside, eyes wandering as he took in my living room. I closed the door and moved toward the kitchen. "I'm going to make some coffee. Would you like some?"

"Yeah." He followed me into the kitchen and took a seat on one of the two bar stools I had bought for my kitchen island.

I turned on my coffee maker and it began gurgling. As it brewed, I went over to my fridge and started pulling eggs, cheese, and sausage patties out. I glanced over my shoulder at Creed, who was silently watching me. "Do you like breakfast sandwiches?"

"Yes."

I piled everything on the counter next to the stove and bent over to grab some pans from the lower cabinet.

"Nice PJs."

I was wearing silk Batman pajamas. The shirt was a solid black crop top with a large yellow Batman logo on the front and the bottoms were high-waisted shorts that were patterned with the same Batman logo and had yellow drawstrings.

I set the pans on the stove. "Who doesn't love Batman?"

I caught his small smile before I went back over to the coffee pot and poured some into a mug for him. "Cream and sugar?" I asked as I set the mug in front of him.

"Black is fine," he said, scooping it up to take a sip.

I made myself a cup of coffee with cream and went back to

work on breakfast. I decided to make enough sandwiches for Creed's brothers, too. We didn't talk much. Just hung out in comfortable silence.

After giving him his sandwich and sitting down next to him at the island, I watched him dig in. He took a big bite and his brows lifted as he chewed. He gave me a nod of approval and I beamed, happy that he liked it.

"Do you like cooking?" he asked.

I chuckled at the random question. "I do."

"You smile as you cook."

Huh. I hadn't known I did that. "My mom was a chef," I admitted, and when I didn't become overwhelmed with sadness, I decided to continue on. "As far back as I can remember, she would drag me and my sister into the kitchen with her so she could show us a new recipe. My sister hated it. I loved it. To me, my mom's passion for food was contagious."

"Do you want to become a chef like your mom?"

"I used to."

"What changed your mind?"

I stilled as I was bringing my sandwich up to take a bite. How could I answer that without lying? It had been stupid of me to bring up my mom in the first place, but it felt really nice to talk about her. I set the sandwich back down to my plate as I debated how to respond.

"If you don't want to answer, you don't have to." His tone was nonchalant. His eyes told me different. They thankfully didn't hold any pity. That was the last thing I wanted. In his blue depths I saw understanding. Seeing that eased my nerves and it made it a little easier to find the answer to his question.

"My family is gone," I said in a low voice. "And with them, my dreams and passions. It wasn't until recently that I started reintroducing myself to the things I used to love, like cooking and baking. I find that I still enjoy doing them, but it's not the same. I mean, what's the point in trying a new recipe when I have no one to share it with?"

Creed was quiet for a while and I was beginning to think I'd made him feel awkward. "The weight of their absence will get lighter over time," he said. "And you won't always be alone, Shiloh."

I nodded, not trusting my voice, and finally took a bite of my sandwich.

As soon as I was finished eating, I put together the breakfast sandwiches for Creed's brothers and packaged them up in foil for him to carry back to his house.

"Thank you," I said as I walked him out.

"I think I'm supposed to thank you," he said, holding up a wrapped sandwich.

"I meant for hanging out with me."

He nodded and turned to leave. "See you at school," he shot over his shoulder as he headed back to his house. He was walking down my drive when his brothers Keelan and Knox stepped out of their house, dressed for the gym. They spotted Creed and surprise took over their faces. Then their gazes shifted to me.

Keelan's mouth slowly stretched into a smile. "Well, good morning, Shiloh."

"Morning," I said back.

Knox turned a hard look on Creed. "Did you spend the night over there?"

My cheeks burned, realizing how it must have looked for Creed to be leaving my house this early in the morning.

"No." Creed tossed a sandwich to each of them. "Shiloh made us breakfast. It's good. Eat it," he told them and went into their house.

Keelan held up his sandwich. "Thanks, Shiloh!"

"Welcome!" I waved and escaped inside.

～

"Hey," a voice said as I pulled my textbook for my first class out of my locker. I looked over my shoulder, finding Colt and Creed standing behind me.

I greeted them with a smile. "Hi." I shut my locker and turned to face them.

Their eyes dropped and roamed over my outfit. I had chosen to wear a red sundress that went to my knees and had spaghetti straps. To cover my exposed shoulders, arms, and more importantly, my scars, I'd paired the dress with a long-sleeved, dark-blue-and-white polka dot, shrug cardigan. I'd taken the risk of wearing my black ankle boots with ankle socks, leaving the tops of my scars visible. I had my anklet tracker tucked under my sock. I'd made the mistake of forgetting it at home yesterday and had gotten a huge lecture from Logan last night when he had called me. Apparently, he checked the GPS while I was at school.

I caught Creed staring at the two gold star barrettes in my hair. The corner of his mouth twitched, and I had a feeling he understood the theme behind my outfit choice today.

"Is it just DC or are you into Marvel also?" he asked.

Colt's brow furrowed as he looked from his brother to me.

I shrugged and did my best not to smile. "Maybe."

Colt looked me over again and I saw as he had that light bulb moment. He turned to glare at Creed. "She looks cute. Why are you making fun of her?"

"I'm not," Creed said with a bored tone. "I've just discovered that Shiloh has a slight obsession with superheroes."

"Well, not just the superheroes. I like some of the villains too. No offense to the good guys, but a lot of their stories are the same song and dance. The villains, though...they're different. More relatable, maybe? I don't know. They're definitely entertaining. The Joker is my favorite, followed by—" I slammed my lips closed and cringed when I realized that I'd let my inner geek surface.

Creed and Colt had been listening intently, their smiles

stretching. "Who do you think played the best Joker?" Colt asked and I could have hugged him.

"Heath Ledger," I replied.

Creed's smile dropped. "Joaquin Phoenix played the best Joker."

"I have to agree with Creed. Joaquin was amazing," Colt said.

I shook my head and started walking toward our first class. "He played second best."

Even though the twins and I bickered over the subject all the way to class, I couldn't stop smiling.

8

THE SCHOOL WEEK SOARED BY. DURING MY RUN AFTER SCHOOL Friday, Logan called. He asked me how my week had gone. I was happy to report that I was keeping busy and droned on about the flowers I planned on planting this weekend in the front yard along the driveway. Logan asked if I'd made any friends. I briefly told him about the twins and Ethan. The four of us at school had been inseparable all week. What I didn't tell Logan was I'd had both Creed and Colt over this morning for breakfast. I didn't want Logan to know I had woken Creed up twice this week with my screaming. If Logan knew I was having consistent nightmares again, he'd worry and that was the last thing he needed right now. Besides, it had been really nice to have breakfast with Colt and Creed. Instead of stomping over and banging on my door to complain like last time, Creed had woken up Colt before coming over. I had opened the door to concern instead of irritation. With sleep-tousled hair, Colt had asked if I was alright. The heavy turmoil that usually weighed on me for a while every time after I had a nightmare had receded quicker with that question. Like I had done last time with Creed, I'd offered them breakfast as an apology. They'd both sat at my kitchen island while I'd cooked.

I'd purposely made extra food again and wrapped the leftovers in tortillas, making breakfast burritos for Knox and Keelan.

"You couldn't find any girls to be friends with?" Logan asked, pulling me from my thoughts.

"I haven't met anyone I've clicked with yet. Maybe next week." So far, the girls I interacted with the most were Cassy and her clique of mean friends. They were constantly trying to hang around the twins and their friends. The girls' presence irritated Colt. Creed regarded them with indifference. One would think that anyone with a sliver of self-respect would move on, but the twins' lack of interest in Cassy and her friends seemed to have the opposite effect.

They blatantly hated me. Wednesday, Cassy had rammed her shoulder into mine as we had passed each other in the hall. She'd told me to stay out of her way. I had a feeling she hadn't been referring to when she was walking in the halls. She and her friends had judged, snidely commented on, and made fun of everything and anything to do with me. They'd quickly picked up on the fact that I wore a sweatshirt in gym. Sam, a member of Cassy's posse, had asked if I wore sweatshirts to hide the fact that I was flat-chested. Not that it mattered, but my breasts were not something I would ever feel insecure about. Amber, another member, had said my hair color made me look like a troll. I'd done my best to ignore them. Colt, on the other hand, couldn't. He'd come to my defense a few times. A lot of the girls didn't like that, especially Amber. It was obvious she had it bad for Colt and she saw me as a threat for being his friend. When Creed had come to my defense yesterday after Cassy had made a comment about the scars on my ankles, Cassy had glared at me with this look that had promised I would pay.

"I know you're eighteen and all," Logan started, his tone hinting that he was slightly uncomfortable with what he was about to say. "And you've got a level head on your shoulders, but if you end up liking one of these boys, you know how to be safe, right? I really don't want to give you the sex talk, but if I have to—"

"That won't be necessary," I cut him off. I'd already had *the talk* with my mom. "And like I said, they're just friends."

"Yeah, I had girls who were 'just friends' in high school, too."

I scrunched my nose as I turned down my street. With Logan's call, I'd slowed to a walk and now that I was cooled down, my run was over. "I don't think I can have anything more than friends."

"That's perfectly fine, Shi. Healing isn't a race and if anyone tries to pressure you into anything you're not ready for, just remember what I taught you."

"I don't think stabbing a teenage boy in the carotid is the best course of action."

"You never know." The smile I could hear in his voice caused the corners of my own mouth to lift.

An awkward silence followed. We'd been skirting around the Mr. X topic. Steeling myself, I forced out the question I was dreading to ask. "How...how is *it* going?"

He was quiet for a moment. "We have a possible lead in Mississippi. Ian and I are catching a flight there in about an hour."

If he had more to report than that, I knew he'd tell me, and he wouldn't sugarcoat it, either. That was just who he was. I was grateful for it, but that didn't mean it was always easy to hear.

We hung up not long after that and the music from my running playlist started playing through my earbuds again. As I approached my house, I headed for my 4Runner. Talking to Logan about planting flowers had reminded me that I still needed to get the big bags of soil out of my trunk. Humming to the music, I opened the trunk and pulled out one of the three heavy bags. I grunted as I used my knee to heft the heavy bag further up in my arms.

A hand grabbed my shoulder. I didn't know if it was because I had just talked about Mr. X or what, but fear exploded in my chest and my survival instincts took over. I dropped the bag of soil, grabbed the hand on my shoulder, and threw my elbow back at the person behind me. They caught my elbow with a skilled dodge before it could touch them. So I hooked my foot around their leg and slammed my whole body backward into theirs. With my music still playing, I felt rather than heard their grunt jump in their chest. By the lack of breasts and the masculine smell, I was betting my attacker was male. We both fell to the ground and I rolled off of him with my hands still locked around his. My plan was to hyperextend his arm. As I threw my legs over his neck and chest, my gaze locked with wide, familiar, golden brown eyes. The person I had just taken to the ground was the twins' flirty older brother.

"Keelan!" I quickly ripped my earbuds out and was met with the sound of laughter. Standing in their driveway, Colt and Creed were bent over laughing.

A slow, bright smile stretched across Keelan's mouth. "I think I've met my soulmate." He shifted under me and groaned. "Can I have my arm back now?"

I might have been in shock because I still had his completely tattooed arm clamped between my legs. I quickly lifted my legs off of him and released my grip on his hand. "I'm so sorry, Keelan," I said, scooting away until my head touched the bumper of my 4Runner. I brought my knees to my chest and tried to slow my speeding heart rate. My hands were shaking uncontrollably. Scratch that, my whole body was trembling.

I rubbed my chest as I let out a wobbly breath. I was relieved that it had been Keelan, but fear had taken root. The kind of fear I hadn't felt in a while.

Keelan's eyes narrowed as he studied me. Then he quickly sat up. "Hey, are you okay?"

Not trusting my voice, I nodded.

Worry furrowed his brow. "Shit, I'm sorry I scared you. I

called out to you, but you had your music on. I was seeing if you needed help." He pointed at the bag of soil I'd dropped.

Creed and Colt, who had finally stopped laughing, came over and stared down at us.

Colt gave me a small smile. "I warned him not to sneak up on you because you scare easy." He shook his head, chuckling. "Didn't expect you to ground him, though."

"That was the best thing I've ever seen," Creed said, grinning at Keelan. "How did someone as tiny as Shiloh take down someone who's been learning mixed martial arts since he was six?"

Keelan shrugged. "Once I realized she had some skill, I wanted to see how much she knew." His eyes flicked to me. "How long have you been training?"

"Almost a year."

His brows shot up. "Jiu-jitsu?"

I nodded. "I'm sorry if I hurt you," I said with a shaky voice.

Having noticed, Keelan quickly got to his feet and held his hand out to me with concern etched around his eyes. "It's okay, Shiloh. I'm not hurt."

That was a relief. I took his hand and let him pull me to my feet. I quickly brushed off the dirt sticking to my leggings and the sleeve of my jacket.

Colt scooped up the bag of soil and threw it over his shoulder. "Where do you want it?"

I pointed toward the porch. "Next to the steps, please."

Creed and Keelan grabbed the remaining two bags from my trunk and followed Colt.

"What are you planting?" Keelan asked.

"Flowers," I said, shutting my trunk and pocketing my earbuds. The three of them aligned the bags next to the steps. "Thank you."

Keelan brushed dirt off his hands. "No problem." He eyed my running attire. "Have you eaten yet?"

"Not yet," I replied.

"Perfect. You can come out to eat with us," Keelan said.

The twins frowned at their older brother, giving me the impression that they didn't want me to come.

"I don't want to impose—"

Colt's frown dropped as he looked at me. "You won't be imposing. Knox is the cook in the family, but he's working late tonight. The three of us have to fend for ourselves."

"Plus, we need to make it up to you for making breakfast for us twice this week," Keelan added.

I glanced at Creed to see if he was alright with me going.

He gave a slight shrug. "We were thinking about going to this diner down the road. They have good burgers."

A burger sounded amazing. "Do I have time to take a quick shower?"

"Of course," Keelan said. "Forewarning, though, Creed gets grumpy when he's hungry."

Creed went to punch Keelan in the arm, but Keelan easily dodged and pulled Creed into a headlock. Colt sighed at the both of them and I chuckled as I headed inside.

I took the world's fastest shower. I only had time to smear on some foundation and apply mascara. After running a comb through my wet hair, I braided it to the side. I threw on jean shorts, a black T-shirt, and tennis shoes. On the way out the door I grabbed my purse and sweatshirt. I slid into the latter as I walked next door.

Creed was the one to answer after I knocked on their door. His eyes roamed over me with a look of irritation. "It's hotter than hell out. Lose the sweatshirt."

"No."

Creed held out his hand. "Just take it off."

"Whoa, what are you asking her to take off?" Keelan asked, appearing behind Creed with Colt. They looked from Creed to me.

Colt seemed to pick up on what we were arguing about right away. "Leave her be, Creed. It makes her feel comfortable."

Creed ignored his twin and didn't remove his stern gaze from me. "No one is going to say shit about your scars and if they did, I'd kick their ass."

"Why would she need you to kick someone's ass? She can clearly do it herself," Keelan stated. His flattery was definitely good for the ego.

I held Creed's stare as I debated. He was right about it being hot. Sweat was already rolling down my spine. With each passing day I lived here, wearing athletic jackets and sweatshirts was making me more miserable.

Without backing down from our stare-off, Creed added, "You've got to stop caring about what other people think, Shi."

Hearing my name shortened by someone other than Logan did something to my heart. Woke it up, maybe? Sure, it beat fast when I was scared, and it hurt when I was sad. But I couldn't remember the last time I'd felt the warmth of happiness. Shayla had been the first to call me Shi. As a baby, she hadn't been able to fully say *Shiloh*. Thinking it was cute, my parents and Logan had adopted the nickname as well.

Creed was right. I needed to stop caring what other people thought. Knowing I had him and Colt in my corner made the decision easier. I slid my purse off my shoulder and held it out to him. He took it and I shed my sweatshirt. Keelan's gaze roamed over my scars with a schooled expression. I battled with myself to not care—to ignore the heavy weight of his eyes. Creed saved me from my overwhelming nerves by pulling my focus back to him. He plucked my sweatshirt from my hands, balled it up, and tossed it into their house.

I opened my mouth to tell him that I'd need it back. He cut me off by saying, "One down. Only fifty more sweatshirts to go." Then he handed me back my purse.

"Alright, let's go," Keelan said before I could tear into Creed, who had the audacity to smirk at me as we all walked over to Keelan's silver Jeep Wrangler.

The diner had a fifties theme, and all the waitresses were wearing poodle skirts. "Can't Help Falling in Love" by Elvis was playing in the background as we were seated at a half-circle booth. I slid along the rounded bench seat first and ended up sitting between Keelan and Colt.

"Oooh, I'm getting a milkshake," I said as I read over the menu. "Chocolate or strawberry? Hmm...I can't decide."

"How about you get one and I'll get the other and we'll share?" Colt suggested.

I beamed. "Okay."

Because Creed had said they had good burgers here, I ordered one and so did the guys. Once the waitress left after having taken our orders, Keelan looked at me. "So where did you train?"

"I didn't learn in a class setting," I replied.

"Where, then?" Creed asked.

"My uncle taught me in the Alaskan wilderness."

Keelan's curiosity was clearly piqued. "Have you thought about joining a class? We offer some at the gym."

"You work at Desert Stone, too?" I asked him.

Keelan gave me a confused look and opened his mouth to respond.

"Yes, Keelan works there, too," Creed said before Keelan could.

I felt like I was missing something. "That's nice that you all get to work together."

Keelan grinned at his brothers. "Yes. I suppose it is nice that we all get to work together. Knox works there, too."

"I've been there a few times now and I haven't seen any of you," I said.

Keelan turned his grin on me. "Knox and I were there the day you signed up. I spotted you when you were getting the tour with Becky, one of our personal trainers."

"Why didn't you tell us Shiloh had signed up?" Colt asked.

Keelan shrugged.

The waitress returned with our drinks. She set the strawberry shake in front of me and the chocolate in front of Colt. Keelan and Creed had ordered Cokes. Before the waitress could take off, Colt asked for extra straws. After she placed them on the table, Colt quickly unwrapped four straws and put two in each of our shakes. I couldn't help but smile as we went to take sips of our shakes.

"Mmm," I hummed. The strawberry was really good and creamy. After I was done taking a drink of my strawberry, Colt slid his chocolate shake over to me.

"Jealous you didn't get a shake to share with Shiloh?" I heard Keelan ask Creed.

I glanced over at Creed to see him glaring at his older brother. "Shut up," he grumbled.

Keelan just smirked.

9

Sunday, I went to the gym when I knew the twins were working. I spotted Keelan the moment I walked inside. He was talking to another employee near some of the weight machines. I had a feeling the other employee might have been a personal trainer by how buff he was, and he also wore the same dark navy polo with the Desert Stone Fitness logo on the breast pocket that all the other employees wore. Keelan, on the other hand, wasn't wearing a polo. He was wearing a black gi.

As I went to pass him, heading toward the locker room, he saw me. "Shiloh!"

I stopped walking. He quickly parted ways with his coworker and walked over to me. I smiled. "Look at you," I said, gesturing to his gi.

Keelan put his hands on his hips and glanced down at his outfit. "I'm filling in for another instructor who's out sick today. They teach a jiu-jitsu class for beginners and it's about to start if you want to join?"

I adjusted the strap of my gym bag on my shoulder. "I'd love to, but I think I'm a little too advanced for a beginner's class."

"How advanced do you think you are?"

I winced. "I'm not entirely sure."

"Hmm." He appeared to contemplate something. "If you truly want to take some classes, I could set aside some time to work with you to determine the best placement for you."

"Really?" I beamed, beyond thrilled.

"Yeah. Let me look over my schedule and I'll text you?"

"Sure."

"Great. I have to get to that class. I'll talk to you later," he said, and we parted ways.

I locked up my gym bag before starting my stretches by the indoor boxing ring. I did some lunges with side bends, then worked on my quads and hamstrings. As I was bent over touching my toes, two sets of shoes came into view. I had a feeling I knew whose feet they belonged to.

"You shouldn't be allowed to stretch in public," Creed said.

"What?" I stood up straight. As soon as I saw them, or should I have said what they were wearing, I gaped. "You both look adorable!"

And they did. Both of them had on the navy Desert Stone polo with black pants. A couple of guys stretching a few feet away chuckled. Creed, who was already frowning, folded his arms over his chest. Colt scrunched his nose.

"What?" I asked again.

"Guys don't like to be referred to as adorable," Colt explained.

Oh. "Would you have preferred handsome?"

"Or hot," Colt supplied at the same time Creed said, "Or sexy."

I snorted. "Noted."

Creed's frown lessened. "Are you planning on going up to the track?"

I nodded.

He held out his hand. "Jacket."

My stomach dropped. I was only wearing a sports bra underneath. The scars on my arms, I could suck it up and deal with the stares. It was the scars on my stomach and shoulder I refused to have people gawk at. I had been lucky so far that the guys hadn't asked how I'd gotten the others, but if they saw the ones on my stomach, they'd ask. How could they not? "I can't take off my jacket."

"You'll overheat," Creed argued.

"I *can't* take it off, Creed."

"Why?" Colt asked.

I sighed and stepped closer to them. "I'm only wearing a sports bra underneath. I'm not comfortable running around in just that."

They both stared at me, surprised, then Creed said, "I'll be right back," before walking away. I gave Colt a questioning look and he shrugged.

Creed returned pretty quickly with a navy T-shirt that had *Desert Stone Fitness* written on the front. He held it out to me. "You can wear this while you run."

I took the shirt. "You can't just give this to me, Creed. I need to pay for it."

"We'll take care of it," Colt assured.

I looked back and forth between them. "Are you sure?"

Colt grabbed me by my shoulders. He turned me around to face the locker rooms. "Yup, go get changed and we'll see you after your run."

I returned to the locker room and replaced my athletic jacket with the Desert Stone T-shirt. It fit perfectly. After locking up my jacket, I headed up to the track.

I ran for a little over three hours. To cool down, I walked one more lap. Movement to my right caught my eye and I glanced to see there was a good-looking guy walking next to me. He was tall and had, despite being a little sweaty, silky brown hair. He smiled at me, revealing a dimple. I pulled out one of my earbuds.

"Are you training for a marathon?" he asked me.

I was breathing heavily but I still managed to get out a, "No."

"Really? I think you should consider it. You ran for a long time."

Did that mean he'd been watching me the entire time? I gave him a tight smile.

"I'm training for a half marathon that's next month and I'm hoping I'll be ready for the full one by next year," he told me, and he continued to follow and talk to me even as I veered off the track toward the cubbies, where people kept their water bottles. I scooped up my bottle and began chugging it.

"I'm Jacob, by the way," he said, holding out his hand.

I didn't want to be rude and not shake his hand, but something about this guy didn't sit right with me. He was coming on too strong.

"Shiloh," a deep, rumbly voice said. I turned and to my utter surprise, I found Knox standing by the stairs. He was wearing the same Desert Stone polo as the twins, but with khaki dress pants and black dress shoes. His hands were in his pockets and he held a cold expression as he looked from Jacob to me. "It's time to go."

I was slightly unsure whether he was kicking me out or giving me an escape. Either way, I was relieved. To be polite, I said goodbye to Jacob and scurried over to Knox. He stepped out of the way so I could go down the stairs. Once back on the main floor, I turned to face him. His attention was fully on me. Gosh, he was intense and seemed even bigger up this close. He made me feel incredibly small as he stared down at me.

"Thank—"

"Colt and Creed are waiting for you at the front desk," he cut me off, and then he walked away.

I tried not to scowl at his back. Colt had warned me that Knox was a thousand times pricklier—my words, not Colt's—than Creed.

Air from a vent directly above me blew over my exposed neck

and arms, giving me goosebumps and reminding me that I was soaked with sweat. I quickly grabbed my stuff from the locker room and headed for the front desk. Colt and Creed were sitting behind it. They had changed out of their uniforms and were now wearing T-shirts and basketball shorts.

As I approached, I saw the pretty blonde receptionist sitting with them blush and laugh at something Colt had said. Creed spotted me first and got to his feet. "All done?"

Colt got up next. Both him and Creed slung their gym bags on their shoulders and made their way around the desk.

I nodded.

"Good, let's go eat," Creed said as they came to stand next to me.

I gaped at him. "Can you not see me? I'm soaked and I'm pretty sure I stink."

"We can stop at home real quick for you to shower," Colt said before his twin could argue.

Thank goodness because I really did stink. "Alright, what are you buying me for dinner?"

"Buying?" Creed scoffed. "Who said we were buying?"

I grinned and started for the exit. "Well, since you didn't give me any say in the matter..."

Colt chuckled. "She's got us there." He gave a small wave to the receptionist, who had been watching us. "Have a good night, Stephanie."

"You too!" she said enthusiastically.

Once outside, I glanced at Colt. "I think she likes you."

His brows rose. "Stephanie?"

Creed snorted. "Colt isn't the one she likes."

"Yeah, she's had it bad for Knox for a couple of years now," Colt said.

"Really? She blushed when talking to you," I pointed out.

They both laughed. "You blush all the time," Creed said.

"That's because I'm shy," I grumbled as my cheeks scorched.

Creed gestured to my face, laughing harder. "You're like an innocent cherry tomato."

My mouth fell open slightly as I gawked at the both of them. Were they making fun of my height? I might have only been five-four, but that wasn't that short. I wasn't going to even attempt to decipher the innocent part.

"Whatever," I grumbled and tried to veer off toward my car.

Colt grabbed my hand and pulled me back to them. "We think it's adorable that you blush."

I frowned. "I understand your reasoning for not wanting to be referred to as adorable."

"Would you prefer hot?" Colt asked and Creed followed with, "Or sexy?"

Even though they were teasing me, I couldn't stop myself from laughing no matter how hard I tried.

10

I had gone to the twins' practice on Monday. I'd been impressed. They had been so fast, they'd soared through the water like torpedoes. I wanted to go to their practice today, but I had some errands to run, like grocery shopping. I was embracing my old love for cooking and there were a few recipes I'd seen on the Cooking Channel I wanted to try. I also needed stuff to make my lunches with. It wasn't that I had anything against what they served at the cafeteria, but a lot of their food was deep-fried and, I dared say, terrible. Yes, I was a food snob. Cafeteria food grossed me out, which was why I had bought a prepackaged sandwich my first day of school. I also avoided fast food like the plague as well. I didn't fault others who enjoyed fast food, like the twins, but I just couldn't. To me fast food was too salty, made with cheap and fatty cuts of meat—if it was real meat at all—and it was too greasy.

Colt had been bummed that I wasn't going to their practice. That had made me feel bad, which was how I had ended up promising to make him and his brothers the new lasagna recipe I was currently putting together. I shook my head, smiling at the memory, as I set down the last layer of pasta, ricotta mixture, and sauce.

I covered the lasagna with foil and put a sticky note on top with instructions to bake it at three hundred and fifty degrees for thirty minutes before eating. I also wrapped up some homemade garlic bread and Caesar salad. It was a complete dinner. Reaching into my pocket, I pulled out my phone.

Are you home? I texted Colt.

Pulling into the neighborhood.

After reading his reply, I scooped up their food and headed for the door. I was making my way down my driveway when the twins pulled up in Creed's black F-150 Raptor.

"How was practice?" I asked as they climbed out of the truck. Both had wet hair from their showers after spending the past couple hours in our school's giant pool. Colt took the food from my arms.

"Same old shit," Creed grumbled as he slammed his truck's door.

That didn't sound good.

Colt sighed. "Ignore him."

"Well, I hope you're hungry. This is the biggest tray of lasagna I've ever made. I'm sorry to say I stereotyped you boys. I kind of assumed you four are bottomless pits and I got worried I wasn't going to make enough."

"Is that why you sent Colt home with two huge containers of baked goods?" Creed asked.

He was talking about the day Logan had left. "Uh, no. I just made a lot and begged Colt to take most of it home. I would have been upset if it all went to waste. I was having a bad day and kind of went overboard with the baking."

Colt plastered on a smile. "It didn't go to waste. Between the four of us it disappeared quick." That was good to know. I'd had to throw most of my portion away. "Do you have plans for dinner?" Colt asked.

"I have my own small tray of lasagna in the fridge. I was just going to eat that and binge watch the Food Network."

"Why don't you eat with us?" Colt asked.

I looked to Creed. He didn't seem put off by the idea.

"Um…okay," I said, suddenly feeling nervous.

I followed them inside their house. Similar to my house, the front door opened to their living room. Theirs was almost twice as large as mine. They had a large leather sectional curved in front of the biggest flat-screen TV I'd ever seen mounted on the wall, which was surrounded by a giant entertainment center filled with gaming consoles, games, and movies. The whole setup screamed bachelor pad. Straight past the living room, there was the dining room and to the right of the dining room appeared to be the kitchen. There were hallways off of the left and right sides of the living room, giving me the impression that this house had a split floor plan.

I stuck close to Colt as he headed straight for the kitchen. On the way there, both guys tossed their backpacks on the dining table, which was already covered with clutter. Once inside the dining room, there was a direct view into a somewhat open kitchen. It was U-shaped with an island in the center. Their appliances were all black, the countertops were speckled tan granite, and the cabinets were espresso-colored wood.

Seeing my note on the top of the lasagna, Colt set the oven to three hundred and fifty degrees. Looking around, I was unsure what I should do. I'd never been to a guy's house before. I'd also never had friends who were guys, either. It wasn't like being over at a girl's house, and even though the guys were just as much my friends as a girl would be, it still felt different. Plus, our friendship was still new. "Is there something I can do? I can help clear the table."

Colt was leaning against the counter next to the oven while Creed was bent over the island, resting on his arms. Both were watching me as I internally freaked out. I was cursing my recluse lifestyle up until now. Mostly, I blamed Mr. X. It was my fear of him watching me and following me wherever I went that kept me home. When and if I had gone to the movies or walked around the mall with the few friends I'd had, I'd always gotten pictures of myself in the mail the next day with a disgusting letter telling me how beautiful I was and what he wanted to do to me.

"Are you nervous, Shiloh?" Colt asked.

I winced. "Yes."

Colt and Creed shared a look.

I picked at the end of my sleeve, in an attempt to busy myself. Today, I had worn a maroon, long-sleeved V-neck and dark blue, ripped jeans. "If you give me something to do, I'll feel better. Want me to set the table? Are your brothers eating with us?"

Colt walked over to me and put his hands on my shoulders. "Deep breath. There's nothing to be nervous about." He squeezed a little. His touch was calming. It was like his hands were sucking away my tension. "Besides, we don't really eat at the table." The oven beeped loudly, notifying us that it'd reached the set temp. Colt stepped away from me to put the lasagna in the oven.

"You guys don't sit down at the table for family dinner?" I asked.

Creed was silent as he watched us.

Colt shook his head. "No, we're a 'grab a plate and eat in front of the TV' type of family."

What a shame. They didn't know what they were missing. Then again, not everyone was the same. Everyone liked different things.

Creed pushed away from the island, scooped up their bags from the table, and disappeared down the hallway on the left side of the house.

"What time is your swim meet on Thursday?" I asked Colt.

"It starts at five. You're still coming, right?"

"Yup. I lost that bet with Ethan and have to flaunt my team spirit, remember?"

A slow and downright naughty smirk took over his face. "Oh, yeah. You have to be our personal cheerleader."

The way he looked should have been a sin. It made me feel like my stomach was full of anxious butterflies trying to fight their way out. I nodded. "I'm either going to embarrass the crap out of you guys or you're all going to have a good laugh. Either way, I might end up scarred for life."

Creed came back before Colt could say more and started clearing the clutter from the dining room table. He caught both Colt and I watching him. "You want to help me with this?" he asked Colt.

Appearing a little surprised, Colt began helping with clearing the table.

Creed then pointed at the cabinet next to the fridge. "There's plates in that cabinet and silverware in the drawer just below if you want to grab what we need to set the table."

I turned on my heel to do as he said, grateful to be put to work. It also allowed me to give him my back so I could hide my smile.

I assumed their brothers were going to join us and I collected five plates and five sets of silverware before carting it all over to the table. The three of us were setting the table when the front door opened.

"We're home!" Keelan shouted as he removed his gym bag from his shoulder and tossed it on the couch. Knox walked through the door next while going through a stack of mail.

"Good. Dinner's almost ready," Colt announced.

Both Keelan's and Knox's heads whipped in our direction. Their gazes immediately landed on me. Keelan smiled charmingly while Knox schooled his face to look impassive. It reminded me of the way Creed regarded Cassy.

"Hey, Shiloh," Keelan said and strutted into the dining room. He took in the set table before his eyes met Creed's and I could see the question pass between them.

My attention shifted to Knox, who slowly walked over after setting the mail down on a small table they had near the front door. He hadn't removed his eyes from me. I could tell he wasn't happy that I was there.

Colt brought in the lasagna and set it down in the middle of the table. He noticed Knox staring and frowned. "Shiloh was nice enough to make us dinner. We're going to all sit down at the table and eat like a *family*." He put extra emphasis on the word *family* and his tone was firm.

Both Knox's and Keelan's brows rose, clearly surprised. Keelan was the quickest to recover. "That sounds like a great idea. It smells amazing, Shiloh." He walked to the other side of the table and pulled out a chair.

Colt and Knox seemed to be caught in a stare-off. I looked at Creed, already forming an excuse to leave. He startled me a little by putting one hand on my shoulder and the other on my back. Pushing me forward gently, he steered me over to one side of the table, across from Keelan. He pulled out a chair and gestured for me to take a seat. I stiffly plopped my butt in the chair, while Creed sat in the seat next to me. I glanced over my shoulder at the two remaining brothers standing.

Knox sighed before walking over to the head of the table. "Thank you, Shiloh," he said tightly as he sat. Colt took a seat at the other head of the table, to my left.

"You're welcome. I hope it's good. I was trying a new recipe," I rambled. Everything was at the table—the salad, garlic bread, serving utensils. Creed was the first one to cut into the lasagna and to everyone's surprise he put the first piece on my plate. "Thank you," I mumbled. That seemed to break the ice of awkwardness and everyone started piling food onto their plates. Everyone's first bites had me grinning happily. More than one of the guys murmured that yummy *mmm* sound.

"How was practice today?" Knox asked the twins.

"Coach was up our asses the entire time," Creed answered. "It's like the rest of the swim team doesn't even exist."

I glanced at Creed. He sounded really pissed off. I guessed that was what he'd meant earlier by *same old shit*.

"Coach Reed always was an asshole," Keelan mumbled around his food.

"Are you guys coming to the meet Thursday?" Colt asked. Both Knox and Keelan nodded. "Good. Shiloh can sit with you."

"I promised to sit with Ethan," I said quickly. I didn't want his brothers to feel obligated.

"Are you dating Ethan?" Knox asked me.

His question appeared to blindside everyone at the table, because Keelan and the twins gaped at him. Again, Keelan was the quickest to recover, smirking as if he was privy to something the rest of us were not.

I shook my head. "No. Ethan is my friend. My obnoxious, doesn't-know-when-to-shut-up, womanizing friend."

Colt and Creed snorted.

Keelan outright laughed. "That sounds like Ethan. I bet his ego is suffering with you around."

Colt nodded. "You should have been there when they first met. She put him in his place before he could even introduce himself. Poor guy didn't know what to do."

"You're a senior?" Knox changed the subject, his attention fully on me.

"Yes," I answered.

"How old are you?"

"Eighteen."

"The house next door is your uncle's?"

Wow, this was feeling like an interrogation. Instead of feeling nervous, my hackles began to rise. What the heck was his problem? "No. I own it."

"You're still a child and still in high school," he said harshly.

"Why aren't you living with your uncle or another adult? It's not safe for someone as young as you to be on their own."

"Knox, that's none of your business," Colt snapped. I really liked that he defended me, but that didn't mean I wasn't capable of taking care of myself.

Knox shifted his attention to Colt. "It is my business because you're my business, especially if you're going to be bringing her around here."

I had often wondered why the four of them lived together and where their parents were. I hadn't asked the twins because I was afraid they'd ask about mine. Listening to Knox, I either figured they were deadbeats or had passed away like mine.

I understood where Knox was coming from. It wasn't easy to find that understanding under the cloud of my anger. If my sister were still alive, I had a feeling I'd be just as protective. Taking in a deep breath, I put a comforting hand on Colt's arm. I might as well get this over with.

"My uncle is a U.S. Marshal, and his current assignment requires him to travel a lot. He took something like a sabbatical last year to take care of me after my parents and sister died. Now that I'm eighteen, it was time for him to return to work. I didn't want to travel with him. I wanted to finish my last year of high school without interruptions. I don't live with another relative because I don't have anyone else. I chose to move to Arizona by closing my eyes and putting my finger on a map of the U.S. I wanted to move somewhere new because I wanted to start over and find a way to move on. I bought the house next door with my family's life insurance money. My birthday is July twenty-seventh. I've been a straight A student all my life. My favorite food is popcorn. I hate the color pink. I'm currently trying to quit smoking. I haven't had a cigarette in over a week. Only reason I picked up the disgusting habit was because my family had just died and drowning myself in alcohol and smoking seemed like better vices than drugs. I dyed my hair this strange color because my sister used to dye her hair wild colors all the time and it's my own way of honoring her. Plus, whenever I look in the mirror, for just a minute, I forget that it's me standing there." I looked to Colt, then Creed, who were wide-eyed. "I used to be a twin," I said, my voice just shy of a whisper.

I might have overwhelmed them with the information overload but once I'd gotten started, I hadn't been able to stop. It had felt good to vent, yet at the same time it had made me feel sick to my stomach. The table had gone dead silent. I stood from my chair while staring at the floor. "I hope you guys enjoy the rest of your dinner. Please excuse me, I have to go." No one tried to stop me as I left.

A few hours later, after a long steamy shower, I was relaxing on the couch in short pajama shorts and a tank without a bra. I had popcorn popping in the microwave and the gorgeous Bobby Flay barbecuing on the TV. This was how my evening should have started. The microwave beeped, signaling the popcorn was done. As I got up to head into the kitchen there was a knock at the door. Cautiously, I looked through the peephole. It was Colt and Creed.

I opened the door. Colt was the one standing right in front of the door with his hands in his pockets while Creed was off to the side, leaning on the railing surrounding my porch. They both looked apprehensive, but that unease lessened as both of their gazes tracked down my body. Glancing down, I was reminded of my lack of bra and the fact that my bottoms were practically booty shorts. *Crap.* I crossed my arms over my chest to somewhat cover up.

"We came to apologize. Knox is an asshole to everyone and when he wants to know something, things like tact go out the window. Not that I'm making excuses for him," Colt said, rubbing the back of his head. "I figured you had lost your parents. You had the look I've seen on myself and my brothers. It's why I haven't pried. Our mom passed away from cancer when Creed and I were six and our dad died in a car crash three years ago. Knox and Keelan took on the responsibility of taking care of us. They sacrificed a lot, and we were lucky to have them because I can't imagine going through that on my own."

I looked from him to Creed, who was quietly watching me. "You don't need to apologize," I said. "I get that Knox is looking out for you. That's what you do for the ones you love."

Colt nodded. "So we're still friends?"

I smiled. "Of course we're still friends."

His shoulders slumped. "Phew, that means I can do this." He grabbed my elbow, pulling me close to hug me.

My nose met the center of his chest. I inhaled. His scent was soft like clean linen and smooth like musk. My hands fisted the back of his shirt, absorbing how good his embrace felt. Then I remembered Creed was there. I turned my head to the side so I could see him and rested my cheek on Colt's chest. Creed tried to appear bored, but I could sense that wasn't the case. I let go of Colt's shirt with one of my hands and held it out to him. He stared down at it before his eyes jumped up to meet mine, frowning. *Just hold my hand, you jerk.* I eyed him challengingly.

As if it was the most inconvenient task in the world, he relented and put his hand in mine. I squeezed it lightly before the three of us released each other.

"Want to carpool with us tomorrow?" Colt asked.

I didn't know if it was his question or the hug, but the loneliness that weighed heavily on my heart seemed to lessen.

"Sure."

11

"HE SENT ME A VIDEO. IT WAS OF HER CHANGING IN HER BEDROOM. *That bastard sat right outside her window and watched my little girl. He's probably home jerking off to it right now. When are they going to catch this sick fuck?!" my dad yelled, followed by the sound of glass shattering.*

"Jonathan, please!" my mom hissed. "The girls will hear you."

Too late. We'd heard him when he'd come home, stumbling drunk. Shayla and I sat on the staircase listening as my parents talked in the kitchen.

"He left the video on the windshield of my car at work, Heather. What if someone else had grabbed it?"

My eyes stung and my shoulders shook from my silent sobs. When was this going to end? When was this monster going to leave me alone? Shayla's hand enveloped mine and she squeezed it tightly. I stared at her with apologetic eyes.

"What if we considered moving? I spoke to Logan again and he offered to help spirit us away or something—get us set up somewhere new," Mom suggested.

Shayla gasped, jerking back with surprise. Some of her cotton candy pink hair fell forward. Moving would be her worst nightmare. She loved her life here and would miss all her friends.

She glared at me. "If I hadn't bitched in public to my friends the next day about moving, Mr. X wouldn't have found out and slaughtered us a week later." Her voice became raspy toward the end and a red line appeared around her throat before blood sprayed out of it, soaking me.

My eyes ripped open and I sat up quickly. It was dark. The only light came from the TV, playing infomercials. *I'm safe*, I reminded myself.

I was in my living room. I had been sleeping there for the past couple of nights because I didn't want to wake Creed with my nightmares. I picked up my phone from the coffee table and saw it was three-thirty in the morning. It was going to be dark for another hour, not that it mattered. I was still going for a run. It being dark out just meant I needed to carry a gun. I still had that small holster Logan had given me and I'd make sure I had my anklet tracker. Hopping off the couch, I dashed into my room to get ready for a run.

I ran for three hours. I didn't pace myself like I normally did. I pushed myself until my muscles felt like they were going to explode. I relished the pain because it temporarily diminished the pain in my heart. I was paying for it now. My legs were killing me.

Today, I dressed in a jean skirt with a tucked-in, long-sleeved, black blouse. Underneath, I was wearing my favorite Superman panty and bra set. I wasn't the typical fan who collected the comics or action figures. Nope. I had a decent collection of shirts and pajama sets, but my obsession showed in the amount of superhero lingerie I owned. I was pretty sure I had a lingerie set to represent almost all the characters in the DC and Marvel universes. A lot of it had been special-ordered from online sites and adult sex stores, but all my sets were cute and tasteful. All I needed now was a phone booth and I could be Sexy Superman. *More like Stripper Superman,* I snickered to myself.

Walking out the front door, I was glad I'd decided to put my hair up in a ponytail today. I'd discovered this morning on my run that it had rained last night, and it was humid out. The smell of rain here was different. It smelled stronger and almost sweet. It was addictively good. The need to know why had pushed me to research it as I'd brushed my teeth this morning. Apparently Arizona had a desert bush called creosote that secreted an oil that smelled like sweet rain. When it rained, that oil wafted into the air, giving it an intense smell.

Trying my best not to limp, I made my way next door. All four of the Stone brothers were walking out the front door as I was walking up their driveway. I wasn't sure if it was the wet ground or the weakness in my legs, but my foot slipped forward and backward I fell. I yelped as one of my legs shot up in the air and I landed on my butt. "Ow," I groaned.

All four of them were there in an instant. Colt leaned down behind me and lifted me up to my feet from under my arms like I weighed nothing. "Are you okay?" Colt asked.

"Yeah. More embarrassed than anything. I think I just flashed everyone," I said as I pulled down my skirt.

"No," Colt said at the same time Keelan and Creed said, "Yes."

Keelan looked to Knox. "I have the sudden urge to binge watch all the Superman movies."

I blushed big time.

Creed shoved Keelan's shoulder in an attempt to defend me, but I could see him trying not to laugh.

Knox sighed at his brother, then looked at me. "You were walking funny."

"Uh, yeah. My legs hurt from my run this morning."

He gave me a single nod before looking to Keelan. "We need to get going."

I stiffly turned and winced with each step as Creed, Colt, and I walked over to Colt's blue Charger. "I'll sit in the back," I said, and I opened the door to the backseat. "Cheese and rice. Cheese and rice," I hissed repeatedly as I slid in.

The twins were both turned around in the front seat by the time I got in and were staring at me with matching perplexed expressions.

I sighed. "My mom always said a lady never swears. Because I'd been the good child who was too afraid to disappoint her, I learned how to be creative. The habit stuck," I explained.

Creed snorted before turning around.

"Do you want us to stop and get you something for the pain?" Colt asked, giving me a sympathetic look.

"I have ibuprofen in my bag. I'll take it after I buy a water bottle at school."

Creed leaned forward and I heard him unzipping his bag. He produced a water bottle and offered it to me.

I took it with a grateful smile. "Thank you." I had a feeling I'd proven myself worthy to Creed because he had been showing me his sweet side more and more lately.

"Admit it, you like her," I said as Ethan and I walked out of biology. I'd repeatedly caught Ethan staring at this girl, named Isabelle, who sat in the front row of our class.

"I don't know what you're talking about," he grumbled.

"Huh," I said as I studied him. What had happened to the boisterous and flirty Football God I'd come to know?

He gave me the side-eye. "What?"

"You *really* like her."

He sighed, obviously feeling embarrassed or exasperated with me. I was going with the former.

"Why haven't you asked her out?" I asked.

"I have. She turned me down," he admitted.

"Huh."

This time he looked at me fully. "Why do you keep doing that?"

"I'm surprised. When you asked her out, did you—"

A shoulder collided with mine. With my legs still being sore, I couldn't stop myself from falling into Ethan. Thankfully he caught me before I could hit the floor. The same couldn't be said for my textbook and folder.

The sound of girls giggling had me looking for the source. Amber and Sam were a few feet away, wearing matching evil smirks.

"Watch it, Troll," Amber said as she flicked back her platinum blonde hair before continuing on down the hall, arm in arm with Sam.

"What a bitch," Ethan said as he scooped up my stuff off the floor.

I couldn't have agreed more.

Going outside literally felt like stepping into an oven. As the day went on, the temperature reached over one hundred and ten degrees. In gym class, the coaches made us stay inside the gymnasium for safety and everyone was required to play volleyball.

"Shiloh is going to be on our team," I overheard Colt say.

I glanced up from where I sat on the bleachers retying my shoe. Colt was standing with Creed, Ethan, and two of their friends, Gabe and Daniel, discussing who would take what position. Daniel was the tight end on the football team with Ethan. Gabe was on the baseball team and was Cassy's cousin. I shouldn't have been surprised. They resembled each other, with the same tawny hair and honey-colored eyes. He hadn't been friendly either when Colt had introduced us. Being a jerk must run in the family.

Creed came up next to me and glared at my sweatshirt. Yes, I'd agreed that I shouldn't care what other people thought about my scars, but I hadn't found the courage to go without covering my arms at school yet. Thankfully Creed seemed to understand that. "How are your legs? Do you think you'll be up for this?" he asked, bringing my focus back to the volleyball game.

The stiffness in my legs had loosened up as the day had gone on. "As long as I'm not forced to run a mile, I think I'll be fine. But you should also know, I'm not the best volleyball player," I said as I got to my feet.

Creed shrugged. "Not everyone here is."

"Thanks for the pep talk," I deadpanned, which earned me a chuckle.

Our team faced off against another group of six students that included Cassy and her minion, Amber, who happened to be on the girls' volleyball team. *Great.*

I did my best to help from my position in the back center. Colt, Creed, and Daniel were in the front row. Ethan and Gabe flanked me in the back. As the game proceeded, both of our teams seemed to be evenly matched. Each time our opponents gained a point, Cassy would give Creed a taunting look from where she stood directly across from him on the other side of the net. Creed ignored her, which thoroughly pissed her off.

The game was neck and neck. The guys became really determined to win, especially Gabe. He was insanely competitive. He openly complained about me hitting the ball incorrectly and just now, we'd run into each other as we both tried and failed to hit the ball before it touched the ground.

"Next time just stay out of the way," he snapped at me.

"Gabe, relax," Colt snapped back at him.

"If she doesn't know how to play right, why is she even on our team?" Gabe snarled.

Creed whirled around and gave Gabe a disapproving look. "It's just a game. Quit being an ass."

I caught Cassy smirking. Amber leaned close and whispered in Cassy's ear. Cassy's smirk stretched to an evil smile and they got back into position to serve one last time. The final round would determine which team would win. The ball was hit back and forth, until Cassy tossed the ball straight up and Amber hit it over the net toward me. I put my wrists together, intending to go for the ball. A body slammed into me, knocking me to the floor. I hit the ground hard, landing on my left hip. Pain zapped from my hip bone down my thigh, making me whimper.

"Shiloh!" Colt ran over and knelt next to me. "Are you hurt?"

Biting my lip because I refused to cry, I shook my head, lying. Cassy and her friends laughed, pointing at me.

"What the hell is your problem?" Creed yelled at Gabe.

Gabe shrugged. "I told her to stay out of the way."

Before I could protest, Colt slid his arms under my legs and around my back. He lifted me with ease.

Fear of being dropped had me gripping his shirt. "I can walk."

"I have a feeling you can't," he said, anger seeping into his voice. Colt had always been kind, sweet, and the peacemaker. To hear his tone turn so cold left me stunned.

"I saw you go after her, Gabe, not the ball," I heard Ethan argue.

"You fucking shoved her?!" Creed yelled.

Colt set me on the bottom bench of the bleachers. "I'll be right back," he said tightly before heading back over to where Creed was now up in Gabe's face.

Gabe straightened his stance. "Get out of my fucking face." Then he shoved Creed.

Before Creed could react, Colt came up behind Gabe, jerked him around by his shoulder, and punched him in the face. The impact and force behind the punch made Gabe crumple to the ground.

"What the fuck!" Gabe roared and scrambled to get back up to his feet.

Colt shoved him back down and cocked his arm back to hit him again. Creed grabbed Colt from behind, locking his arms around Colt's. Colt struggled to get free as Creed pulled him away from Gabe. I jumped to my feet and winced when pain flared in my hip. I didn't think anything was broken. I was definitely going to have a nasty bruise, though.

Colt eventually stopped fighting once Creed and he were standing in front of me. "I'm good," Colt snapped, and Creed released him.

A whistle was blown, startling us all. Coach Dale, a tall, bald man who was one of the gym teachers as well as one of the coaches for the football team, stormed over. He looked from Gabe, who was climbing to his feet with the help of Cassy, to Creed and Colt. "What is going on over here?"

No one said anything.

I watched Colt's fists clench and unclench. His knuckles he'd used to hit Gabe with were bright red. Hesitantly, I reached out for his hand. I would've been lying if I'd said I wasn't nervous. The tips of my fingers lightly brushed over the back of his hand. He glanced down, then over his shoulder at me. I forced a small smile. He surprised me by wrapping his hand around mine and lacing our fingers together.

"Well?" Coach Dale pushed.

Cassy stepped forward. "Just a little accident on the court, Coach. Some players slammed into each other when trying to hit the ball."

Coach Dale eyed everyone skeptically. "Is that right?"

Everyone murmured in agreement.

Coach Dale shook his head. "Go to the nurse, Gabe. Get some ice on that cheek."

Gabe nodded and left, while rubbing his already swelling face.

Ethan came over to stand by us. "Are you okay?" he whispered to me.

"Yeah," I lied again.

Coach Dale blew into his whistle. "Put the balls away and go get changed! Class is over!"

Ethan left to help a few other students put the volleyballs away while everyone else made their way toward the locker rooms. Creed and Colt turned, catching me rubbing my hip gently with my free hand.

"Did you land on your hip?" Creed asked.

I quickly dropped my hand from my hip. "I'm fine. You don't have to worry—"

Colt squeezed my hand. He had yet to let it go. "You don't have to play it down, Shiloh," he said calmly. The anger in his voice was slowly receding. "If you're hurt, just tell us."

"I'm fine." I wasn't. Today had utterly sucked. It had started off bad and only proceeded to get worse. I wanted to go for a run. It was my escape and I really wanted to escape what I was feeling right now. With how badly my hip hurt, I knew that wasn't an option and wouldn't be for a while.

"No, you're not," Creed argued.

"Yes, I am." Why couldn't they let this go?

"Why are you lying?" Creed snapped.

"Because if I say it out loud, it makes it real," I snapped back.

"What?" they asked at the same time.

Frustrated, I rubbed my sternum. "I can't get hurt, alright? I just can't. Because if I do—if I truly get hurt—who would I call? Logan's on the other side of the country, therefore, I can't call him. So who would I call?" I shrugged with my arms out as my eyes filled with tears. "I don't have anyone. It's just me," I said bitterly. "And today—falling—was just another reminder of that." I was having a bad day and I had no one to talk to about it. I couldn't go vent to Shayla about Cassy and Amber and how terrible they were. And if I had broken my hip, I couldn't have called my mom or dad for help. The people I needed most—the people I relied on—were gone. I was on my own and today had rubbed my nose in that fact.

They both stared at me with stunned looks on their faces.

A couple of tears escaped and rolled down my cheeks as I glanced down at the floor, feeling mortified. They probably thought I was crazy. They didn't know that things had been building up, causing me to explode. They were seeing a girl completely overreacting after falling and getting hurt. "I'm sorry."

Colt stepped closer, bringing us chest to chest, or more accurately, my nose to his chest. He wrapped one arm around my lower back and released my hand to bring his up to cup the back of my head. "Don't apologize." His embrace tightened and my nose became buried in his chest.

Feeling the comfort his strong arms provided, I slowly began to calm, and my body loosened against him. I wrapped my hands around his waist and allowed a few more tears to leave my eyes.

"It's alright to tell us stuff, Shiloh," Colt said as his fingers began to knead the back of my neck. "I get that it hurts you to talk about your family, but you can't keep it all bottled up. You can talk to us and we'll listen."

I was happy he didn't think I was crazy, but was I that transparent?

"And you can call us," Creed said. Like I had yesterday, I turned my head, resting my cheek on Colt's chest so that I could see Creed. He was staring down at me with a tight expression. "If you ever get hurt, you can call us."

I sniffled. "Don't say that just because you feel sorry for me."

"I wouldn't have made an offer like that lightly," he assured.

A smile slowly stretched across my mouth. "Does that mean you like me?"

Colt's chest bounced as he chuckled.

Creed scoffed, slightly shaking his head. "Yeah, Shi, I like you." His admission gave me that warm feeling in my heart again.

I released a heavy sigh. "I landed on my hip," I finally admitted and pulled back from Colt. "It's not broken, but it hurts. I'm not going to be able to run for a while."

Colt took a step back. "Can you at least walk?"

"I think so," I said. Colt took a few more steps back and I walked to him with a limp.

"Why don't you go grab your stuff and we'll take you home?" Creed offered.

I shook my head. "You have swim practice. Your meet is tomorrow."

"So?" Creed drawled.

"Coach Reed will be pissed, but he won't bench us for the meet if that's what you're worried about," Colt said.

"You shouldn't miss practice because of me. I'll go and watch you, like we originally planned." With them driving to school today, we had already discussed me staying after to watch them practice.

Colt shook his head. "You're not going to sit on a metal bench for hours in pain."

I opened my mouth to argue.

"Shi, if you don't let it go, I'm going to throw you over my shoulder and carry you to the girls' locker room to get your shit," Creed threatened in a deep, firm voice.

It was two against one. I let out a long sigh and began limping toward the locker room to get my stuff.

12

Colt parked his Charger in front of my house. After I slowly climbed out of the car, Creed scooped me up. Having experienced being carried already once today, I wasn't as startled this time around. I still hooked my arms around his neck, holding on tight as we headed toward my house.

Colt walked behind us, carrying my backpack. "Are your keys in your bag?"

"Front pocket. I have an alarm," I warned Colt. I wasn't supposed to tell anyone the code. I hesitated for a second as I debated, then remembered I could always change it later if I had to and told him the code.

As Colt pulled my keys from my bag, Keelan's Jeep pulled up their drive.

"Why aren't you at practice?" Knox asked loudly as he and Keelan climbed out.

"Here we go," Creed grumbled under his breath, then shouted over his shoulder, "We didn't go!"

Colt dashed ahead of us to unlock my front door.

Knox slammed the Jeep's door and stormed around it to stand along the oleander bushes that separated our properties. "Please tell me you didn't ditch practice so one or both of you could try and get between Shiloh's legs?"

My breath caught in my throat as my cheeks began to burn. Creed paused at the top of the porch steps, his jaw clenching. He started to turn us slowly to face Knox. With the rage burning in his eyes, I knew he was about to explode on him, and it wasn't going to be pretty.

Colt's hand landed on Creed's shoulder. "Take Shiloh inside. I'll deal with this." Colt didn't wait around for a reply and pounded down the porch steps. Creed listened to his twin and carried me inside.

We were only a few steps inside when we heard Colt growl, "That was fucked up, Knox. Even for you."

"You two aren't being smart," Knox growled back.

"Why? Because you think we skipped practice to get laid?" Colt snapped. "Way to fucking assume the worst, as usual. Shiloh is our friend and—"

"I've seen the way you both look at her," Knox cut him off.

Creed's arms tightened around me. I hesitantly glanced at him. His jaw was clenched, and his gaze angrily bored into the floor.

"Alright, that's enough," Keelan said, his voice taking on a serious tone. "Colt, why did you and Creed skip practice?"

"A guy at school shoved Shiloh and she got hurt," Colt answered.

"Is she alright?" Keelan asked.

I didn't get to hear Colt's response. Creed hiked me up to restrengthen his hold of me. "Where do you want me to take you?" he asked, his tone coming out sharp.

I was dying to change out of my jean skirt and into some loose shorts. I pointed to the hall just off the living room. "In my bedroom."

I felt the tension ease a little from his body. Looking at his face, I caught the corner of his mouth curling up. "Oh, really?"

I frowned, confused. "Yes. I really need to get out of this skirt."

Creed chuckled as he headed for my room.

I replayed what we both had said in my head and my blush that had yet to fully recede flared again. "Oh." Then I ended up chuckling, too.

Creed carried me down the hall to my room. He gently set me down on my bed. As his eyes roamed around my room, I lay back across my bed with a sigh. I didn't have much that was personal in my room besides a few knickknacks and my jewelry box sitting on top of my dresser. My furniture in my room was espresso-colored and the linens on my bed were teal and white. I hadn't gotten around to putting my stamp on the space yet.

"You don't have any pictures," Creed pointed out.

No, I didn't. I wasn't allowed to have anything out that might give away my true identity. The few pictures I did have had been approved by Logan and they were only on my phone.

"I haven't gotten around to hanging any yet," I lied, staring up at the ceiling. I hated lying to him. I let out a heavy sigh and I felt fingers touch my bare knee.

"Are you alright? Is it your hip?"

I internally grimaced. Shayla had always said I was a crappy liar. I never could master a poker face. I looked down where my legs hung off the side of the bed. Creed was standing there staring down at me. I shook my head. Before he could push further, I changed the subject. "Knox was really upset."

This time Creed sighed and plopped down on the bed next to me. He lay on his side, propped up on one elbow, his hand supporting his head. "He'll get over it."

I met Creed's aquamarine eyes. My breath hitched as his fingers brushed a few stray hairs away from my forehead that had escaped my messy bun. "Your roots are brown."

I leaned in close and whispered, "That's because I have brown hair."

He rolled his eyes. "No shit, smart ass. What I meant to say is that I didn't know you had brown hair."

I laughed and he watched me with a tiny smile.

"You're so beautiful when you laugh," he said, and with a featherlike touch, he ran his finger from my temple to the corner of my mouth. "Your whole face lights up." His eyes dropped to my mouth and he slowly trailed his finger along my bottom lip. "Your smile is the best part."

Butterflies went wild in my stomach.

"Then we should make her laugh more often," a voice said.

Creed dropped his finger from my lip and we both looked toward the source and found Colt leaning against the doorframe. His eyes took us in, lying next to each other, with an unreadable expression.

"I should let you get changed," Creed said as he sat up and clambered off the bed.

"Would you mind grabbing me a pair of pajama shorts from my dresser? They're in the second drawer," I asked Creed, as I sat up slowly. The movement caused a little discomfort. Scooting to the edge of the bed made me hiss.

Creed made his way over to my dresser and as I saw him start to pull the second drawer open, I realized my mistake. "I meant the third drawer!"

I was too late. Creed pulled the drawer all the way open and gaped down at all my superhero lingerie. I had forgotten that I'd had to move my pajamas down a drawer when I'd realized one drawer for my underwear wouldn't suffice. And if I'd thought the situation couldn't get any worse, Creed plucked one of my Spider-Man bras out and began looking it over.

"Creed, you can't take shit out of a girl's underwear drawer and look at it like a creeper," Colt admonished.

Creed looked at his brother with a stupid grin. "Shiloh has a naughty collection of superhero lingerie."

That took the frown Colt had right off his face and replaced it with a look of intrigue.

I was undoubtedly red as a freaking tomato. "It's not naughty. They're cute!"

Creed laughed and turned back to the drawer. Without shame he began rummaging through it. "She's got Captain America, Batman, Robin…"

Colt took a step toward his brother with a torn expression.

"Creed, stop going through my underwear!" I yelled and threw a decorative pillow from my bed at him. "How would you feel if I went through yours?" The small pillow bounced off his shoulder and dropped to the floor.

Creed briefly glanced at the pillow, unfazed. With a sigh, Creed closed the drawer and opened my pajama drawer. "Feel free to go through my underwear all you like. They're all in the top drawer of my dresser," he shot over his shoulder. Once he found the Batman pajama set I'd worn that first morning I'd cooked him breakfast, he held both the top and bottom out to me. He smirked. "But my underwear isn't nearly as sexy as yours."

Feeling flushed from head to toe, I snatched my PJs from his hand. "Thank you."

"After you change, you should really get some ice on that hip," Colt said.

I nodded. "I have a few ice packs in the freezer."

"Let's order some food and watch a movie," Creed suggested.

Colt looked to me. "Chinese or pizza?"

"Ooh! I want Chinese food." I beamed.

"It's a date," Creed said and pushed Colt out into the hall before shutting the door behind them.

A date? I mused to myself, then shook my head and began changing.

〜

A swim meet was exactly like I'd pictured it would be. Bleachers on each side of the gigantic pool, filled with families and fellow students here to show their support. Ethan had been right. The swim team was a big deal. There were a lot of people here.

Walking along our school's side of the pool. I scanned the crowd for Ethan. When I spotted him two rows up, I noticed he was already sitting with Keelan and Knox. All three of them saw me at the same time. Ethan took in my appearance and threw his head back laughing. I put my hands on my hips and cocked an eyebrow at him.

Ethan stood up. "Do a twirl, Shi."

Before I humored him, I unzipped my black sweatshirt and slid it down to the crease of my arms, so he could see the back of my shirt. As I twirled, he laughed harder.

I was dressed to the nines as a cheerleader, colors and all. I'd lost a bet and now it was time to pay up. Last week, I had stopped by the school's student-run store to purchase our swim team's T-shirt and a jersey for the football team. Both were dark blue with gray lettering. The swim team's shirt had the team's name and mascot on the front. I'd enhanced it by turning it into a crop top. On the back, across the shoulders, I'd ironed on gray letters, spelling out *Team Stone*—the twins' last name. I'd paired the shirt with a high-waisted, pleated miniskirt I'd had to order online. The color was the same shade of dark blue and had a single gray strip an inch from the bottom. I'd put my hair up in pigtails. They curved out on the upper sides of my head with black, blue, and silver ribbons tied around my hair ties. The strands of the ribbons hung along with my hair.

"What's the verdict?" I asked.

Ethan gave me a smile. "Adorable, yet sexy."

I snapped my fingers, mocking disappointment. "Darn, I was hoping to embarrass. I guess I'll have to try harder for your game tomorrow."

Ethan chuckled. "I can't wait."

I made my way up the bleachers slowly because my hip was still hurt. Ethan stood, offering the spot between him and Keelan.

"Hi," I greeted Keelan and Knox shyly before taking a seat. They both were staring at me. Keelan was looking at me all over, probably taking in my outfit, and Knox...well, he was frowning. I wondered if he was still upset about yesterday.

"Shi, do you want to fix your sweatshirt?" Ethan asked as he pulled up the sleeve that had fallen down to my wrist, revealing my long, nasty scar on my inner arm.

That drew Keelan's and Knox's attention. Keelan had already seen my scars, but Knox hadn't—at least until now. He might have just gotten a glimpse of the scar before Ethan could cover it.

I tried not to feel embarrassed. In fact, I forced it down with all my might. I didn't want to ruin this evening with my insecurities. I give Ethan a grateful smile. "Thanks."

He grinned back. "I'm assuming you're wearing a jersey to my game. Did you put my name on it, too?"

"Not exactly." I pulled out my phone. "Since you pretty much figured it out, I might as well show you." I went to my pictures and found the one with the dark blue jersey. I showed him my phone.

He burst out laughing. "No, you didn't!"

Yes, I did. Instead of his name on the back of the jersey, I'd ironed on *Football God* over his number on the back.

"This is the best thing I've ever seen." He beamed.

"Did you invite Isabelle to the game?" I asked him. Isabelle was the girl I had caught him staring at in biology yesterday. We hadn't been able to talk about her again until today. I'd tried to give him advice and suggested that he invite her to his game.

"Yeah, but I don't know if she'll show up," he said.

"You didn't act like a horndog when you asked her, did you?"

"I was respectful," he deadpanned. "She said she would think about it."

"Did she say anything else?"

He shook his head.

I bumped his shoulder with mine. "She'll be there."

He shrugged, not completely convinced.

Ethan was a sweetheart when he wasn't acting like a woman-izing fool. She would be a fool not to show.

"Do you want some popcorn, Shiloh?" Keelan asked me.

Surprised, I turned to look at him, then over his shoulder to see a student selling popcorn and drinks while walking up and down the steps of the bleachers. "Yes, please. I love popcorn."

Keelan waved at the student and bought two slim, red-and-white-striped cartons of popcorn and a water. I reached into my pocket to get him some money. Keelan put a hand over mine, stopping me. "I got it," he said, handing me a carton of popcorn.

"Thank you." Popcorn was my favorite. It was my go-to when I was sad, happy, or bored.

The meet started shortly after that and everyone really got into it. Even I was cheering on the twins as they soared through the water. They kicked butt and smoked the competition. Ethan had to leave when the meet was over. Keelan, Knox, and I stayed behind, sitting on the bleachers waiting for the twins to come out of the locker room after showering.

Mostly everyone had cleared out, except for a few waiting like us. Creed walked out of the locker room first, Colt following closely behind. I hopped up from my seat. Ignoring the slight zap of pain in my hip, I made my way down the bleachers to the ground next to the pool. Colt grinned at me and Creed smirked at my appearance.

"That was exciting. Good job, guys," I gushed.

Creed held out his hand. "Take the sweatshirt off."

I looked at Colt. He had his hand over his mouth in an attempt to hide his smile as he stared down at me. I glanced around quickly out of habit before sliding my sweatshirt off and handing it over to Creed. I did a slow twirl, like I'd done for

Ethan. By the time I completed my turn, both were smiling broadly but didn't comment as to what they thought.

I put my hands on my hips. "Ethan said I looked adorable."

"He also said sexy," Keelan said as he approached with Knox.

I scrunched my nose at that and went to grab my sweatshirt.

Creed held it out of my reach. "No way are you covering up."

I glanced at Knox. He was glaring down at my wrists. I had the strong urge to hide them.

Colt grabbed my hand, lacing our fingers, and pulled me along toward the exit. "Ethan texted me saying I'm going to be jealous when I see your outfit for tomorrow. What did he mean by that?"

"I don't know why he would say that. All I did was show him a picture of the jersey I'm going to wear. My phone is in one of my sweatshirt's pockets if you want to see it."

Before I could even finish telling them that, Creed was pulling my phone out from my sweatshirt he was carrying as he followed. He tapped and swiped at my phone. "Why does it say Football God?" Creed asked.

Colt stopped walking. "What? Let me see?"

Creed handed over the phone to Colt. He looked at the picture for a minute before laughing. "It's a joke between them. Don't read into it. Ethan is just trying to stir shit up," Colt told his brother.

"Are we going to be let in on why Shiloh is dressing like a cheerleader?" Knox asked.

Creed and Colt stared at their brother and then at each other. "No," Creed replied.

I shook my head at them. "Don't be mean."

Creed's brows shot up. I was just as surprised as he was that I'd defended Knox.

"I lost a bet," I told Knox.

Him and Keelan wore the same *ah* look, like the twins placing bets was a regular occurrence.

The five of us made our way to the parking lot. Colt's Charger was parked right up in front and Keelan's Jeep was parked in the back of the lot. I was among the unlucky bunch who'd had to park in the neighborhood next to the school because the lot had been overflowing with cars by the time I'd shown up.

"Where's your car, babe?" Colt asked, looking around the lot.

I didn't react to him calling me *babe*. I liked it. "I had to park in the neighborhood down the street."

Colt squeezed my hand. "We'll drive you to pick it up."

"You don't—"

"It's dark out and you shouldn't be walking alone," he said in that firm tone.

I wasn't going to point out that I ran when it was dark out most of the time. Then again, I took a gun with me when I ran that early. All I had on me now was my tracker tucked in my sock. I didn't argue and climbed into the backseat of his Charger. Like his new term of endearment, I liked that he worried about me.

13

"SHILOH, A WORD," MR. X SAID AS I TRIED TO DASH OUT OF THE classroom.

I squeezed my textbook tightly in front of my chest as I spun on my heel, with a polite smile plastered on my face. "I have to catch the bus, Mr. X," I said, hoping he'd let me leave. Mr. X made me feel...unsettled. I didn't like the way he watched me or found ways to touch me. Shayla had laughed it off when I'd tried to talk to her about it. She'd said that I was imagining things—that there was no way our high school's beloved English teacher would be interested in a freshman girl.

"It won't take long," he said from where he sat behind his desk.

I stayed rooted where I was standing near the exit. My panic built and built with each student that left the class.

After the last student exited the classroom, Mr. X stood from his desk and walked over to the door. He toed the door stopper out from under the door and I watched, trying to stay calm as the door closed with a snick.

Mr. X put his hand on my lower back, making me jump a little, and ushered me further into the classroom. His hand slid down slightly as we walked. When his fingers flexed over my butt, bunching up the skirt of my uniform in the process, I quickly tried to step to the side and out *of his reach. His hand locked around my upper arm and yanked me around until my backside met the front of his desk.*

"Why are you shying away from me?" he asked, stepping close and trapping me between him and his desk. He put his hands on my shoulders and ran them down my arms. "We've shared so many moments. Are you mad I didn't give in to you sooner? I've needed to be discreet in showing my affection for you. No one else will understand our need for one another."

Tears filled my eyes as he yanked my textbook, my only shield, from my arms and tossed it to the floor. "Mr. X, please," I pleaded, tears rolling down my cheeks. My whole body shook with fear.

"Shh, it's alright. I'm giving in. I can't take that look of longing you've been giving me any longer." He stepped even closer, molding the front of his body with mine. "I'm going to give us what we both want." Then he rubbed his erection in his pants against my stomach and I felt the urge to vomit.

I didn't know what he was talking about. I'd never given him a look. "No," I said firmly as I tried to shove him back.

He grabbed me by my wrists with a chuckle and forced me to turn around. "Now, Shiloh, if you're going to be naughty and play hard to get, I might have to punish you." He held my hands together behind my back tightly and forced me to bend forward over his desk. His foot kicked my feet apart.

I cried out as he lifted my skirt over my hips. "Please stop!"

Please, someone save me!

Feeling defeated, I took a seat on the curb along the street in front of my house. I was tired and my hip was still sore. The bruise I had was large and ugly. As much as I wanted to run, my body was protesting. I itched to have a cigarette. It'd been weeks since I'd last had one and I was determined never to smoke one again. I had school in a few hours. So drinking was out of the question. My nightmares were only getting worse. Maybe it was time to go back to therapy. I quickly shoved that idea away. Therapy was the last thing I wanted to do.

My nightmare hadn't woken me up too early this morning. The sun was already peeking over the mountains. I supposed I could go back inside and watch some TV.

"No marathon today?" someone said.

I glanced over my shoulder and found Knox standing behind me. He was holding a coffee mug. With his disheveled hair and sleepy eyes, he appeared to have just rolled out of bed. He was wearing black basketball shorts that hung low on his hips and a white tank that showed off his bulky muscles. The Stone brothers had the uncanny ability of looking gorgeous after just waking up. I hadn't seen Keelan yet, but I was sure he was just as blessed. It was kind of unfair.

I looked away. "My hip is still sore." Silence fell between us and I slipped into a daydream while staring out into the street.

"Want some breakfast?" he asked.

I peered back over my shoulder, a little skeptical I'd heard him right.

"The twins don't normally like to get out of bed for another hour or so, but when it comes to you, they make an exception." He was referring to the times the twins had come over for breakfast after I had woken Creed with my nightmares. "You can have the privilege of waking them."

"Are you afraid of waking your little brothers?" I taunted with a smirk.

His eyes narrowed slightly. "No."

"Hmm, sounds to me that you want to have a family breakfast and you need me to be the sacrificial lamb that has to wake the two sleeping demons," I teased. I knew it probably wasn't a good idea to poke the bear, but I was feeling testy this morning.

"Is that a yes?" he asked, trying to sound bored.

"Yes," I said and bit my lip in an attempt not to smile. I stood stiffly from the curb and brushed the back of my purple leggings. My top was a matching sports bra I'd covered with a dark gray athletic jacket. I followed Knox inside and into the kitchen.

"There's coffee, if you want some. Mugs are in the cabinet above the coffee maker and there's creamer in the fridge," Knox said while pointing to where things were before opening the fridge to pull out eggs, milk, and bacon, then headed over to the pantry and grabbed pancake mix.

Coffee sounded wonderful. I busied myself by fixing myself a cup. They had vanilla creamer in the fridge. I grabbed that. I was stirring a little bit of creamer into my coffee when Keelan zombied into the kitchen, rubbing his eye.

I had to fight to keep my face blank. There was nothing I could do about the blush that was working its way up the back of my neck. He was in red shorts, but he was shirtless. I tried not to stare at all his golden skin, chiseled muscles, and *oh my,* he had a lot of ink. There were tattoos sprinkled on his chest, ribs, hips, and his one arm that I already had seen. Only the upper portion of his other arm had a few tats.

Once he finished rubbing his eye, he noticed me. His brows shot up with surprise as he took me in, standing there trying not to gawk, before he looked at his brother. A Cheshire grin pulled at the corners of his mouth. "Good morning, Shiloh."

"Good morning," I said before taking a sip of my coffee. I sighed softly as the liquid caffeine went down. I hoped it kicked in soon. My body needed the boost. I took one more sip, then set my mug down on the counter and turned toward Knox, who was opening the bacon. "Would you like some help?"

His intense brown eyes met mine for a moment. "I just need you to be my sacrificial lamb."

Knox was an intimidating creature. He was obviously a "take me or leave me" type of individual like Creed. Even though he had shown me repeatedly how much of a jerk he could be, I had a feeling it was a shield. Like Creed, Knox had a worthiness test. I wouldn't be worthy in Knox's eyes based on my character, which was how Creed decided. Knox challenged and pushed at people with his jerkish behavior. It was only a guess, but I believed that by not backing down, I might eventually get past Knox's shields to see his good side. I refused to believe that someone who had taken on the responsibility of raising his brothers after their parents had died and helped raise them to be kind and wonderful was a bad person.

"Point me in the right direction and I'll go wake up the Sleeping Beauties," I said.

Keelan chuckled. "Good idea, sending her to wake them. She has a better chance of making it back alive."

Knox pointed toward the hallway that was off the left side of the living room. I should have guessed because it was the side of their house that was closest to mine. I took off in that direction. Down the hall, I found three doors. One led into the bathroom and I assumed the other two would take me to each of the twins' rooms. I tapped lightly on the first closed door before poking my head in, then walking in fully. *So this is what a boy's room looks like.* It smelled masculine and it was tidier than I'd imagined it would be. Apart from the very full laundry basket of dirty clothes, the room was spotless. The room had a desk with a laptop, a dresser, and a queen bed pushed up against one side of the room. Creed was lying on his stomach, face pointed at the wall. He was shirtless and his faux hawk was smushed in different directions. I walked over to the bed and lightly touched his bare shoulder. "Creed, it's time to wake up," I said softly.

Creed groaned. "Fuck off," he grumbled, making me laugh.

I climbed up onto the bed, leaned over his back, then lightly brushed my finger down the arch of his nose, tickling him. "Good morning, Sunshine. It's time to open those pretty eyes."

His nose scrunched before his hand reached up to capture mine, stopping me from tickling him anymore. "I don't want to wake up. I'm dreaming about a pretty girl lying on top of me," he mumbled with a tiny smile, then opened one eye to peek up at me. My cheeks became hot. His body shook underneath mine as he chuckled huskily. "You're too cute," he said with a tired voice. He pushed up from the bed without releasing my hand and turned just enough to wrap his free arm around my waist.

The next thing I knew, I was on my back and under him. His chest slightly squished mine as he burrowed his face into the crook of my neck and pretended to go back to sleep. His breath tickled my neck, making me giggle. I found bare skin when I grabbed his bicep with one hand and used the other to push up on his chest. "It's time to wake up. Knox is making breakfast and I still need to wake up Colt."

Creed pushed up onto his elbows and hovered above me. His eyes traveled to the clock on his nightstand before returning to look down at me, taking in my appearance. "Did you not go for a run this morning? And why are you waking me up at five-thirty?"

Without thought I brushed his blond locks away from his eyes. "My hip is still bothering me. Knox found me pouting on the curb and asked if I wanted to come over for breakfast."

Creed pushed off of me and knelt by my legs as he frowned at my hip. "Do you think you need to get it looked at by a doctor?"

I shook my head. "It's just sore and I have a huge bruise."

His frown didn't lessen. "Can you show me?"

I hesitated as I thought it over. It wasn't like I would be showing him anything private and my jacket would still cover the scars on my stomach. I hooked my fingers into the side of my leggings and pulled them down past my hip bone, revealing the dark purplish bruise that was the size of my hand.

Creed hissed as he looked it over. He lightly trailed his fingers along the edge of my bruise, causing me to gasp. His eyes flicked to mine. "Did I hurt you?"

I shook my head.

His fingers trailed to the arch of my hip bone and the butter-flies in my stomach fluttered. A look flashed across his face that I couldn't decipher as he glanced back down at my hip. His pointer finger drew small circles, tickling me.

A giggle slipped out of me and Creed smiled. He pulled the side of my leggings back up and sat back on his haunches. "You should probably go wake Colt. I'll be out in a minute."

I sat up and clambered off his bed. I walked across the hall and gave Colt's door a light tap before entering. Colt's room was set up the same as Creed's room only mirrored, with the same furniture. The only differences I noticed were that Creed's room was decorated with darker colors and black bedding and also had a couple of posters on his wall. Colt's room had lighter colors and blue bedding. Instead of posters, Colt displayed his medals and trophies he had earned from swimming. I wondered why Creed didn't display his.

Colt was asleep on his back and was also shirtless. I sat next to him on the bed with my legs hanging off the side. He looked like a sleeping angel with the morning light hitting his golden hair and skin. I shook his shoulder gently. "Colt, wake up."

His forehead scrunched as he groaned before his eyes squinted open. His eyes registered that it was me and the corners of his mouth curled up. "Hey, beautiful. What are you doing here?"

"Knox invited me over for breakfast."

His brows rose. "Knox did?"

"I'll explain at breakfast." Playfully, I tugged on his hand.

He chuckled as he laced his fingers with mine and threw off his covers. Holding hands, we left his room for the kitchen.

The dining table was already set and Keelan, who was still shirtless, was carrying food to the table while Knox finished up at the stove. I was transfixed by the way Keelan's muscles flexed a little as he leaned over the table to place a plate stacked with pancakes and a large bowl filled with scrambled eggs.

"You're drooling," a voice whispered next to my ear.

Letting go of Colt's hand, I whipped around to find Creed

standing behind us. Embarrassment consumed me but externally I tried to keep my cool. I put my hand on my good hip and stared Creed down. "Can you blame a girl for looking? Keelan is very pretty."

"Thanks, Shiloh," Keelan said, his tone hinting that he was amused.

My back was to him now and even though I was displaying fake bravado, there was no way I would've been able to look him in the eye right now without blushing like crazy. "You're welcome," I shot over my shoulder.

Both Colt and Creed frowned.

"I've tried to tell them that I'm the prettiest, but they've never believed me," Keelan said.

Colt rolled his eyes and reclaimed my hand. He led me over to the chair I'd sat in last time I'd attempted to have a meal over here. Fingers crossed, things would turn out better.

"Why don't you go put a shirt on, gorgeous?" Creed grumbled at Keelan as he made it over to the chair on my right. Colt snorted from where he sat on my left.

Keelan arched a brow at Creed. "You and Colt aren't wearing shirts."

"Maybe we should all put our shirts on," Colt suggested. "I don't want Shiloh to feel uncomfortable."

The three of them glanced at me.

"I'm fine," I assured. "Don't feel the need to put your clothes on because I'm here."

Knox erupted with laughter from where he stood at the stove, followed by Keelan and the twins. I gaped at all of them as they laughed, even Knox as he brought a plate of bacon to the table while shaking his head with a smile.

"Thanks for the permission to be naked, Shiloh," Keelan said as his laughter settled.

"I—" Then it clicked. "Oh."

That caused another round of laughter.

"Alright, that's enough," Knox said. "Let's eat."

Creed was the first to scoop up some scrambled eggs and put them on my plate, serving me like he had with lasagna the other night. Knox and Keelan watched in fascination as Colt reached across me to grab a bunch of bacon. He dropped some on my plate before plopping the rest on his.

"Thank you," I mumbled and took a sip of my coffee that was already waiting for me at the table. I was more than capable of serving myself, but because I weirdly kind of liked that they did it, I stayed quiet.

The five of us ate, enjoying the food.

"I was going to text you the day you got hurt about getting together," Keelan said to me. It took me a second to figure out what he was referring to. We had talked about him working with me to determine the best level of jiu-jitsu classes to take. "If you're up to it, I have time this weekend," he offered.

I opened my mouth to agree, but Creed spoke before me. "Her hip is still hurting her."

"Sparring could make it worse," Colt added.

They were right. If I pushed it, I might have to go longer without running. Then again, Keelan was nice enough to take time out of his schedule.

"Do you two speak for Shiloh now?" Knox grumbled.

Creed frowned at his brother and Colt gave me an apologetic smile.

"I might be well enough by Sunday," I offered.

Keelan shook his head. "There's no rush. Besides..." He gave me a mischievous grin. "I need you at one hundred percent to see all that you got."

14

For Ethan's game, I wore my dark blue Football God jersey with black shorts. My hair was back up in pigtails with the gray, blue, and black ribbons. Using black eyeliner, I made those black grease marks footballs players put under their eyes, and with white eyeliner I spelled out *Go* within the black mark on one cheek and *Team* on the other.

When I was all set to go, I made my way next door. Keelan answered the door. His eyes did a slow descent and he whistled. "Looking good, Shiloh."

I smiled. "Thank you."

He stepped aside for me to come in. Knox and Creed were sitting on the couch. Both looked in my direction when I entered. Knox's brows shot up when he saw me, but Creed's eyes narrowed.

"Colt!" he yelled before standing.

Keelan chuckled as he sat on the couch next to Knox. "This should be entertaining."

Creed came to stand in front of me, arms crossed over his chest.

I frowned. "What?" I knew I looked ridiculous, but was it really that bad?

Colt walked into the living room from the hall that led to his room. He noticed me and smiled. As his eyes took in my outfit, his smile dropped.

"What?" I repeated with a little bit of bite.

Colt looked to Creed. "Fuck Ethan, let's just stay in and watch a movie."

What?! "We can't do that. He's our friend and we promised him we'd go to support him."

"I agree, fuck Ethan," Creed said, siding with his brother.

That made me glare at both of them.

"I bet this makes you wish you had gone out for football instead of swim, now doesn't it?" Knox said and chuckled. Finding what he said funny, Keelan chuckled, too. Creed and Colt scowled at their brothers.

I breathed in through my nose and out through my mouth to calm myself. "I don't go back on my promises. If you're embarrassed to be seen with me like this, then we don't have to go together, but I'm going regardless of how absurd I look to support my friend."

All four of them went quiet. My eyes dropped to the carpet as I tried to keep my hurt from showing.

"You got it all wrong, baby girl," Keelan said, making me look back up at him.

Before I could ask him to elaborate, Colt stepped toward me. "I know you find it hard to believe, but you're extremely beautiful, Shiloh," he stated and rubbed the back of his neck—his nervous habit. "You could dress up like a clown and still look gorgeous. We aren't embarrassed to be seen with you. We're just…"

"You're wearing another man's jersey, looking hot as hell, and we don't like it," Creed said bluntly.

My brows shot toward my hairline. "But this is my jersey. Not Ethan's."

Creed shook his head. "Doesn't matter. It has his number on it. You might as well be advertising to the whole school you two are dating."

Staring at Creed, I squared my shoulders. "What about not caring about what people think? Ethan's seen the jersey and loved it."

"We know. He's been gloating about it since last night," Creed grumbled.

I didn't back down. "I'm not changing." Creed and I glared at each other, neither one of us wanting to give in.

Colt sighed. "We better get going or we're going to be late."

Creed broke the stare-off to frown at his brother. "Fine," he said and dove for me.

I yelped as I was thrown over his shoulder. "You better not drop me!" I yelled as he carried me out of the house and over to his truck.

The bleachers were packed when we got there. Thankfully, we managed to snag a good spot toward the top on the home team's side of the field. The only problem was the small section of bench available—it was only big enough for two. The twins didn't see anything wrong with it and both sat down before Colt wrapped his arms around my waist and pulled me into his lap.

I didn't know much about football. Colt and Creed did their best to explain how the game was played and what things were when they popped up throughout the game. It was a little confusing, but I still had fun. After the game ended, we waited around for Ethan and a few of the twins' other football friends to come out of the showers. Excited, I kept my eyes glued to the locker room door. I didn't want to miss Ethan's reaction when he saw who else was waiting for him.

As soon as he came out, he spotted us right away and began heading over. He noticed me staring at him and I tilted my head to the right. His eyes moved in that direction and I had the pleasure of watching his face light up when he spotted Isabelle standing a few feet from us. He beelined for her with a big smile on his face. He invited her to hang out with us and our group moved to the student parking lot. Once we got there, our group almost doubled as more football players joined us. I couldn't remember most of their names. Daniel was the only one whose name I remembered. That was because he was in our gym class and had played volleyball with us the other day.

I was flanked by the twins as we all talked. Well, all the guys were talking about the game while I tried to get to know Isabelle. She was about my height and had long, straight, dirty blonde hair. She was a little shy and had a genuine sweetness about her.

"I like your nails," I told her. They were painted yellow with black stars.

"I like your jersey. Is that Ethan's number?" she asked as she eyed it.

I smiled because it was a good sign that she remembered Ethan's number. "Yes. I lost a bet with the guys and had to show up as their personal cheerleader."

"Oh," she responded, which made me remember what the twins had said about what wearing Ethan's number would imply.

"It's all in good fun. The guys are *just* friends," I said, hoping she'd understand.

She gave me a small smile and Ethan inched closer to Isabelle. "Are you hungry?" he asked her.

Wanting to give my friend a little privacy, I moved away, bumping into Colt. He gave me a smile and wrapped his arm around my lower back, pulling me even closer. His eyes flicked over to Ethan and Isabelle, who were now walking away toward

Ethan's car. *Yes!* I felt so happy for Ethan, but it was short-lived when Cassy and her friends showed up.

"Hey, guys," she practically purred as she hung an arm on Daniel's shoulder. Cassy didn't even acknowledge my existence. Amber, standing next to her, was glaring at Colt's arm around me.

Cassy stared at Creed with a predatory obsession in her eyes. Seeing that gave me the overwhelming urge to put myself between her and Creed. Then I glanced back at Amber. The desire to stay by Colt's side was just as strong.

"I'm having a party tomorrow night, are you gentlemen coming?" Cassy asked. I liked how she'd excluded me from that invite. Not that I'd ever go to her party.

"Can't. We have to work this weekend," Colt said.

She gave a flippant wave of her hand. "Your brothers own the place. I'm sure they'll give you the time off."

What?

Creed completely ignored Cassy and looked to me. "You ready to go?"

I nodded and the two of them said their goodbyes to their friends, while Cassy stood there fuming.

Once in Creed's truck, I asked, "Knox and Keelan own Desert Stone Fitness?"

Both of their shoulders slumped.

"Does it really matter?" Creed asked with a bored tone, which I'd realized he used when he didn't want you to know what he was truly feeling.

"It doesn't," I said a little defensively. "I just don't understand why you both didn't tell me." I was a little hurt. Then I felt like a hypocrite. I didn't share everything with them. Maybe they had their reasons.

"We didn't tell you because most people bug us for free memberships or discounts when they find out," Colt explained.

"I would never do that."

I caught Creed smiling through the rearview mirror. "We know that now."

~

"I don't own a swimsuit," I said as Creed practically dragged me into their house after we got back from the game.

"You don't need a suit. Just go in your underwear. That's just as revealing as a bikini," Colt said over his shoulder as he walked ahead of us.

Knox and Keelan were still on the couch but playing video games. At the mention of underwear, they both glanced in our direction.

"But I'm not wearing any underwear," I said with all the seriousness I could muster.

Colt stopped walking to turn and look at me, eyes wide, and Creed's hands on my shoulders stopped pushing me forward. Knox and Keelan were very quiet as they watched us, their video game playing on without them.

"I guess you could go naked. I doubt anyone here will complain," Creed said from behind me.

I whirled around. "Creed!"

He just smirked down at me.

"I'm wearing underwear," I grumbled. He held this cocksure smirk that told me he knew I had been teasing them and he had successfully turned the tables on me. I crossed my arms over my chest. "If I had known you two would be making me go swimming later, I would have worn granny panties."

Creed's head fell back and his laughter filled the room. "Only you would want to go swimming with us in granny panties." He spun me around and started pushing me forward again.

"My, someone has a big ego," I mumbled as I dug my feet into the floor, stopping us from moving toward the back door just off the kitchen. "I'm not going swimming in my underwear," I said firmly. I wasn't embarrassed of them seeing me in my underwear. That wasn't the issue.

"A night swim sounds like fun. I think I'll join you," Keelan announced as he stood up from the couch. "I can give you a shirt to wear to go swimming in, Shiloh." He tossed his controller on the couch and headed down the hallway on the right side of the living room.

Colt glanced over at Knox. "Does that mean you're coming, too?"

Knox turned after switching off their video game and shrugged. "Why not?"

Keelan returned and held out a black T-shirt to me.

"Thank you," I said, feeling relieved. I took it and let Creed lead me to the bathroom to change while they went to their rooms to put their swim trunks on.

I stripped down to my underwear. I was wearing my Harley Quinn set that was half black and half red and had black sequin diamonds on the red sides. Using toilet paper and a little water from the sink, I wiped away the black marks on my cheeks. I removed the ribbons and took my hair out of the pigtails. I slipped Keelan's shirt on and it was large enough to end at mid-thigh.

His shirt smelled good. It was a perfect mixture of masculine and laundry detergent. I opened the door to Colt and Creed waiting in the hall. Both were shirtless, wearing their swim trunks. I folded my arms across my chest, feeling a little nervous when their eyes dragged over my body.

As if noticing, Colt held out his hand to me. "Ready, babe?"

I nodded and put my hand in his.

Their backyard was like an oasis and gave me the motivation to work on mine, which was just an embarrassing patch of dirt. In the center of their backyard was a rectangular pool with a stone-step waterfall on the side. Just as you stepped out the back door and to the right was a U-shaped outdoor cooking area equipped with a grill, mini fridge, and sink, all surrounded by stone tile high-top counters and four bar stools. On the left side of the yard was a large outside seating area with a wicker L-shaped sectional that curved around a table with a fire pit in the middle. Even though it was dark out, the yard was perfectly lit with landscape lighting surrounding the pool and the string of lights hanging from the rooftop over the outdoor kitchen.

Knox and Keelan were already in the inviting dark water. Colt let go of my hand with a mischievous smile and he ran toward the pool, flipped, and cannonballed into the pool, splashing his brothers.

Knox and Keelan wiped water from their faces, chuckling. "Show-off," Keelan said and splashed water at Colt when his head popped out of the water.

As I took a step in the direction of the pool's steps, strong arms scooped me up. I let out a yelp, drawing everyone's attention. "What are you doing?" I asked as I circled my arms around Creed's neck tightly. He gave me the same mischievous smile Colt had before he started running for the pool.

"Creeeeeeeed!" I squealed as he jumped off of the ledge of the pool. He tucked his legs in, turning us into one giant cannonball, and we hit the cool water, plunging deep in liquid darkness. We separated and swam to the surface. Laughter greeted me when I popped above the water.

"I'm surprised there's any water left in the pool after that," Keelan teased and Creed pounced on his back, dunking him under the water. Keelan easily threw Creed over his shoulder and they began to wrestle.

I laughed and I tried to swim away from them. Their wrestling was a little too close for comfort. An arm wrapped around my middle and jerked me in the opposite direction. I barely saw Creed's body land in the water where I had just been as my back hit a muscular chest.

I was shocked to hear Knox's voice rumbling from behind me. "Hey, shitheads!"

Both Keelan and Creed froze.

"You almost landed on Shiloh," Knox explained.

Keelan and Creed broke away from each other, mumbling their apologies while looking contrite. Still in disbelief, I peered up at Knox over my shoulder. His gaze flicked down to mine for only a moment before he released me and swam away.

"You okay, babe?" Colt asked as he pulled me close. His hands slid up my back, under the T-shirt.

"I'm fine." Having a mind of their own, my legs wrapped around his waist and he swam effortlessly while holding me above the water.

Creed swam up behind me and sandwiched me between them. His hand flattened on my bare stomach, making me jump. "Want to race? Four laps back and forth," Creed asked.

Colt's brows rose, looking intrigued. "What are the stakes?"

I rolled my eyes. "I think you two have a gambling problem."

They both looked at me.

"You're not going to race with us?" Creed asked. "We had to race on your turf. It's only fair you race on ours."

"You guys ran against Shiloh? Who won?" Knox asked as he and Keelan swam up to us.

"Colt," Creed and I grumbled at the same time while Colt grinned proudly.

Keelan chuckled at our sour expressions. "Who was last?"

"We tied," Creed answered and looked to me. "What's it gonna be? Are you going to race?"

I laughed dryly. "Why would I enter a race I know I'm going to lose?"

Knox and Keelan murmured their agreement.

Colt's hands shifted to my hips, fingertips touching the swells of my butt cheeks. "What if we gave you a five-second head start?"

I shook my head.

"Ten seconds," Creed countered.

I sighed. "Fine. What are the terms?"

Colt looked at Creed to decide.

"We're going out tomorrow night. Winner gets to pick what we do, losers pay."

Colt and I both agreed and swam to one end of the pool. Knox and Keelan swam off to the side before Keelan counted down, "Ready...get set...go."

I pushed off of the wall, taking full advantage of my ten-second head start. I counted in my head with each arm stroke I took, and I was starting my second lap before I felt them soar past me, going in the opposite direction, starting on their first lap. I pushed on, increasing my speed. They both caught up to me on the fourth lap and I knew I was going to lose. I wasn't going to give up, though. I kicked and stroked with all my might. One second they were passing me with ease and the next I was passing them, and I finished the race when my hand touched the wall. I surfaced, panting, looking for Creed and Colt, who I assumed would be right next to me at the wall, but they weren't there. The sound of splashing water caught my attention. I turned, finding them being held back by Keelan and Knox.

"That's cheating," Creed griped as he struggled against Keelan's hold around his neck.

"Quit whining. Shiloh won," Knox said as he released his hold on Colt.

Keelan released Creed next. "It would have been a dick move to make her pay and a gentleman would have let her win."

"We wouldn't have made her pay and she would have been pissed if we let her win," Creed said.

I nodded, confirming that was true.

Colt sighed. "Shiloh wins this round. We'll rematch without an audience next time."

15

I spent the next morning marinating a log of filet mignon. While waiting impatiently for the right time to cook it, I surfed the internet for ideas on what I should do with my backyard. After last night's swim, I was a little envious of the guys' personal backyard oasis. So far, I knew I wanted a bench swing for the back patio and some twinkly lights to hang up on the awning. As for the yard, which was a patch of dirt, I was unsure. There was no rush. I'd start with the patio first and I was sure inspiration for what to do with the yard would come to me.

After hours of marinating the filet, I decided to start cooking it close to lunch time. I was trying a new steak sandwich recipe I'd seen on the Cooking Channel along with a roasted vegetable salad as a side. Humming while I worked, I pulled my skillet with the filet log from the oven, waited for the meat to rest, then sliced it up.

I made too much, like always. At the time of buying every-thing I'd figured I could just eat the leftovers over the next few days. After the first delicious bite, I was bummed I had no one to share it with. My thoughts immediately traveled to the guys and with a smile I pulled out my phone.

Four words...the BEST steak sandwiches :) I texted Colt and Creed in our group message before going back to eating.

New recipe? Creed texted back a few minutes later.

Yup. Have you four had lunch yet? I made too much and want to share.

We haven't eaten yet. You're gonna bring us food, babe? Colt answered.

Yup. Be there in 30 mins, I replied.

I made quick work of wrapping four individual sandwiches in foil and split the rest of the veggie salad into four separate plastic containers. I placed all the food in a picnic basket along with forks and napkins, then dashed to my room to change into my workout clothes. My hip was feeling a lot better and I figured I might run the track for a while.

～

With my hair up in a high ponytail, dressed in turquoise leggings and a matching athletic tank, I walked into Desert Stone after sending a quick text telling the guys I was here. I was being brave today by not wearing a jacket.

I went straight up to the front desk to wait and was immediately greeted by Stephanie, the pretty receptionist. "Hi, how may I help you?" she said, eyeing the picnic basket I was holding.

"I'm just waiting for my friends."

She opened her mouth to say something, but Keelan and Knox chose that moment to walk out from the hallway behind the front desk.

"Hey," I greeted them.

Keelan made his way over by going around to the front of the desk while Knox held back by the hall, texting on his phone.

"Heard you were bringing us lunch?" Keelan said.

I held out the picnic basket in front of me. "I tried out a new recipe. Want to be my guinea pig?"

Keelan smiled brightly and held out his hand to take the basket. "When it comes to your cooking, I'd happily volunteer as tribute." He tilted his head in Knox's direction. "We're all going to hang in Knox's office."

I nodded and followed him around the front desk.

Knox looked up from his phone as we approached. "What'd you make?" he asked me.

I met Knox's intense eyes as I hiked the strap of my gym bag further up my shoulder. "Food."

My response made Keelan snort. Knox, on the other hand, narrowed his eyes. Yet again, I was playing with fire by messing with the eldest Stone brother. I couldn't seem to help myself. It was too much fun.

I held his stare and the corner of his mouth lifted ever so slightly. As soon as that tiny hint of a smile appeared, it was gone, leaving me doubting it had actually happened. His attention flicked to Stephanie. "We're all taking our lunch, Steph." He didn't wait for her response before taking off back down the hall.

Knox's office was pretty big. There was a giant wooden desk facing the door right when you walked in and off to the side as you went deeper into the room was a long conference table that had ten chairs surrounding it.

Keelan set the basket on the center of the table before opening it up and pulling everything out. "It smells really good, Shi. Thank you," he said as he worked.

"You're welcome," I mumbled sheepishly as I took a seat at the table. "Where are Colt and Creed?"

"They're finishing up a tour with some new members," Knox answered as he sat at the head of the table.

"Are you not eating, baby girl?" Keelan asked as he set four sandwiches and four containers in front of him and Knox and two empty seats, I assumed for the twins.

I shook my head. "I already ate at home. I figured I'd head upstairs for a run after I dropped off the food."

Keelan pulled out the chair next to me and took a seat. "How's your hip? You're not pushing yourself, are you?"

"It's a lot better today. I figured I'd stop running if it begins to bother me," I replied.

The door to the office opened and the twins came strutting in. Colt smiled when he saw me. "Sorry we're late, babe."

Creed glared at Colt. "If you weren't so polite, that chick wouldn't have assumed she had a chance with you. I swear I've never seen someone hint at how available they were so much in my life. The woman was so desperate it was fucking annoying."

"Aw, is someone jealous?" I teased Creed.

Creed turned his glare on me, and Colt's smile widened.

"I'm surprised she didn't try for both of you," I said to them. "Whenever Shayla and I were out and about together, pervs would ask if we were a package deal."

They all went quiet and I caught Colt and Creed exchanging a look. I was just as surprised as they were that I'd talked about Shayla. It showed that I was beginning to feel comfortable around these guys and that I'd need to be careful with what I revealed moving forward. It was alright to share some things about my past, but the whole point of WITSEC was to protect my true identity. If anyone found out, Logan would relocate me, and I'd have to start over again somewhere new. Alone. I didn't want to risk that. Colt and Creed were…important to me and I would miss them. I also had this fear that if they did find out, they wouldn't want anything to do with me anymore. Who could blame them? Would anyone really want to be friends with someone whose family was murdered by an obsessed, crazed stalker who was still out there looking for her? No, they wouldn't. If the guys ever found out, I would lose them.

Colt masked the slight surprise that was showing on all of their faces. "Shayla was your twin, right?"

"Yeah." I took a deep breath. *I can do this.* "Would you like to see a picture of her?" I asked timidly and pulled out my cell phone from the thigh pocket of my leggings. I tapped on my album app and I scrolled through the few pictures Logan had said I could keep until I found one. It was one of the last pictures we'd taken together. We were at the beach on the last family vacation we'd ever take. Shay and I were dressed similar, wearing jean shorts, bikini tops, and flip-flops. Shay's hair was blue and styled up in a bun, whereas my brown hair was in two long braids hanging down my chest. The two of us were posing on a pier with the ocean showing in the background. Shay had hopped on my back and was smiling with her arms in the air while I held her legs and laughed. We looked so happy. Carefree.

I offered my phone to Colt. He took it and held it out so all his brothers could see. At the same time, small smiles pulled Colt's and Creed's lips. "Shayla has the blue hair, right?" Creed asked.

"Can't tell the difference?" I teased with a smile before nodding.

"Look at all that brown hair," Keelan said as his eyes roamed over the picture. "How old were you?"

"Sixteen."

"You looked really happy," Creed mumbled, and his brothers all stiffened. Colt cleared his throat before handing me back my phone. The twins walked around the table. The moment their butts hit their chairs, they all began peeling back the foil around their sandwiches and dug in. The room filled with groans and I smiled.

"Have you thought about what we're going to do tonight?" Colt asked.

I sighed because I had been thinking about it. I just couldn't come up with anything. "I know I want to get ice cream," I said.

Creed frowned. "We have to do more than just go out for ice cream."

"I know. I'm still thinking," I grumbled and opened the internet app on my phone to look up stuff to do in the area.

"What about a movie?" Colt suggested.

That wasn't a bad idea. I was about to ask them what movie they'd want to go see when a cell phone started ringing. All the guys checked their phones before looking at me. That was when I realized the ringing was coming from my gym bag. I scrambled quickly by ripping back the zipper, rummaging through the inside of the bag until I pulled out my burner phone. My heart sped up with panic. It was an unknown number. I looked up at the guys and they gave me confused looks as they stared at both phones in each of my hands. I didn't have time to explain.

"I need to step outside," I said and flipped open the burner phone, answering it before turning to head for the door. "Logan?" I said into the phone.

"Shiloh," a familiar voice spoke on the other end.

I froze just before reaching the door leading out of Knox's office. "Ian?"

"Hey, kid."

The tone of his voice made my legs feel weak; I had to put my hand out to brace myself on the door. There was only one reason Ian would call me instead of Logan and that was to tell me Logan was dead.

"Where's Logan?" It took everything in me to ask that because I was falling apart on the inside, waiting for him to tell me.

"He's busy in the other room," he replied and a wave of relief washed over me.

Regaining my strength, I opened the door and stepped into the hallway. "You just scared the crap out of me!" I whisper-yelled into the phone. "Why are you calling me and not Logan?"

"Logan wanted me to give you a heads up before this shit hits the news. He couldn't call you himself because he's currently wrapped up in giving his report to our superiors," Ian explained.

"What happened?"

~

After my phone call with Ian ended, I numbly walked back into Knox's office to grab my bag and told the guys I was going to head upstairs for a run.

Colt studied me. "You okay, babe?"

I forced a smile. "Yeah," I lied and left.

I ran that track for almost four hours, pushing past the irritation in my hip and the new fiery ache in my legs. The only reason I stopped was because everything I'd eaten that day was making its way back up. I beelined for the trash can by the stairs. I barely made it before I knocked the lid off and heaved into it. Up came my steak sandwich and I had to clutch the sides of the dirty trash can to hold myself up as spots dotted my vision. I felt a hand begin rubbing up and down my spine and then my hair, dangling from my ponytail that was barely missing being soaked with vomit, was pulled away.

"I think I'm going to pass out," I cried and heaved again. Great, now I was crying and puking.

"Focus on breathing." It was Knox's voice.

Whimpering, I did as he said, forcing myself to breathe in through my nose and out through my mouth, but each exhale came out as a pant. My whole body wouldn't stop shaking. *Cheese and rice.* This was the worst I'd ever felt after a run. I had done this to myself. I hadn't been able to stop until my body had made me stop. My phone call with Ian had gutted me. The guilt was too much. The memories were too much. I had just wanted an escape until I was ready to deal with it—to face it. Apparently I was never going to be ready, with how far I'd pushed myself.

That poor girl.

Ian had called to tell me that they had found the body of a high-school girl who had looked similar to me. She had been a victim of Mr. X. How they knew that was because he had stapled a picture of my face to her face and they'd found his DNA—a polite way of saying his semen—all over her body. She had been tortured and raped repeatedly over the span of four days.

She was dead now because he couldn't find me. I was here, safe and hidden, while he was out there preying on girls who looked like me. *How do I live with that?* How was I supposed to move on or start over or whatever the heck I was doing, knowing that? I felt like I was on borrowed time and that time had to come from somewhere…or someone. Four days. Was that how much time I'd received in exchange for her life? How much time would the next girl grant me?

I hated it.

It made me sick.

I made me sick.

I shouldn't have fought so hard.

I should have never made it out of that house.

I should have let him have me because I would never be free of him.

A sob ripped from me and my knees gave out. Knox caught me. "I got you," he told me as he slowly eased me to the floor. My tears fell from my eyes as if a faucet that controlled the flow had been twisted open to the max.

"What happened?" The voice belonged to Creed. Not that I could confirm that with flooded eyes.

"She overdid it," Knox answered. "Can you toss me her water bottle that's in her bag over there?" Once Creed retrieved my water, Knox took it from him and held it up to my mouth. "Small sips."

I did as he instructed, swallowing the small sips of water he poured into my mouth between my panting breaths.

I heard footsteps rushing up the stairs before Keelan's voice joined us. "I got a cold washcloth to help cool her down." He came into view when he knelt down next to me. He pressed the wet cloth to my forehead and slid it down the side of my face, then to the other side before sliding to the back of my neck. I let out an embarrassing groan and I couldn't find it in me to care. It felt that good.

Colt was the last to show up. "What happened? Why is she crying?" He sounded equally concerned as he did angry. *I must look as bad as I feel.*

Ignoring his brother, Knox asked Keelan, "Can you help her back to my office and put her in the shower? I'll meet you down there as soon as I get this cleaned up. Colt, you can help him. Creed, go fetch me another trash bag," Knox ordered.

"I'm going to pick you up and carry you," Keelan told me before scooping me up bridal-style.

I rested my head on his shoulder. "I'm sorry," I whispered.

"It's okay, baby girl," Keelan reassured.

"Are you sure you got her?" Colt asked, sounding on edge. I didn't like him upset, even more so knowing that I was the reason.

"I got her. Can you grab her bag?" Keelan nodded at my bag on the floor, then started walking toward the stairs.

I had been too upset to remember to lock it up in the locker room. Not caring, I'd dropped it next to the stairs and taken off down the track. I hadn't even bothered to put my earbuds in to listen to music.

Back in the office, Keelan walked past Knox's desk and the big conference table, toward a door I hadn't noticed earlier. It led to a full-fledged bathroom with a spacious tile shower. Keelan set me down on the closed toilet. He opened the glass door to the shower, turned on the tap, and held his hand under the spray, feeling the temperature. Colt followed us in shortly with a yellow sports drink and knelt down in front of me. He unscrewed the cap before placing the drink in my hand.

"Take small sips," he ordered and began untying my tennis shoes. "We're going to put you in the shower to help cool you down," he explained.

I numbly took a small sip, scrunching my nose while I did it. I hated the taste of sports drinks.

"You going in with her?" Keelan asked Colt.

Colt pulled off my shoes, followed by my socks. "Yeah," he said, and I felt his fingers fiddle with my anklet. I looked down as Colt tilted his head up, giving me a questioning look.

"It's a GPS anklet tracker. If I'm ever taken, Logan can use this to find me wherever I am as long as I have it on," I explained.

Colt's eyes shifted to Keelan, who had been quietly listening. In the back of my mind, I knew I probably shouldn't have told them that. It would only create more questions, but I didn't have the energy to care.

With a heavy sigh, I reached down to take it off. I hated getting it wet. The anklet was waterproof, but water got trapped between my skin and the bracelet and that irritated my skin.

"Babe," Colt said gently. "Why would you worry about being taken?"

After stuffing my anklet into one of my shoes, I met Colt's eyes. "Are you using one of your five questions?"

Colt stared back at me and I could tell he was considering it. When he finally came to a decision, he rose to his feet and pulled off his shirt. I closed my tired and puffy eyes, relieved.

Colt stripped down to his boxers. "Do you want to get in with your clothes on or do you want to go in your underwear?" Colt asked.

I waited for the panic to surface, but I couldn't feel it through everything else overwhelming me.

"Whatever you're comfortable with, Shi," Keelan said at my hesitation.

"I have more scars," I admitted, looking down.

"Hey." Colt's hands cupped my cheeks and made me look at him. "We don't care. You might have heat exhaustion and all that matters right now is that we cool you down."

I gave him a tiny nod and curled my fingers around the bottom of my shirt. I lifted it over my head. Keelan helped me stand on shaky legs. Colt slipped his fingers inside the waistband of my leggings and pulled them down my legs. I hissed as I went to step out of them. Colt worked quickly to unhook each pant leg from around my ankles.

After I was stripped down to my black sports bra and matching boy shorts, they both helped me get into the shower. With each step I took, the muscles in my legs spasmed and flared with sharp pain.

Pulling me against his chest, Colt hugged-slash-held me up under the spray. I wrapped my arms around his neck and rested my cheek over his heart. Listening to it beat, I closed my eyes and enjoyed the cool water cascading down my body.

16

It wasn't long after getting into the shower that I had to sit down. I couldn't bear to put any weight on my legs anymore. The pain in them was so bad, the soreness in my hip was barely a blip on my metaphorical pain radar.

Colt sat with his back to the tile wall and I lay back against him, in between his legs. Cool water continued to pour on us, which had long since cooled my body down. Colt rubbed his hand up and down my arm soothingly while holding me against him with his other.

My eyes were closed. I was fighting sleep. Kind of. My thoughts wouldn't let me drift off completely. Being held by Colt had helped calm me greatly and I had been able to pull myself from the toxic spiral I had fallen into. I knew I wasn't being fair to myself. That girl's death hadn't been my fault. I was not responsible for a psychopath's actions. But even though I tried to remind myself of that over and over again, a tiny part of still me didn't listen.

Colt's hand stopped rubbing my arm and his fingers brushed some stray wet hairs from my forehead before I felt his lips press against my temple.

"Is she asleep?" I heard Creed ask.

Colt sighed. "I think so. She wore herself out."

"We should get her out and dried off," Creed said. A gush of cold air hit my body, indicating the shower door had been opened. Next, the water was turned off. "Shi."

I forced my eyes open. Creed was in the shower, squatting in front of us. His eyes dropped to my bare stomach. I knew what he was staring at. To the right of my belly button were two jagged, three-inch scars. Mr. X had stabbed me repeatedly. Both wounds had almost killed me and required hours of surgery to repair the internal damage.

"Think you can stand?" Creed asked, his eyes flicking up to meet mine.

I nodded tiredly.

Mustering what little energy I had left, I sat up from Colt's chest. Creed helped me get to my feet by putting his arms under mine and practically lifting me. I wrapped my arms around his neck and smothered a pain-filled groan in the crook of Creed's neck on the way up from the shower floor. I plastered my wet body against his, trying to hold myself up. "I'm sorry," I said with a sniffle. More tears were already filling my eyes again. I didn't deserve what they were doing for me.

Creed's arms circled my back and he held me closer, if that was even possible.

"It's okay, Shi." Bending down slightly, his hands traveled to the backs of my thighs. He lifted me up and my legs weakly wrapped around his waist. He stepped out of the shower and he sat me down on the counter next to the sink. He pulled away and looked into my eyes. His brow furrowed. "We're not mad, if that's what you think."

"I don't want to burden—"

"You're not a burden," Colt interrupted. He pulled two towels from the wall rack and tossed one to Creed. Creed did his best to dry me off. Once he seemed satisfied I was dry enough, he wrapped the towel around me and pulled me forward, hugging me tightly. Fisting the back of his shirt in my hands, I laid my head on his shoulder, absorbing the comfort he was offering, and my eyes drifted closed.

Creed's body began shaking with silent laughter. "She's out."

"Shi, let's get you in some dry clothes and then you can sleep, okay?" Colt said.

I opened my drowsy eyes, finding Colt standing next to us. "Mhmm," was all I could get out as lifted my head.

Colt picked up a men's T-shirt and basketball shorts from the pile of clothes sitting on the back of the toilet. He looked at the clothes in his hands, then at me. "Can you stand long enough to change yourself?"

I supposed I was about to find out. Creed took a step back, allowing me room to slide off the counter onto my feet. I hissed when the pain ripped through my muscles. I only lasted a few seconds before I reached out for Creed, fearing my legs were going to give out on me. His arms shot out quickly and held me steady.

Colt sighed. "Babe, I know it's not ideal, but if you let us help—"

"I can do it!" I exclaimed, feeling irritated.

"You're going to fall on your ass," Creed said. "We won't look."

"Everyone looks," I grumbled. I took a moment to weigh my options. I didn't have any. I was in pain and exhausted both emotionally and physically. I just wanted to get this over with so I could get off my legs and rest. I let out an annoyed sigh. "Just don't look."

"We won't," they said at the same time.

Colt knelt in front of me, his eyes on the floor as he pulled down my underwear. He pulled the soaked, skin-fitting material down my hips, baring to the world a part of me I hadn't let anyone else but my doctor see. Colt's eyes stayed glued to the floor as he worked to get my feet through the holes of the basketball shorts and as he slid them up my legs. When I was covered, his eyes lifted up to meet mine. They were guarded as he pulled on the drawstrings, tightening the waistband so they wouldn't fall, and tied the strings into a bow. Creed helped me sit back on the counter. Colt stood with the T-shirt in his hand. Without really thinking, I pulled my sports bra over my head. When I had it off, I found them both staring at my chest.

I crossed my arms over my breasts. "Don't look!"

"There was no warning!" Creed argued as he spun around.

Colt averted his eyes to the ceiling. He cleared his throat and held out the shirt. "Sorry."

I took it and quickly put it on. Creed spun back around after I told them I was decent. He stepped between my legs and pulled me to him.

"No peeking, babe," Colt teased just before he shoved down his wet boxers. He obviously wasn't shy. I got a glimpse of his butt before my wide eyes shot to the ceiling.

Creed chuckled, drawing my attention to him. "I guess you two are even."

Heat bloomed in my cheeks, which made him laugh some more. I laid my head back on his shoulder and closed my eyes.

"Hey, Shi." I felt a hand shake my shoulder.

I groaned and opened my eyes. At first all I saw was Keelan standing above me. *What is he doing here?* I thought, then my eyes drifted around the room, taking in the posters on the walls, the black comforter tucked around me, and the familiar smell. I was in Creed's room.

"Are you hungry? Dinner is almost ready," he said.

After my brain was finally awake enough, everything that had happened today came back to me. My sore legs were a big memory-jogger. The last thing I could remember was falling asleep in the back of Colt's Charger on the way home. The twins must have scooped me up out of the car and carried me inside. "How long have I been asleep?"

"A few hours. How are you feeling?"

"Honestly, like an idiot," I said. I knew better. I knew what my limits were, and I'd pushed past them anyway because the pain that had followed was better than the pain I was feeling.

"I get it. We all do," he said. "I know you have Colt and Creed, but if you ever need to talk, I'm a good listener."

I nodded even though I'd never be able to talk to him or the twins. Until Mr. X was caught, it'd never be safe for me to talk to anyone.

"Knox is cooking dinner. It's going to be ready soon. If you're hungry, you're welcome to join us," he offered.

"Okay, I'll be out in a minute."

Keelan left and I hobbled stiffly across the hall to the bathroom. Looking into the mirror, I sighed. My hair was a frightening sight. Most of it had fallen out of my hair tie, which was now on the side of my head. I pulled the elastic tie from the rest of my hair, finger-combed it the best I could, and pulled it all back up in a messy bun on the top of my head. I splashed some water on my face and pinched my cheeks to bring some color out of my pale complexion. After doing my business in the bathroom, I hobbled down the hall and made my way into the kitchen. The aroma coming from whatever was cooking smelled mouthwatering. Knox was at the stove while Keelan filled a glass with water from the fridge.

Keelan hurried over when he saw me. "Here, take this," he said as he offered the glass of water with one hand and held out two white pills in his other.

I took the pills and water from him. "Thank you."

At the sound of my voice, Knox turned from the stove. He watched as I put the pills Keelan had given me into my mouth and chased them with the water.

I walked my pathetic limping butt to the kitchen island and set my glass down. "Can I help with something?" I asked.

Knox didn't say anything and continued to stare at me. I just cocked a challenging eyebrow at him. The corner of his mouth pulled into a small smirk and Keelan, who'd been watching, chuckled.

"How can you help when you can barely walk?" Knox challenged.

My eyes narrowed. "My legs are sore, not broken."

"She's a stubborn little thing, isn't she?" Keelan commented with laughter in his eyes. The way he stared at me was like I was the most enticing thing he'd seen all week.

Knox crossed his arms over his chest and stared me down from across the island. He gave me an *I'm not going to budge on this* look. "Everything is done. We're just waiting on the twins to return."

Now that he mentioned it…

Keelan shook his head, snickering. "I think she just realized they weren't here."

Just after he said that, we all heard the front door open. The twins walked into the kitchen with grocery bags in hand.

"Hey, how are you feeling?" Colt greeted as he set his bags on the island and Creed followed suit.

Eyeing the bags, I said, "Better. Where'd you guys go?"

Creed smirked and started unpacking what was in the bags. He pulled out container after container of different ice cream flavors, followed by different toppings like sprinkles, chocolate sauce, and caramel. I couldn't hold back my huge happy grin. When Colt pulled the very last item from the last bag, I laughed. Popcorn. "We didn't know what flavor you liked," he said, explaining the five different flavors of ice cream. "You said you wanted ice cream."

My smile dropped. "I'm sorry. You guys wanted to go out…"

They both shrugged at the same time. "We can go out another

time. We'll stay in and watch a movie tonight," Creed said and started stuffing the ice cream into the freezer.

My smile returned. "Okay. What are we going to watch?"

"What about something scary?" Creed suggested as he finished putting the last of the ice cream away while the rest of the guys started carting plates and dishes of food to the table.

"No!" I blurted loudly. Everyone froze and my cheeks burned. "Nothing scary, please," I said in a normal volume. I couldn't handle the suspense. Especially when it came to slasher or home invasion horror movies. They triggered episodes of PTSD.

Everyone slowly recovered from my outburst and they finished setting the table for dinner. Creed walked up to me and put his hands on my shoulders. "Okay, Shi. Nothing scary."

We debated over movie choices all through dinner and ended up going with the TV show *Game of Thrones* instead. None of us had seen it and we'd all heard it was awesome.

I went home to shower and change into my own clothes really quick. The pain medicine Keelan had given me and the hot shower had done wonders for my achy legs. I put on my Wonder Woman pajama set. The shorts were cobalt blue with white stars and the tank was red with a gold Wonder Woman logo. I tossed my hair back up in a messy bun and slid into flip-flops before heading back over. All the guys smiled at my pajamas, even Knox.

"Popcorn or ice cream, baby girl?" Keelan asked.

"That's a difficult question to answer," I replied, making them all laugh.

Keelan tossed the box of popcorn at Colt. "Both it is," he said and started pulling out all the ice cream from the freezer. While the popcorn popped in the microwave, we all made our own sundaes.

After the sundaes were assembled, we took our ice cream and the popcorn to the living room. Colt and Creed made me sit between them on one end of the couch and Knox and Keelan lounged out on the other end. Knox started the first episode and all of us were instantly engrossed. The opening scene of the show was quiet and of men on horseback. Then ominous music started playing and my back went a little stiff.

Colt put his hand on my thigh and leaned close. "You alright?" he whispered in my ear. I nodded and put my hand onto his. Knowing what I wanted, he flipped his over and laced our fingers together. He held my hand until the suspenseful scene ended. It hadn't been that bad, but it was nice to have the support nonetheless.

After the first episode ended, we had to watch the next one and the one after that. Six episodes later, it was one in the morning and I was tired.

"Just stay over," Creed pleaded as he fought to keep his eyes open. Halfway through the last episode he'd stretched out on the couch and laid his head in my lap. I had run my fingers through his hair, loving the way the silky strands had felt slipping between my fingers.

"I can't," I said, wishing I could. They had dealt with enough of my drama today. The last thing I wanted to do was freak them all out with my nightmares.

"I'll walk you home," Colt said, standing from the couch.

Creed let out an exaggerated sigh and sat up. "Alright, I'm coming, too."

"You'll have to come over tomorrow night so we can binge some more episodes. I don't think I can wait long to find out what happens," Keelan said.

I smiled at him. "I'll be here." Before I left, I said goodnight to him and Knox.

Colt and Creed walked me to my house. They stayed with me as I unlocked my door and turned off the alarm. The house was dark. "I should have left a light on," I mumbled, hating that I felt scared.

Colt stepped inside and disappeared into my dark living room. A few seconds later he flicked on the lamp next to the couch. Creed came inside, too. He shut and locked the front door behind him. I didn't question why he had done that. I was happy they were willing to stay for a while.

Colt walked ahead of us to my bedroom and turned on my bedroom light. I sat on my bed with a tired sigh. Looking equally as tired, Creed walked around to the opposite side of the bed, pulled the covers back, and climbed into my bed. Colt and I watched as he adjusted a pillow before lying down and closing his eyes.

I chuckled. "What are you doing?"

Creed opened one eye, then shot up, grabbed me, and pulled me down to lie next to him. "We're having a sleepover," he mumbled.

"You don't want to sleep with me," I said.

Both he and Colt snorted.

I frowned. "What?"

"Nothing," Colt said.

"Let's just go to sleep," Creed whined as he snuggled me with his arm around my waist.

"I have night—"

"Nightmares?" Creed finished for me. "We know. Stop worrying. You're not going to scare us away, Shi."

"Unless you're uncomfortable with us staying over?" Colt asked.

I looked from Creed to Colt, feeling equal parts happy and sad. "If you keep being amazing, I don't know how I'm going to be okay sharing you."

They gave me confused looks. "What do you mean?" Creed asked.

I scratched one of my blushing cheeks. "I doubt you two are going to be single much longer," I said. "A couple of girls are going to snag your attention one of these days and I don't know how I'm going to handle it. I guess that makes me selfish."

Colt sat on the edge of my bed. "You're not selfish."

Creed chuckled next to me. "I think what you're really feeling is jeal—"

Colt punched him in the shoulder before Creed could finish. "Shut up," Colt snapped.

Maybe I was jealous. Jealous of the time and attention I'd have to give up to other girls. Just imagining it made me sad.

I climbed under the blankets and took off my bra from under my shirt. I didn't care if my friends were guys. I refused to sleep in a bra. They watched as I tossed it across the room toward my laundry basket.

"You matched your underwear to your pajamas?" Creed mumbled tiredly.

"I was feeling Wonder Woman vibes this evening and wanted to represent with every layer," I said as I lay on my side facing Colt. "Will you get the lights?" I asked him.

Colt nodded and left to turn off the living room light. Creed scooted closer, spooning me. He let out a big yawn before burrowing his nose against the back of my neck.

Colt returned, flicked off the bedroom light, and slid into bed. He lay down on his side facing me. The only light we had was moonlight shining in from the window. After my eyes adjusted to the dark, I could see his outline. He scooted closer, until his body brushed up against mine.

"Thank you for today," I whispered. I had a feeling Creed was already asleep.

I felt Colt's fingers lightly run up my arm to my shoulder, leaving goosebumps in their wake. His fingers didn't stop at my shoulder. They followed my collarbone to the hollow at the base of my throat. His touch did something to me. It made my heart pound in my chest. The butterflies in my stomach were going crazy and flying south, causing an ache—a needy pressure between my legs.

He leaned his face closer. "You're welcome," he whispered, and I could feel his breath on my lips. His fingers moved down from my throat. They paused at the top of my breast as if to give me the chance to stop him from going further. I didn't want to stop him.

When I didn't say a word, his fingers continued their descent. I gasped as they grazed over my nipple at the same time his lips pressed against mine. His lips were soft, and the kiss was gentle but restrained, as if he was holding back for me to respond. Colt had always gone out of his way to make sure that everything was my choice. Even now. Which was why I felt comfortable and confident enough to kiss him back.

That seemed to be all Colt needed. He went from gentle to passionate as he deepened the kiss. His tongue slid past my lips and stroked mine. My hand fisted the front of his shirt, pulling him closer, wanting more. His wandering fingers were replaced with his whole hand, cupping my breast, then squeezing.

Creed's arm that was still around my waist tightened and he shifted behind me. The movement had the same effect on me as being splashed with a bucket of ice water.

What am I doing?

I broke away from our kiss, breathing heavily. How could I be so stupid? I was kissing my friend while my other friend was sleeping behind me.

Colt let go of my breast to cup my cheek. "You alright?"

I nodded. "Yeah."

He brushed his thumb across my cheek. "Okay. Let's get some sleep."

I took his hand in mine and forced my eyes closed.

17

I COULDN'T LOOK AWAY FROM MY DAD'S MUTILATED BODY. I TOOK A step back. Then another. A hand touched my shoulder and I let out a scream. That hand quickly went to my mouth to try and silence me.

"It's me." It was Shayla. I whirled around to face her. Her cheeks were streaked with tears and fear had seeded deep within her eyes. "We need to leave. He's in the house," she whispered.

I didn't need her to tell me who "he" was. I nodded frantically. Holding hands, we took a step to leave. A crash came from the other side of the house, followed by our mom's scream that sent a trembling wave of fear through every bone in my body. The sound of running on the hardwood floor echoed through the house next. The running sounded closer and closer. Shayla pushed me back, further into the living room, and pulled me to the floor behind the couch our dad's corpse was lying on.

It was a second later when panting breaths and my mom's pain-filled yell sounded in the room. Shayla squeezed my hand as we listened to wrestling. The lamp was knocked over, but it didn't break. My mom cried out before a thud vibrated through the floor.

I knew I shouldn't have looked but I couldn't stop myself. I peeked around the side of the couch. My mom was on the ground, crying as she stared up at Mr. X, who was straddling her. He had her pinned with a large, bloody knife at her throat. A gasp escaped me. It hadn't been loud, but it caught my mom's attention. Our eyes met for only a moment before she forced herself to look back at Mr. X. In that brief moment her emotions switched rapidly. First there was surprise to see me, then worry. Both had been shadowed with terror.

"Where is she?" he growled.

My mom's expression hardened, as if determined.

"Where is she?!" Mr. X shouted in her face.

"Go to hell!" she wailed as she thrashed at him.

Mr. X lifted the knife from her neck, rose it high above his head, and brought it down. My mom's breath hitched, eyes wide as the knife plunged into her chest. Mr. X withdrew the knife and brought it down again, stabbing her over and over.

≈

"Shi."

I opened tear-flooded eyes to a blurry shadow in the shape of a man holding me in their arms. Panic seized my heart. "No!" I cried out and pushed at their chest to get away. He let go and I scrambled to my knees.

His hand locked around my arm. "Shi, it's me," he said at the same time the light flicked on, revealing Creed kneeling in front of me.

My fear-induced adrenaline began to fade as I glanced around. Colt was standing next to the bed with sleep-tousled hair. I looked back at Creed. The movement of my eyes caused more tears to fall down my drenched cheeks. "I'm so sorry," I whispered, my gaze dropping. This would be it. I knew it. This would be what scared them away. I had too many issues—too much trauma that I was failing to deal with. Who would want to put up with that? I covered my face with my hands as sobs rattled through my body. I was beginning to hunch over, wanting to cave into myself, and my forehead met a chest.

Creed wrapped his arms around me. "It's okay."

I shook my head. "No, it's not."

Creed's hands moved to my wrists and pulled my hands away from my face. "Hey," he said, trying to get me to look at him. I couldn't. I was afraid of what I'd see. His fingers curled under my chin, forcing me to look up at him. I met his beautiful aquamarine eyes. Concern was etched around them. "Talk to me," he pleaded.

"I'm a fucking mess," I forced out with a wobbly voice. "I'm waiting for you to realize it and walk away."

Creed's eyes went wide. "You just said 'fucking.'"

The bed dipped behind me. "What are you talking about, babe?" Colt asked, putting his hand on my back.

"I'm still dealing with the loss of my family. I have moments or days where I can't hold myself together. Yesterday is a perfect example of that. It's not fair to either of you to be burdened with this—with me." I squeezed my eyes shut, trying to find the strength to say what I needed to next. I opened my eyes again with a little determination and a whole lot of heartache. "You two should go." They both looked stricken. "If you don't go now, I'll grow more attached."

Neither of them moved.

"Please!" I cried. "I'm more trouble than I'm worth. I cry more than I smile. I have nightmares—"

Creed grabbed my face with both hands and slammed his lips onto mine. At first, I was so taken aback that I was frozen like a statue. Creed pulled back a little to look me in the eye. "I'm already attached," he said before returning his lips to mine.

My body slowly softened, and I kissed him back. Creed wasn't gentle. His lips demanded everything I could give and when his tongue slipped past my lips to taste mine, he groaned, pushing me backward. My back collided with a chest.

I broke our kiss as Colt's hands went to my hips. I froze again, unsure what to do. I had kissed him last night and had just kissed Creed right in front of him.

Creed's gaze met his brother's over my head. He shrugged. "She was freaking out. I panicked."

Colt sighed behind me. "Did you not think for a moment that kissing her might freak her out more?"

"Why?" Creed smirked. "Because you kissed her last night?"

I desperately wanted to curse again.

"Yes, because I kissed her last night," Colt snapped. "She's not ready—"

"Oh-my-lanta, please don't fight," I begged. "I'm sorry. We won't kiss ever again. We should chalk up all the kissing to curiosity amongst friends. Or better yet, how about we forget any kissing happened at all?"

They both frowned at me. "Why?" they asked at the same time.

Frustrated, I rubbed my cheeks dry. "You know why. There's two of you and one of me. You're going to make me choose and I refuse to do that."

Creed opened his mouth to say something, but Colt spoke before him. "We'll circle back to the kissing situation at a later time. Right now, we need to talk about you pushing us away."

Tired of standing on my knees, I plopped down on my butt. "Like I said, I'm a mess."

I desperately wanted to move on with my life. It was why I'd been so happy when Colt and Creed had come into my life. I hadn't thought that becoming closer with others would grant them the ability to see things about me I'd thought no one would ever see. I had been naive to think I could hide it.

"Everyone is a mess. Some are just better at hiding it than others," Creed said.

I shook my head. "You're both perfect."

They both scoffed and shook their heads.

"I promise, babe, we're not," Colt said.

I gave them a doubtful look.

Creed sighed and sat next to me. "I hate being on the swim team. Actually, no, I hate competing. Our dad died the first time we competed at state during our freshman year." As he spoke, he got this sad, faraway look. "It's a high achievement to make it to state," he continued. "I remember looking out at the stands, feeling angry that he wasn't there to support us. He'd never missed a competition and it pissed me off that he was missing what I thought would be the most important competition in my life. We both came home with medals around our necks to find out that he'd been on his way to see us compete, but never made it. Someone had sped through a red light and T-boned him. His car had been reduced to a crushed tin can and he'd died instantly."

I took his hand, then Colt's and gave them a little squeeze.

"I've hated competing ever since," Creed continued. "I do it because it's what he would have wanted, and it will help me get into college and all that bullshit. But...whenever we're at practice and Coach is yelling at us to do better, I just want to scream that I don't care. I don't care if I win or I lose. My life isn't 'live and breathe swim' anymore."

"What do you live and breathe for now?" I asked.

He shrugged. "I don't know. I haven't found it yet."

"We still have bad days and we're still dealing with his loss," Colt said, sullen. "We were kind of young when our mother died, but Keelan and Knox weren't. They took her death really hard and losing our dad..." Colt trailed off, looking away with pain in his eyes. He cleared his throat. "What I'm trying to say is that the four of us know what it's like to struggle in the trenches of our grief. It's how we know that's what you're going through now."

"And why would you want to deal with that?" I asked. "Most people would walk away."

Colt frowned. "Would you walk away from us?"

No. I wouldn't.

Colt had made a point. I wanted to be reassured, but without knowing the full extent of my trauma, they didn't truly understand what they were getting into with me. That thought made me sick to my stomach.

They didn't want to leave, and even though I knew things between us would eventually end, I couldn't bring myself to be the one to walk away. That left me with one choice. I was going to cherish every moment I had with them, for however long our friendship lasted.

I looked at Creed. He had shared something that I knew must have been hard for him to share. I owed it to him to share something. "I was dreaming about my mom. That night…" I paused, thinking over my next words carefully. "I had to watch her—" I looked toward the ceiling to keep more tears from falling. "I had to watch her die, unable to do anything."

I saw the question they were getting ready to ask. It was written all over their faces.

"Please don't ask me how. I can't. I just…can't," I begged, and they kept quiet, waiting for me to continue on. "I was reliving that moment in my dream and it felt so real. It always does when I dream about that night. The smells. The sounds. What I felt in that moment, only it's a thousand times worse because I already know what's going to happen and I'm helpless to stop it." A few tears escaped my eyes and I quickly wiped them away. "She was so scared." My voice broke and I took a minute to regain my composure. I couldn't tell them any more. I'd probably already said too much. Thankfully, they didn't push for more.

"What time is it?" I asked them.

Colt reached over to my nightstand where his phone was. "It's just after six."

"We don't have to go into work until nine," Creed said.

Colt looked to me. "Why don't we try to get a few more hours of sleep?"

I was itching for a run. I needed to escape the anguish that weighed heavily on my heart. However, running wasn't an option. My legs were still sore.

"You're not going running, babe. I can see you thinking about it," Colt said. "Don't do that to yourself. It'd do your body good if you got some more rest."

I nodded "I know."

We crawled back under the covers, with me lying between them. Creed pulled me close until my head was resting on his chest and Colt curled up behind me, with his arm around my waist. Being sandwiched between them wasn't an escape, but I felt my sorrow and fear slowly seep away. Being held by them was better than an escape. It was relief, and for the first time in what felt like forever, it was a little easier to breathe.

18

"SHI, YOU READY TO GO?!" I HEARD CREED YELL FROM THE FRONT of the house. He was putting the emergency spare key I'd given the guys a few days ago to use. I'd decided to give them a key after they had slept over. Something had slightly shifted that night and after that horrible day at the gym. They had really been there for me and that had deepened our friendship. So it had felt right to give them a key to hold onto in case I ever lost my own or was ever locked out. However, Creed using it this morning gave me the impression that the twins had other plans for it.

"Almost, I'm back here!" I shouted. I returned my attention to my bathroom mirror and continued applying a dark magenta lipstick. I'd decided to dress a little brave today by wearing a white, off-the-shoulder romper with beautiful magenta flowers on it. My scar on my shoulder was barely covered. The scars on my wrists and the one going up my arm were on display. Well, one wrist was covered. I'd put on my sister's rose gold cuff. I'd paired the romper with nude peep-toe wedges that had straps that covered my ankle scars perfectly. I had my anklet tracker tucked into my bra. It wasn't an ideal place to put it, but it would be visible with my shoes and I didn't want anyone asking me about it.

I had my lavender hair down and straightened. It was getting really long—almost reaching to the middle of my back. My lips were bold to match the flowers on my romper. The rest of my makeup was shimmery and light.

I was finishing the last little touches to my makeup when Creed appeared behind me in my bathroom mirror. I smiled at him. His brows rose as his eyes trailed from my head to my toes. I turned around to face him. "I just need to grab my backpack."

He nodded as he continued to stare at me.

"What?" I asked.

"I'm trying to think of a way to get you to lift your kissing ban," he said, taking a step toward me.

I took a step back, bumping into the counter. "We can't kiss."

He put his hands on my hips, molding the front of his body with mine. "Do you want to kiss me?"

My heart began to pound in my chest. I did want to kiss him. Badly.

But…Colt.

He stared at me with desire. It was kryptonite to my restraint. "Creed," I begged, sounding a little breathless. I was hoping he would be the strong one.

He let out a heavy sigh and released me. "Go get your bag."

I had to squeeze by him because he didn't move out of the way. He followed me into my room. I grabbed my backpack off my bed, and we headed out.

Colt was already in the car waiting for us. "Hey, babe," he said distractedly as he tapped away on his phone when I slid into the backseat.

"Hey," I greeted back, but I didn't think he heard me.

Colt cursed, tossing his phone in the cup holder in the center console before shifting the car into gear and driving off.

"What's up?" Creed asked him.

"Daniel went to Cassy's party last weekend. All she did was talk shit to anyone who would listen," he grumbled angrily.

"About?" Creed asked.

I caught the look Colt gave Creed. It didn't take a genius to figure out that Cassy had been talking crap about me.

"Why is he only telling you about this now?" Creed asked angrily. "It's already Wednesday."

I sighed. "What does it matter?"

Creed turned in his seat. "It doesn't bother you that she and her friends are complete bitches toward you?"

Of course it sucked. "I thought I wasn't supposed to care what other people thought of me?"

"This is different, babe." Colt's hands white-knuckled the steering wheel as he spoke. "She's saying shit to hurt you and we're allowed to not like that."

The rest of the drive to school was in silence.

As soon as we were parked in the student lot, I hopped out of the car and grabbed Colt's hand, stopping him from walking away. He was surprised at first and then his eyes danced all over me.

"Please don't be upset," I pleaded. "I can handle Cassy and her crap. I cannot handle seeing you upset. So please bring happy Colt to the surface." I heard a snort behind me, and I knew it was Creed.

Creed scoffed, "You make it sound like he's got multiple personalities."

"Well, when he's mad, he reminds me of the Hulk," I teased and they both laughed. The softer side of Colt resurfaced and the tension around us seemed to disappear.

"You look really beautiful today," he said to me.

Instead of feeling embarrassed, I smiled.

"I'm starting to miss the sweatshirts," Creed mumbled.

Surprised, I turned. "Should I put one on?"

His eyes raked over me again before he looked up toward the

sky, as if to curse the heavens. "No. I don't want you to ever feel self-conscious, but at the same time, I'm a selfish bastard."

Did that mean he didn't want anyone to see me but him? I wasn't given the time to think it over. Colt pulled me by my hand and from my thoughts and the three of us headed inside.

Like every morning, the guys walked with me to my locker before class. As we turned down the hall where it was located, a crowd blocked our way. Colt and Creed walked ahead of me to clear a path. Once past the crowd, we soon realized the reason why there was one. Spray-painted in bright neon purple across my locker was the word **WHORE** and taped all around the word were opened and stretched-out condoms.

"Stay with her. I'm going to go report this," Colt told Creed.

As he went to leave, Ethan appeared and stopped him. "I already reported it to the office. Someone's coming to clean it up," he explained.

Okay, I would admit that having my locker vandalized more than sucked. I really, really hated the attention and there was stuff I needed from inside. I was going to have to suck it up and walk in front of everyone with my head held high. I squared my shoulders, imagining myself putting on my big-girl panties, and took a step forward. A hand landed on my shoulder, stopping me, and Colt walked past me, up to my locker. He spun the dial, entering my combination—he'd seen me spin it from over my shoulder a handful of times—and unlocked my locker. Creed left me with Ethan to join Colt and they both started grabbing everything out of my locker. It was just a few textbooks, some notebooks, and a toiletry bag. Colt slammed my locker and glared at someone standing in the crowd to the right. I leaned forward and saw that it was Cassy and her friends.

"Are you going to write shit on my locker next?" he openly accused her.

Murmuring traveled through the crowd. Cassy just glared at Colt. She opened her mouth to say something, but he took a step forward, startling her. He didn't stop walking until he passed her and he was down the hall, standing in front of his locker. Creed followed him, shooting Cassy a scathing look as he passed.

I glanced at Ethan, who mirrored my surprise. Without speaking, we made our way through the crowd and over to Colt's locker. Creed was helping Colt put my stuff in his locker, leaving out the textbooks we'd need for our first class.

Colt shut his locker to face me. "I'll text you the combination."

I gave him a tiny smile. "I already know it."

Later that day at home, there was a knock on my front door. After a quick look through the peephole and seeing that it was a delivery man, I felt like my day was finally looking up. My bench swing for my back patio was here. Excited, I opened the door and signed for it.

The delivery man took off, leaving me with a very large brown box. I bent to lift it and grunted when I felt the weight. It was so heavy I couldn't even get my fingers underneath. Next, I tried pushing it. It moved a few inches. I glanced over at the guys' house. Colt and Creed were at practice and Keelan's Jeep was gone. Knox was home. Staring at their house, I debated going over and asking for help.

Nope.

Knox and I weren't that close. Besides, I was independent. I could figure this out on my own.

"Right, I got this." I tried to hype myself up and went back inside the house for a knife. I'd cart everything to the back porch a piece at a time.

After about twenty trips back and forth, I had everything that had been in the box laid out. All that was left to do next was put it all together. My shoulders slumped a little. I was hot and sweat was already dripping down my face. I went back inside, figuring

I'd take a little break to cool down and get something to drink. I guzzled a whole glass of water, refilled it, and went to go sit in the living room.

Just ten minutes, I mused as I sat on the couch. I was halfway done with my second glass when something moving across my floor in front of the TV caught my attention. I had to do a double take to convince my brain I was indeed seeing an eight-legged arachnid monster.

I screamed and jumped on top of my couch, panic taking hold of me. "What do I do?!" I yelled from where I stood at the furthest corner of the couch.

I was seriously debating burning down my house as the tarantula continued to make its way across the floor. Its slow, hairy legs made my whole body shiver with the heebie-jeebies. Then it stopped. As if sensing me, it turned in my direction and picked up its speed.

I screamed and leaped off the couch toward the front door. Feeling as if the tarantula was going to get me at any second, I swung the door open and ran next door.

I banged on the guys' front door nonstop. "Knox!" I yelled.

The door ripped open. Knox stood there, taking me in with wide eyes. Without permission, I ducked under his arm and went into their house.

"What's wrong?" he demanded.

I had the heebie-jeebies so bad I wiggled my arms out to get relief before hugging myself. "There's a giant tarantula in my house."

He stared at me for a moment and then the corners of his mouth slowly started to lift.

I glared at him. "Don't you dare laugh at me."

He snorted.

"Knox, it's not funny," I snapped.

That just set him off and he started laughing.

I put my hands on my hips, fuming, and waited for his laughter to stop. "When is Keelan going to be home?"

Still grinning, he shut the front door and headed over to the couch. "Not for a couple of hours."

Crap. The twins would be at practice for at least another hour. I glanced at Knox. He was sitting on the couch staring at me. By his smug look, he knew that I was going to ask him for help.

"Knox," I said with a sigh.

He waited.

"Will you please help me get the tarantula out of my house?"

"Are you sure you don't want to wait for one of your boyfriends to help?"

"The twins and I are just friends," I said quickly.

He gave me the look, one that screamed *sure.*

I counted to five in my head to stop myself from going off on his giant butt. "I will cook you whatever you want for dinner tonight," I pleaded, sounding exasperated. "Heck, I will make you a freaking cake. Just please get the tarantula out of my house."

He didn't respond. Instead, he reached under the coffee table and pulled out a pair of sneakers. I patiently watched him put them on and stand. "Where in your house did you see it?"

My body sagged with relief and I explained where I'd last seen the tarantula as we walked back to my place. Knox walked right into my house without a shred of fear. I tip-toed behind him, scared the eight-legged nightmare was going to pop out at any second.

Knox knelt down and looked under the TV stand, the couch, and the coffee table using the light on his cell phone. I thought he had seen it under the coffee table because I saw him pause, but he eventually stood.

"It's not in here," he said.

We moved to the dining room next. Knox pulled out all the chairs and looked under the table. Feeling a little brave, I went ahead of him to look in the kitchen. I rounded the island and there it was, on the floor, right in front of my kitchen sink. I let out an embarrassing scream and spun on my heel to book it out of the kitchen. I slammed into Knox's chest, who I didn't know was right behind me. He caught me around my waist before I could fall back. The panic and need to get away overtook me so much so that I jumped onto him and clung to him like a koala bear.

"It's over there! It's over there!" I repeated in a high-pitched voice as I tried to climb up his tall and very bulky body.

Knox let out a grunt when the heel of my shoe hit him in the butt. Other than that, he just stood there and let me scale him. "Shiloh," he said calmly.

I was a panting mess as I clung onto him for dear life. I had managed to get one hand on his shoulder. The other was fisting the back of his shirt. I had one leg wrapped around his hip and the other around his upper thigh. I really needed to do upper-body strength training at the gym.

"Please don't let it get me." I knew I sounded pathetic, but I didn't care.

Knox's hands went to my hips and lifted me up. I wrapped my arms around his neck and locked my legs around his waist. He carried me to the living room and sat me on the couch. "Do you have a broom?" he asked, and I told him where I kept it. Knox disappeared back into the kitchen. I heard small noises followed by the back door being opened and closed.

Knox returned. "I got it out of the house."

I relaxed back. "Thank you so much."

He nodded and his expression turned serious. "I need to ask you something."

My relief instantly evaporated. "What?"

"Why is there a gun taped under your coffee table?"

I forgot how to breathe for a good minute.

Sitting up straight, I regained my composure. I couldn't tell him the truth. I couldn't tell any of the guys the truth. For my safety and because I didn't want them to think I was a freak. But I didn't want to lie to them either, even to Knox. It would feel like a betrayal somehow. Lying period was a betrayal. So I needed to evade as much as I could.

"I'm a young woman who lives alone."

His gaze moved to the control panel for my alarm on the wall by the front door. "You have a security system with cameras."

"Cameras and alarms don't stop someone from getting in," I said with a little bit of bite. "Does it make you uncomfortable knowing that I have it? Because if so, I'm going to be honest and tell you that it's not the only one I own. I'm eighteen, still in high school, and have no one left in this world apart from my uncle, who is on the other side of the country. When I moved here, I had zero connections. No one who would notice if I went missing. To someone who's paying attention, I'd be the ideal target to be taken, raped, or killed. I know this might seem excessive to you, but it makes me feel safe and helps me close my eyes at night."

He was quiet for a moment, processing everything. "It doesn't make me uncomfortable," he finally said. "It makes me wonder what happened to you that you think you need all of this to feel safe."

My heart rate became rapid as I scrambled to think of something to say to steer him away from the questions I could see forming in his eyes.

I saw a flicker of surprise flash in his eyes. "Something did happen."

"Please don't ask me," I begged.

He frowned and opened his mouth to ask anyway.

"Please, Knox. Don't."

His eyes bored into mine, searching. For what, I didn't know. He gave me a single nod and headed for the door. When he opened it, he paused. "Pork chops and mashed potatoes," he said. "That's what I want for dinner."

"Do you want them cooked a certain way?" I asked.

He glanced back at me. "Cook them however you want."

Already making a grocery list in my head, I stood. "Alright."

"If it's easier for you, you can use our kitchen," he offered before he left.

By the time Colt and Creed got home from practice, I had already returned from the store and was finishing up all the prep work that needed to be done before I began cooking. Per Knox's request, I was making pork chops, but I was putting my own spin on it by serving them with a bacon jam on top. Keeping me somewhat company, Knox sat at the kitchen island, texting someone on his phone.

"We're home," Creed yelled out.

"How was practice?" I yelled back as I plopped all the potatoes I'd just finished cutting into a large stock pot of boiling water.

There was a silence on Colt and Creed's end. I had a feeling they were surprised to hear my voice. Not more than a second later, they walked into the kitchen.

"Hey, we were just about to come over," Colt said as he came up to me. He gave me a kiss on the temple and rubbed his hand down my back. "What's going on here?" Both him and Creed looked from me to Knox.

"I'm cooking you guys dinner," I replied. "Knox requested pork chops and mashed potatoes."

Creed crossed his arms over his chest. "Why does he get to pick?"

Knox set his phone down. "Because your girlfriend ran over here, hysterical, and begged me to remove the tarantula that got into her house."

My mouth fell open. "I was not hysterical."

Knox gave me a look that begged to differ.

I sighed angrily through my nose. "Because Knox graciously helped me get rid of the tarantula and I didn't have to bribe him or anything." My voice was chipper and my words dripped with sarcasm. "As a thank you, I offered to make him whatever he wanted for dinner."

One side of Knox's mouth lifted. "I would have done it for free, but I was enjoying watching you squirm with having to ask me for help."

I counted to ten in my head so I wouldn't smack that stupid smirk off his face with a spatula. "It isn't wise to mess with people who handle your food. Keep it up, Knox, and I might burn your pork chop."

His smirk only broadened as he stood from the island. "Go ahead," he said and turned to leave. "Might be a better flavor than that jam you're making," he shot over his shoulder.

I had a spatula raised above my head so fast, I shocked even myself.

Colt grabbed my wrist. "Whoa, there. Why don't we put the spatula down?" Colt took the spatula from my hand, allowing Knox to leave the kitchen safely.

Creed chuckled, his eyes filled with mirth. "You should have let her chuck it at him. I would have laughed my ass off if she managed to clock him with it."

The twins were better company to have as I cooked. Keelan got home right as dinner was served.

"Dinner is on the table right when I get home? Nice!" Keelan beamed as he sat at the table. Everyone piled food onto their plates. The guys tried my bacon jam with the pork chops, even Knox, and all of them groaned when they took their first bites.

I, on the other hand, sat back and watched Knox's reaction. When he noticed me staring, I arched a brow. "What do you think of my bacon jam now?"

He kept his face impassive and just cut off another bite of pork chop with extra bacon jam on it.

"Thought so," I mumbled to myself triumphantly and began digging into my food.

Keelan looked around the table, confused. "What'd I miss?"

Colt and Creed laughed, then gave Keelan a play-by-play of the verbal showdown Knox and I had had earlier.

19

"Did you see her wrists?"

"Look at her ankles."

"Someone likes to be tied up. Slut."

Deep breath, Shi. Just ignore them. I inhaled deeply as I tied my sneakers in the girls' locker room. I could do this. I wasn't going to care what they thought.

Ever since my locker had been graffitied yesterday, I'd been stared at and talked about at school and no one was very discreet about it when I walked by, either. The weekend couldn't get here fast enough. At least today was almost over. The twins had a meet tonight, but it was at another school.

Holding my head up high, I got up and made my way out into the gym. We were spending today inside playing volleyball again. It was a record one hundred and fifteen degrees out.

Colt, Creed, and Ethan were already standing on the other side of the gym. I began walking in their direction when I was cut off by Cassy, Amber, and three of their friends.

"What the fuck is up with your wrists and ankles?" Amber asked. "One of your clients get a little too rough?"

I didn't engage and tried to appear unfazed as I attempted to step around them. They closed ranks and blocked me from getting away.

"Don't you have something better to do?" I bit out, my irritation quickly building. "You all need to get a life and stop obsessing about mine."

Amber stepped closer. "Don't think you're better than us, you stupid whore," she snarled and shoved me. I stumbled back a few steps. I caught an evil smirk on Cassy's face before my eyes leveled with Amber's.

"You just put hands on me," I said directly to Amber and loud enough for others to hear. "If you do it again, I'll make you eat the floor." I was strangely calm standing against five girls who were undoubtedly getting ready to attack me. Maybe it was because I'd survived something so much worse or maybe it was because I knew I would not be a victim in this fight. I knew how to defend myself. That gave me a little bit of confidence and a sense of control I wasn't used to having.

Amber didn't heed my warning. When she went to shove me again, I stepped out of the way, latched onto her wrist with one hand, yanked her forward while I hooked my foot around her ankle, propelling her face first to the floor. It happened so fast that she didn't have time to brace herself. She hit the floor with a hard thunk. Blood gushed from her nose onto the tan gym floor.

After the shock wore off, the other girls tried to come after me, but Colt and Creed appeared, jumping in between us, blocking them from me.

A whistle blared, echoing throughout the gym. Coach Dale and Coach Ross came running toward us.

"Break it up!" Coach Dale yelled.

We all stepped away from each other. When they approached us, Coach Ross knelt next to Amber while Coach Dale looked between us all before pointing at Cassy and her friends. "You four! Go to the principal's office right now!"

"What?!" Cassy screeched in disbelief.

"I said right now!" Coach Dale yelled. Cassy and her posse reluctantly turned and left. Then Coach Dale looked at me. "Miss Pierce, come with me."

I followed Coach Dale out of the gym toward his office next to the boys' locker room. He pointed to a chair outside his office. "Take a seat." I did as he said and he walked into his office, shutting the door behind him.

I didn't know how long exactly I sat there, but it had to have been more than thirty minutes. It wasn't until the principal, Mr. Morgan, showed up that Coach Dale finally popped out of his office and gestured for me to come in. I took a seat in one of the chairs in front of Coach Dale's desk. Coach Dale offered his desk to Mr. Morgan to sit at while he stood off to the side.

Mr. Morgan sighed as he sat behind Coach Dale's desk. "I just want to start off by saying, we have zero tolerance for violence at this school—"

"Your zero tolerance didn't stop five girls from cornering me in the gym," I snapped. Stewing for thirty minutes hadn't calmed me down. If anything, it had pissed me off more and I was on the defensive.

"And why did they approach you?" Mr. Morgan asked.

"They were making fun of my scars," I answered honestly.

Their eyes dropped down to my wrists. "I see," Mr. Morgan said. "And what did they say about your scars?"

I fidgeted in my seat. "Amber implied that I provide sexual services and asked if one of my clients got a little too rough. They've been calling me a whore every chance they get for the past couple of days."

"How'd you get your scars?" he asked bluntly.

Logan and I had gone over a fake history I was to tell if anyone were to ask me questions. That was the whole point of WITSEC. I wasn't supposed to be me, and no one could find out the truth. I was Shiloh Pierce now and I would tell them her story. "My family and I were in a car accident a little over a year ago. My parents and sister were killed. I was the only one who survived, but I didn't walk away from the accident unscathed."

Mr. Morgan cleared his throat. "I'm sorry for your loss."

I nodded.

"I interviewed some of the other students who had witnessed the altercation. All stated that Amber shoved you and that you told her not to do it again or you would kick her ass," Mr. Morgan said.

"To clarify, I said I would make her eat the floor. Not kick her...butt," I corrected.

"Well, you certainly did as promised." His eyes squinted slightly as if he wanted to laugh, but he remained professional. "Because Amber shoved you, she is being suspended. The rest of the girls received detention. As for you..."

I narrowed my eyes. "You're going to punish me for defending myself?"

"With our zero tolerance for violence, my hands are tied," Mr. Morgan said.

I was floored. "May I ask what you would have done in my situation, Mr. Morgan?"

"You could have yelled out for help," he suggested.

Really?

Mr. Morgan released a heavy sigh. "With the policy in place, I don't have a choice...but I'm willing to make a deal with you," he said, and I waited for him to continue. "It's been reported to the office that your locker was vandalized yesterday and just this morning your name was graffitied in every boys' bathroom. Both incidents were reported by someone other than you. I could only assume you were afraid to come forward. Which is why I had planned on calling you into my office tomorrow morning." Mr. Morgan paused. "If you explain what's been going on, I'll lessen your punishment to lunch detention tomorrow."

"Why?" I was skeptical.

"Because I think you're being bullied, Miss Pierce, and believe it or not my number one priority is to protect my students. Not just punish them."

I sat back in my chair and chewed on my bottom lip. "If I tell you, what will happen?"

"That depends on what you tell us, but having all this documented could protect you and could help us prevent things from escalating."

I didn't want things to get worse, that was for sure. "I have an idea of who vandalized my locker, but I don't have any proof, and as for the boys' bathrooms, I wasn't even aware of that. So I don't know what I can tell you that will help me."

"Why don't you tell me what's been going on and let me be the judge of that?" he said.

Fine. I began with my very first interaction with Cassy.

"You did the right thing," Keelan said from the passenger's seat of Knox's red 1970 Camaro SS. It was the old car they all had been working on when I had seen them for the first time. The twins had told me their dad and Knox had shared a passion for fixing up old cars. Knox's Camaro had been the last car he and their dad had been working on before his fatal car crash. It was a beautiful car with its buttery black leather interior, hot rod red paint, and white racing stripes.

Knox, Keelan, and I were driving to the twins' swim meet. Keelan had texted me and asked if I wanted to ride with them. With Knox driving and Keelan next to him up front, I sat in the back staring out the window. We were driving in a new area of town for me and I wanted to see what was around. The first topic of conversation was what had happened in the gym today. The twins had blabbed.

"I didn't really have a choice. It was either tell the principal what's been going on or get suspended," I grumbled.

"Morgan is a good principal. He could have just suspended you, not caring to get to the root of the issue like a lot of principals," Knox said while staring at me through the rearview mirror. He had a point. All Mr. Morgan had done was document everything I had said. Like I'd told him, there wasn't any proof Cassy had been behind the vandalization of my locker or the boys' bathrooms, which I'd promptly asked Colt and Creed about on the drive home from school. Apparently, "Shiloh Pierce is an easy fuck but a lousy lay" had been written on the walls in all the boys' bathrooms. They hadn't wanted to tell me about it because they didn't want to see me hurt. As much as it warmed my heart that they were looking out for me, I still wished they had told me.

"Are we going out to eat tonight or do one of you have something planned?" Keelan asked.

"Let's go out," Knox and I said at the same time and we locked eyes in the rearview mirror again.

"Where do you want to go to eat, Shi? We could go to a restaurant or if you want something quick, we could hit a drive-through," Keelan suggested.

"I would love to go to a restaurant. I, ah…don't eat fast food," I admitted sheepishly.

"Really?" Keelan asked.

"It's against my religion," I said, sounding serious.

They both went quiet before Keelan turned in his seat to look at me. "What religion is that?"

I did my best to hold back my smile. "The one I just made up."

Knox chuckled and Keelan shook his head while smiling before turning to sit properly in his seat.

I went back to staring out at the window. "Fast food is nothing but fat, too much salt, grease, and thousands of calories."

"That's what makes it good and you're the last person who should worry about their calorie intake," Keelan said.

I sighed. "I'm a food snob, okay?"

That had them both laughing. "Now that, I believe," Knox said and Keelan nodded in agreement.

20

I was wearing my Team Stone top with high-waisted shorts and my hair was in a loose braid pulled to the side. No pigtails or full-on cheerleader outfit tonight. The guys had decided to cut me some slack and compromised. I had to at least wear the Team Stone top.

Desert Canyon, the high school the twins were competing at, was packed with people. I guessed there was also a play being put on by the drama kids. The parking lot was full to the max and there were people everywhere.

Walking through the parking lot, the guys had me walk between them, like Colt and Creed did. Knox's hand went to the small of my back, steering me out of the way when a car drove by looking for a free spot to park. I tried not to read into it when the car passed and Knox's hand didn't leave my back. My mind and my body were not talking to each other at the moment. My heart rate picked up and my skin tingled, making me very aware of his strong hand touching me.

Once inside, it was crazy packed. It was a miracle we managed to get seats. Just before the start of the meet, the twins came out with their team and I waved at them like a total goof, making Keelan and Knox chuckle. The meet was as intense as it had been last time and my guys kicked butt. I swore they were part fish with how fast they speared through the water. When the meet was over, I sent them a text that we'd wait for them outside, which was where the three of us were making our way toward, moving with the large crowd to the exit. Keelan took the lead with me behind him and Knox behind me. The closer we got to the doors, the more people squished together. Worried we'd get separated, I slid my hand into Keelan's and grabbed Knox's with my other. Surprised, Keelan peered over his shoulder at me, then at mine and Knox's hands together. He didn't say anything or let go. He continued on leading the way.

Outside, the crowd spread out and despite not wanting to, I let go of their hands. People were talking all around us, either about the meet or how hot certain swimmers were, which was the current topic of the conversation the group of girls behind us were having.

"Did you see those twins on the other team?" one of them asked.

"Oh, yeah. I'd totally be the meat in that man sandwich," another giggled.

I snorted in my attempt to hold back a laugh. Keelan smiled at me over his shoulder, obviously listening to them like I was. I looked to Knox. He rolled his eyes. It was downright hilarious listening to the girls go on about Colt and Creed. That was, until one of the girls screamed at the top of her lungs, then giggled because it was her boyfriend who'd snuck up on her. I wasn't really paying attention at that point, though. The damage had been done.

The moment her scream had hit my ears, fear had spiked through me, jolting my heart to pump at a rapid speed. My hands shot up to cover my ears in an attempt to shut out the scream that was currently on repeat in my head. Only the scream didn't belong to that girl, it belonged to Shayla. My whole body froze as that night flashed in and out, causing a shutter effect on my sight of Keelan and Knox, who were starting to give me strange looks.

Deep and slow breaths. It's not real. You're safe. I did as I told myself. I inhaled through my nose and exhaled out my mouth. I tried to fix my eyes on Keelan as my mind toggled between him and standing in the dark at my old house. Keelan's mouth moved. He was talking to me but I couldn't hear him. Not over the screaming.

You're safe. It's not real.

You're safe. It's not real.

The more I told myself that, the longer Keelan stayed in my line of sight between flashes. I felt arms wrap around me, hugging me tightly. When my vision shuttered back to reality, I found my face smushed into a chest. The smell told me it was Keelan. I sucked in his scent deeply. His tight embrace eased my anxiety and, like brakes on a car, slowed down my heart. The screaming began to fade until I could only hear Keelan whispering in my ear.

"You're okay, Shi. I've got you. Deep breaths."

I stiffly dropped my hands from my ears and tucked them between us. My whole body was shaking and weak-feeling.

"That's it. You're okay," Keelan said as he ran his hand up and down my back.

I took one more deep breath before I found the strength to pull myself away. Stepping back, Keelan released me. I continued to move backward, putting some space between us until my back bumped into someone else. Hands went to my shoulders. I knew it was Knox. I couldn't look at either of them. For one, I was mortified and two, I didn't want to see what a nutcase they probably thought I was.

"You want to tell us what that was about?" Knox asked from behind me.

My whole body went rigid.

Noticing my distress, Keelan stepped closer. "She doesn't have to answer—"

"Yes, she does," Knox said with a tone that brooked no argument.

I released a shaky breath. "The scream triggered...I—" Tears started to fill my eyes. I closed them and took another calming breath. "I was diagnosed with PTSD after my family died. Some things trigger me to have flashbacks of that night. I've learned to pull myself out when it happens. But this one kind of blindsided me because I haven't had an episode in six months."

They went quiet and it wasn't until I heard nothing but silence that I realized my eyes were still closed. Opening them, I stared at Keelan's shirt. I was still scared to look at them. A huge part of me was waiting to hear them tell me not to come over anymore and to stay away from Colt and Creed. As the silence continued, I found it harder to hold back the tears and they fell one after another down my cheeks.

"That explains why you kept telling yourself that you were safe and it wasn't real," Knox said behind me and dropped his hands from my shoulders.

Unable to bear waiting for them to tell me to hit the road, I wiped my cheeks with the backs of my hands and stepped away from them. "I'm going to order a car service to take me home. You don't have to worry about me bothering you guys anymore." I took another step away. "Who would want a head case hanging around?" I tried to joke. My mind wandered to the twins and my heart hurt with how much I was going to miss them. I went to leave and made it a few steps before a hand locked onto my wrist.

"Did we say you were bothering us?" Knox grumbled.

I was stunned. Of all people, Knox would have been the last person I would have guessed to stop me from leaving.

Keelan appeared in front of me, also preventing me from leaving. "We know you're still healing from the loss of your family," Keelan said and wiped away a tear that was rolling down my cheek with his thumb. "I don't know if the twins have realized this, but Knox and I have picked up on the fact that it was traumatic, especially after what we just witnessed." I felt myself begin to panic again. His hands went to my shoulders. "Breathe," he ordered, and I took a deep breath. "I know you know we lost our parents. I was about your age when we lost our dad. It probably looks like we've got our shit together now, but it's been over three years since he died. Healing takes time. The four of us are very understanding of that." He gave me a sad smile. "None of us want you to leave. Even if we did, the twins have imprinted on you, so we're kind of stuck with each other now." That made me laugh.

"What's going on?" a voice asked. We looked in the direction of the source and saw Creed and Colt standing a few feet away, eyes bouncing between the three of us.

Knox released my wrist, but Keelan just smiled at his brothers. "I think we're about to get into trouble, Knox. We made their precious Shiloh cry."

Creed and Colt looked at me, noticing my wet cheeks and undoubtedly puffy, red eyes. Colt's eyes filled with rage. "You made her cry?" he seethed and stalked over to us. He pulled me away from Keelan into his arms.

"What did you do to her?" Creed growled as he came to stand next to us and glare at his older brothers. Both of whom seemed unfazed. Knox looked bored while Keelan had a mischievous glint in his eyes.

"They didn't do anything," I said.

"I can see that you've been crying, babe," Colt argued.

"Hormones. They got the best of me. Keelan and Knox cheered me up." It wasn't exactly the truth, but it wasn't exactly a lie, either. Keelan and Knox had cheered me up.

"Hormones?" the twins repeated at the same time, sounding identically skeptical.

I nodded. "Where do you guys want to go to eat?" I asked, changing the subject.

"Don't suggest fast food," Knox warned.

The twins looked at their brother. "We know," they said at the same time again.

"We tried taking her to McDonald's for lunch one time and she ordered a salad. She and Creed bickered about her food preferences the entire time," Colt explained, sounding as if it was a tiring memory.

"I guess if she was going to have a weird quirk, it's at least a healthy one," Creed said.

"And my butt thanks me every day," I grumbled.

A smile pulled at Creed's lips. "You do have a nice ass."

To everyone else, it was just a compliment, but I knew exactly what he was hinting at. I narrowed my eyes at him. "You said you wouldn't look."

He shrugged. "Like you said, everyone looks, and don't think Colt didn't, either."

Colt stilled behind me and his silence spoke louder than words.

"Hold on. Are you two saying you saw Shiloh naked?" Keelan asked. The twins went quiet and my whole body flushed. Keelan frowned a little. "I think I'm jealous."

Knox rolled his eyes and smacked him on the back of his head. "You're making her uncomfortable."

"Why do you care?" Creed asked. "Last night, you pissed her off so much, she almost tried to murder you with a spatula."

Keelan laughed as he rubbed the back of his head. "I would have paid to see that."

Knox ignored them and looked at me. "Where are we going to dinner?"

"I don't know of any good restaurants here yet, but I'm craving enchiladas."

All of them mumbled a name that I assumed was a restaurant.

"Then it's decided," Colt said and started pulling me toward the parking lot. "Shiloh's riding with us," he shouted over his shoulder at Knox and Keelan.

21

Saturday morning, I drove to the gym to meet up with Keelan. We were finally going to spar to see how advanced my training was. As I entered the gym, Keelan was sitting at the front desk with Stephanie.

"Do you know what you're doing for your birthday?" I heard her ask him.

"The same thing as last year. A party at the house," Keelan replied.

I set my gym bag and picnic basket down at my feet before resting my arms on the tall counter of the large, L-shaped front desk. "A party?"

Keelan's face lit up when he saw that it was me. "My birthday is in a few weeks. Colt and Creed didn't tell you?"

"No, they didn't," I said, a little sullenly. I wondered why they hadn't.

A stack of flyers dropped down on the counter as Knox appeared next to me. "They probably didn't think to invite you because it's a given that you'd be there. You practically live with us," he said.

"I don't live with you. I own my own home and I sleep in it every night," I argued.

Knox pulled a piece of paper off the stack and began reading it over. "How long will that last, I wonder?" he said distractedly.

I turned to face him fully, my irritation quickly building. "You think I come over too much?"

Knox scoffed as he began signing the paper. "What gave you that impression?" His voice dripped with sarcasm, making my heart sink.

Once he was done signing the paper, he held it out to Stephanie, who'd been quietly watching us. "Can you fax this?" he asked her. She took the paper and he put his hand on top of the stack of flyers. "These are the flyers for the mud run in October." Stephanie nodded and went over to the fax machine at the other end of the desk.

I fought to keep from showing how his words had affected me.

Keelan frowned at his brother.

Knox noticed. "What?"

Keelan's gaze moved to me and his brow furrowed. "He didn't mean—"

"It's fine," I snapped. I bent over to pick up my bag and picnic basket. I had made lunch for the five of us to eat after Keelan and I were done sparring, but now I realized it had been wrong of me to assume they'd want to have lunch with me. I set the basket on the counter. "I made you guys lunch. Don't feel obligated to eat it if you don't want to." I turned and headed for the exit.

"What the fuck is wrong with you?" I heard Keelan say in a low, angry voice just before I walked out of the gym.

By the time I got home I was itching for a run. The only problem was that it was over one hundred degrees out. I wasn't in the mood for heat stroke, so that wasn't an option. Instead, I headed to my back porch where my swing still lay in pieces, waiting to be put together. I did a quick look-around for any little creatures hanging out nearby. I didn't want to have another encounter with any more desert wildlife. When I didn't see any, I sat on the ground and grabbed the assembly instructions that were inside a bag of loose screws, nails, and washers. I flipped it open and glared at the first thing it said: *For safety, two people are recommended for assembly.*

"Well, one is just gonna have to do," I snapped down at the instructions.

A half hour later, I let go of the two heavy pieces I was struggling to put together with a frustrated huff.

"Want some help?" a voice asked, startling me.

I looked over my shoulder, finding Knox leaning against the frame of the back-patio door. "Apparently, I need to remind Colt and Creed that the whole purpose of an emergency key is that it is supposed to be used for emergencies," I said, my tone sharp and evident of my irritation.

"If you truly believed they'd only use it for emergencies, then you don't know them very well."

Of course, I'd known they'd use it. I loved that they used it. Because it meant they wanted to spend as much time with me as I wanted to spend with them. They'd even used the key last night as I'd been getting into bed. I'd received a text from them seconds before I'd heard the front door open. They'd wanted to have another sleepover. As expected, I'd had a nightmare, but Colt had gently woken me from it and held me until I'd fallen back to sleep. I didn't know why I'd complained about my key being used. Scratch that, I did know. I was angry and I was grasping at anything I could use as ammunition against Knox.

I got to my feet and brushed dirt off the back of my leggings. "What are you doing here?"

His jaw clenched and he folded his arms across his chest. I internally scolded myself for admiring the way the muscles in his arms bulged a little, making the short sleeves of his polo stretch tight.

"What I said…" he started to say.

"It's fine."

Frowning, he dropped his arms to his sides and pushed off the door frame. "You're upset."

Feeling hot and thirsty, I walked toward the door that he was sort of blocking. "I'm fine," I said, squeezing by him to get inside.

He followed me into the kitchen. "Stop saying 'fine.' Clearly, it's not," he said as he watched me grab a glass from the cabinet.

I sighed. If I had been a dragon there would have been smoke coming out of my nostrils. I set my glass on the island harshly. I wouldn't have been surprised if I had broken it. Despite my anger puppeteering my actions at the moment, I was thankful it hadn't. Leveling my gaze with his, I asked, "Why does it matter to you how I feel?"

He didn't respond. Instead, the muscle in his jaw went tight as he clenched it.

Shaking my head, I picked up my glass and began filling it from the fridge's water dispenser. "Go home, Knox, and leave my key."

He let out a frustrated noise. "Shiloh—"

"Why should someone have access to my home if they never intend to extend that same trust to me in return?" I interrupted him.

"Is that what I need to do to fix this? Give you a fucking key?" he snapped.

I fought not to roll my eyes and focused on taking a big gulp of cold, delicious water instead.

Keys jingling sounded behind me. I whirled around just in time to see him take a key from his keyring and slam it down on my island. "Here you go. A key to our house."

I set my water next to the lone key. "I don't want your pity house key."

He squeezed his eyes closed and pinched the bridge of his nose. "You confuse the shit out of me."

"No, you confuse me. A few days ago, you said I didn't bother you, and today you made me feel like an annoyance who had overstayed my welcome," I argued.

"You're not an annoyance, Shiloh."

"Then why did you say that?"

"I didn't mean—"

"Bullshit," I cursed, surprising us both. "You push people away, Knox. It's what you do, and I understand why you do it, but what you did today…you knew how that would make me feel."

His eyes never left mine as his jaw clenched again.

"The four of you have an expiration date in my life," I blurted. "You don't know what it's like to have a ticking clock in the back of your head, counting down until the four of you decide to kick me to the curb. Naively, I hold onto this false hope that you won't, because I hate the idea of going a day without seeing any of you. And yes, that includes you, Knox, the guy who has been a jerk to me ninety-eight percent of the time."

Knox was silent as he held a pensive frown.

His lack of response was all I needed to know. What I felt for him wasn't what he felt for me. The regret of allowing myself to be vulnerable twisted up my insides and the backs of my eyes began to burn. I had to look away. I didn't want to cry. I cried too much as it was, and I was tired of it.

"Don't cry," he said tightly.

I grit my teeth. "Then don't make me cry."

Done with our conversation, I went to storm past him. His hand shot out and locked around my elbow. For a split second I considered breaking his hold. It would have been easy to do. I didn't, though. I let him pull me to him, with a tiny bit of resistance to save face. As my body fell against his, he wrapped an arm around my waist.

"Don't do that. Don't walk away," he said, his livid eyes boring into me. "You talk about how you're worried about us kicking you to the curb, but have you ever stopped to think that we feel you'll do the same? You're not the only one who has had their world shattered from the foundation up. I've done everything to hold my family together. We've worked so hard to repair our foundation and move on with our lives." His nostrils flared as he struggled to contain his rage. "You said I push people away? That's because everyone is a threat to what we rebuilt. You're a threat. You barreled your way into our lives and somehow made yourself important. I don't want to care about you, but I do, and it pisses me off."

I put a hand on his bicep as I stared up at him. "I'm not a threat, Knox. The last thing I'd want is to hurt any of you."

His arms around me flexed at my touch. "You say that now. What happens if you and the twins break up?"

"We're just friends," I said. How many times would I have to tell him? And that was the second time he had implied that I was in a relationship with both of them. Not one or the other.

"You really expect me to believe there's nothing going on with you three?"

"Yes!" I exclaimed.

"The three of you haven't done anything?" His eyes dropped to my mouth. "You haven't kissed them?"

My breath hitched. "They told you?"

A small, proud grin lifted the corner of his mouth. "No. You just did."

I pushed at his chest and he let me go. I put a few steps of distance between us. "Not that it's any of your business, but yes, I've kissed them," I said bitterly. "It was a mistake and won't happen again."

"Why?"

"What do you mean why?" I asked, feeling exasperated. "If we go down that road, I'll have to pick one of them, and that will hurt the other."

He scoffed. "They'd never make you choose."

All I could do was gape at him. Was that why he referred to

both of them as my boyfriends? Oh goodness, he really thought the three of us were in a relationship together. I began to feel flushed at the thoughts that started filling my head. What was surprising was that I wasn't turned off by the idea of being with both of them. It was the opposite, actually. "Have they been with the same girl before?"

He took in my red face and gave me a knowing look. "That's something you should ask them."

"Do you and Keelan...um, share?" I really didn't mean to ask that question, but my curiosity got the best of me.

His brows shot up before he gave me a haughty, male smirk. He stepped closer. "Why?" he asked, his tone full of amusement.

"I—" I took a step back.

He stepped forward again. "You're getting redder by the second."

"I can't help it," I said, taking another step backward, and my back met the front of the fridge.

He closed most of the space between us and flattened his hands on the fridge above my head, trapping me. "Why do you want to know about Keelan and me, Shiloh?"

"I wanted—" Oh, no. Thoughts began to fill my head of the two of them. I couldn't get any redder, could I?

"Wow, what did I just walk into?" a voice asked. I looked past Knox to see Keelan standing in the kitchen's entryway off the living room. He was staring at us, a little wide-eyed. "I thought I'd come here and make sure Knox didn't make things worse."

Knox glanced at his brother over his shoulder. I took that moment of distraction to escape. I ducked under one of Knox's arms and booked it to the other side of the kitchen.

Keelan looked from me to Knox. "What's going on?"

Knox smiled at his brother. "Shiloh asked if you and I share like Colt and Creed do."

Keelan's eyes only widened before he gave me the same stupid smirk Knox had given me. "Are you looking to upgrade from Colt and Creed?"

That made Knox snort.

"Cheese and rice," I cursed, rolling my eyes. "I asked because I was genuinely curious."

"Just because Colt and Creed like to share doesn't mean Keelan and I would be into it," Knox said.

"Speak for yourself," Keelan said.

Knox looked at his brother, clearly surprised.

"If we both loved the same woman and she loved both of us, would you really make her choose at the risk of tearing us apart?" Keelan asked him.

Knox opened his mouth to respond, then snapped it shut.

Keelan shrugged. "It's something to consider."

"I'm not saying it's wrong, but that type of relationship is kind of unconventional," I said.

Keelan looked at me. "Times are changing. People are more accepting and polyamorous relationships are more common than you think."

Knox gaped at Keelan. "You've researched this?"

"I did when the twins started dating that girl Emma last year," Keelan explained. "I was worried about what kind of hardships they'd face by pursuing that type of relationship."

"Emma?" I said out loud and internally cringed at how jealous I felt.

Keelan smiled at me like he knew exactly what I was feeling. "They dated for six months until she and her family moved to Connecticut. She was…nice."

"I didn't like her," Knox said.

"You don't like anyone," I pointed out and then smiled proudly. "Well, except for me."

He frowned. "I said I care about you, not that I like you."

I shrugged. "To-may-to, to-mah-to."

"I guess this means you two worked things out?" Keelan asked.

Knox's and my eyes locked.

"I'm no longer upset with him, if that answers your question," I said, breaking our staring contest to scoop up Knox's pity house key. "Knox gave me a key to your house."

Keelan brows rose. "He did?"

I grinned at Knox. "Yup. He felt it was only fair since you all have a key to my house, right, Knox?"

The corner of his mouth twitched, but his frowny face stayed in place. "Sure."

22

For the most part, school was peaceful this week and flew by. With Amber suspended for a few days and Cassy and her friends being closely watched by Mr. Morgan, I was left alone for the most part. People still whispered about me when they saw me, but my scars were considered old news now that some girl had gotten caught blowing a football player behind the school gym. My lunch detention last Friday had been uneventful. I'd spent the entire time getting ahead on homework.

It was already the weekend. Keelan and I were attempting to spar again. This time I actually made it past the front desk and was in the room where Keelan taught his classes. The room was large and long. The walls and floor were lined with padding. By the door there was a small section of hardwood flooring and shoe cubbies. Keelan had me remove my shoes there before stepping on the padded floor.

"Why don't we start by going over what your uncle has taught you? I know you know some jiu-jitsu. Do you have any other training?" Keelan asked. He was standing in front of me, with his hands on his hips. He was wearing his gi pants and a form-fitting black shirt.

I had chosen to wear red leggings with the Flash's lightning bolt running down the side of the leg and a matching shirt. I liked how I'd gotten a smile from Keelan when he had seen what I was wearing.

"He taught me a little bit of boxing and some judo," I said. "But the majority of what he taught me was jiu-jitsu."

Keelan nodded. "Why don't we start off with holds and how well you can get out of them?"

"Okay." I watched as he came up to me and grabbed my wrist. I frowned up at him. "Really?"

He smiled. "Try to get free." His grip tightened and he started to pull me. With my free hand I grabbed my other and easily yanked my wrist free.

"Good," he praised.

Next, he put me in a standing rear choke hold. To escape, I twisted my body to the side, threw my thigh behind his, and with all my strength, because he was a lot bigger than me, I pulled us backward to the ground. With my thigh behind his, he had no choice but to take the brunt of the fall. As soon as we hit the ground, I was able to slide my head out from under his armpit and get free.

He chuckled as he got back to his feet. "You don't hesitate or hold back. That's good."

His gaze jumped to my ponytail.

I cut him off before he could suggest what we would do next. "If you go for my hair, Keelan, I'll have you face down on this floor and begging in less than five seconds."

My threat only made him grin. "Alright, baby girl. I won't pull your hair...this time."

His tone suggested something other than sparring and my mind filled with filthy thoughts.

My face must have shown what I was thinking, because Keelan smirked. "Sorry. I know I shouldn't tease you, but the way you react is so adorable, I can't seem to help myself."

I put my hands on my hips and tried to look perturbed. "Shall we continue?"

Keelan got back into serious mode and we moved to the floor. I was to lay on my back as Keelan straddled my hips. He started off by pinning my wrists above my head. "Get free," he said, staring down at me.

I brought my feet as close as I could to my butt and thrust my pelvis up, propelling him forward, as I slid my wrists to the sides at the same time. Keelan had two options. One: refuse to let go of my wrists and nosedive into the floor above my head. Or two: let go and catch himself. He chose to save himself. I threw my free arms around his exposed middle, used his body as a way to pull my butt out from between his legs to gain leverage, then hooked my upper arm over one of his as I bent one of my legs again and rolled us until he was the one on his back. I gave him a bright smile. "What's next?"

Keelan tested me again and again until he got a good idea of how advanced my training was, and then we switched to sparring. That was when the fun began. We were both sweaty, breathing heavy, and I had my legs wrapped around his arm and neck. "Quit holding back on me," I growled.

"I don't think that's a good idea," he strained to say. He was having difficulty getting free.

"I'm pretty sure I can take you, pretty boy."

He huffed out a laugh. "Even you talking shit is adorable."

"I'll show you adorable," I grumbled and squeezed my legs.

He tapped my thigh, signaling defeat, and I released his arm and dropped my legs to the floor on either side of him. Between my legs, he sat back on his haunches. For a while we both just focused on breathing.

I tried to sit up and fell back with a groan. "My legs and arms feel like spaghetti."

"What you don't have in strength you make up for in stamina," he said. He cracked his neck. "Man, I'm going to sleep good tonight."

"Does that mean you're too tired for *Game of Thrones* tonight?"

"I won't skip out on our *Game of Thrones* date."

I smiled up at the ceiling. "Good."

"Alright, let's get up," he said, leaning over me. His hands slid under my ribs and up my back a little. I gripped his biceps as he lifted the upper half of my body until we were sitting face to face.

"Can you carry me home, too?" I joked.

He grinned. "You should get with Knox a couple times a week to do some strength training."

I groaned again, this time a little exaggeratedly, making him chuckle. He climbed to his feet and held out a hand to help me to mine.

"So what's the verdict?" I asked.

"I think jiu-jitsu is your strong suit," he pointed out.

"That was the class I wanted to take."

"You have the training and discipline of a brown belt, possibly a black belt. I teach a class for that level. The issue is that it's during the week right as you get off school. We have another class that I don't teach that is an all-levels, but all the students in that are either white belts or blue belts. You won't be challenged in that class."

"I just want to be able to defend myself if I ever need to."

"I'd say you know how to properly defend yourself. What your uncle got you to master in a year is remarkable." He put his hands on his hips and went quiet for a moment. I could tell he was thinking something over. "I can work with you every Saturday at this time."

I scrunched my nose. "One-on-one sessions with Keelan Stone, skilled MMA fighter and one of the owners of Desert Stone Fitness. Hmm, I don't know. You sound expensive," I joked.

He chuckled. "I wouldn't charge you."

I shook my head. "I was kidding, Keelan. Of course you're going to charge me. I would feel guilty not paying."

He shrugged. "You're getting the girlfriend discount."

"I'm not your girlfriend."

"Want to be?" he asked with a charming smile.

All I could do was blink.

He laughed, shaking his head. "So adorable."

He's just teasing me, I mused as I slowly recovered from my stunned state.

"How about this?" he started. "I'm currently teaching a beginners' jiu-jitsu class for just women, but the other instructor who usually teaches the class with me is pregnant and doesn't feel comfortable sparring anymore, even in a teaching setting. I don't have the time to find and hire someone else. I need someone who will demonstrate with me and help me make sure the students are maneuvering properly, because not all of them are comfortable with me being close or pinning them down. Some of them have been through some shit." He paused to see if I caught his meaning and I did. "If you help me teach the class, we'll call it even."

I felt kind of put on the spot, but I was interested. "When is the class?"

"Mondays and Wednesdays at four."

I mulled everything over in my head and couldn't find a reason not to do it. "Okay."

"Great."

We put on our shoes before making our way to his office across from Knox's, who happened to be sitting behind his desk as we walked by.

"What do you have planned for the rest of the day?" Keelan asked as I scooped up the gym bag I'd left in his office.

"I'm going to brave the showers here so I can go to the grocery store," I said.

"Just use the shower in Knox's office," Keelan suggested.

Not wanting to impose, I was getting ready to decline when Knox's voice came from across the hall. "Just use the damn shower, Shiloh."

Keelan snorted and followed me into Knox's office. As we entered, Knox didn't look up from a form he was filling out.

"I'm thinking of making homemade pizzas for dinner. Any requests or can I surprise you?" I asked them and that got Knox's attention.

He looked up and studied me with narrowed eyes. "That depends, are you planning on making something weird you saw on the Food Network and it's going to have ingredients we've never heard of?"

I gave him a sly smile. "Have I made something you've not liked?"

"She has a point," Keelan said. "And I doubt anyone could mess up pizza."

Knox waved his hand flippantly. "Fine, do your thing."

"Yay!" I beamed. "You guys like octopus, right?"

They both went silent and Knox glared at Keelan, like he was at fault. I spun on my heel to head to the bathroom before they could see me smiling.

"Shiloh," Knox said.

Unable to contain it, I laughed as I dashed inside the bathroom.

By the time I was done with my shower and came back out, Keelan and Knox were gone. I pulled out my phone and sent a quick text to all four of the guys in our group chat that I was leaving and that I would see them tonight.

As I stepped out of Knox's office, I ran into Stephanie. "Hi," I said, trying to be friendly.

She looked from me to Knox's office with a frown. "What are you doing back here? This area is for employees of the gym only."

"Excuse me?" I gaped.

"You heard me. Please leave," she said, before squeezing past me into Knox's office and slamming the door.

Confused, I walked down the hall toward the front desk. "What in the H...E...double hockey sticks was that?" I mumbled to myself. I was so befuddled and lost in my thoughts I ran into another person as I came out from behind the front desk. This time I actually collided with them—or more specifically, their chest.

Their hands gripped my hips. "Whoa, there."

"I'm sorry!" I said quickly and glanced up. I fought not to cringe when I saw that it was Jacob, the creepy guy, who I'd met running the track upstairs not that long ago.

"No harm. No foul," he said, smiling. "How've you been, Shiloh?" He said my name with familiarity that didn't sit well with me and he had yet to let go of my hips.

I stepped back until he had no choice but to let me go. "I'm good."

"I haven't seen you running here as much anymore."

"I run at home most of the time."

That made his smile dim a little. "Running on a treadmill just isn't the same."

"I don't have a treadmill." I regretted the words the moment they left my mouth. Why had I been raised to be a polite person?

The spark in his smile returned. "Oh, you run around your neighborhood. It's getting too hot out to be doing that. You must go early in the morning or at night."

The hair on the back of my neck rose. Why did he need to know that? There was a warning going off inside me. It pulled at me to get away from him. I'd ignored that warning with Mr. X. I would not make that mistake again.

I felt a hand touch the small of my back before Colt appeared next to me. "Hey, babe, what are you still doing here?" he asked as he looked from Jacob to me.

I was so happy to see him I could have kissed him. Actually, that wasn't a bad idea. "Hey!" I said, a little high-pitched, pushed up on my tiptoes, and kissed him. He was surprised at first, but he quickly recovered. I slid my hand into his before I broke our kiss with a fake smile. "I ran into Jacob here and we got to talking." I turned my fake smile on Jacob, who didn't seem happy with Colt's presence. In fact, he scowled at him. "I should really be going, though," I told Jacob, regaining his attention. "It was nice talking to you."

Jacob nodded curtly and headed for the exit. I didn't take my eyes off him until he was through the door and walking into the parking lot.

"You're squeezing my hand, babe," Colt said.

I turned to face him. "Please walk me to my car." I hated how there was a hint of fear in my voice.

Anger brewed like a storm in his beautiful aquamarine eyes. "Has that guy been bothering you?"

"No." I grimaced. "He gives me a bad feeling. It's the way he says things like how he's watched me run and brought up how long I run. I run for hours. Does that mean he watched me for the entire time? Then he brought up how I haven't been using the track as much and fished to know what time of day I run around our neighborhood. I know I probably sound crazy, but my instincts are screaming at me that he's no good."

He pulled me close so he could wrap his arms around me. "I don't think you're crazy. If he gives you a bad feeling, that's all that matters to me."

I buried my face in his chest and breathed him in.

"Hey, everything okay?" The sound of Creed's voice made me smile and I turned to lay my cheek on Colt's chest so I could see him.

"We'll talk about it later. Want to take off early?" Colt asked him.

"Sure. We can go with Shiloh to the store and make sure she doesn't buy an octopus."

I giggled. "Did Knox tell you that?"

"Keelan," they both said at the same time.

Colt kissed my temple before reluctantly pulling away from our embrace. "I'm going to go find Knox and let him know."

Creed threw his arm over my shoulders and we watched Colt walk off. "What do I have to bribe you with to get a meat lover's-style pizza?" Creed whispered in my ear.

I laughed. "Hmm…my price would be physical. I don't think you'll want to do it."

He shifted so that we were facing each other. "I think I'll be the judge of that."

I circled my arms around his waist as I stared up at him. "What I want would involve your hands." I brought my voice down to a whisper. "They'd have to do some rubbing and massaging and they might even get a little dirty."

The more I talked, the higher his brows rose. For a moment all he did was study me and it was taking all the willpower I had to keep a straight face. I got to bear witness to his lightbulb moment just before his shoulders slumped a little. "You're talking about kneading pizza dough, aren't you?"

I grinned up at him innocently. "Of course. What'd you think I was talking about?"

23

BY THE TIME WE WERE DONE EATING DINNER, I WAS WIPED OUT. The pizzas I'd made had been a success. Even the one "fancy" pizza, as Knox had called it, had been a hit. It had been a Margherita pizza with chunks of mozzarella, basil, and balsamic drizzle. The other three pizzas the twins had helped me make and to Knox's relief, they had been meat lover's, pepperoni, and supreme.

Even though I was tired, I was determined to watch *Game of Thrones* with the guys. I ran home really quick to throw on pajamas. I chose my Hulk set. The shorts were purple and the top was Hulk green with black writing that read, "Ready for an incredible nap." I returned to the smell of popcorn in the air and Knox, Colt, and Creed were already lounging on the large sectional. Keelan came walking in from the kitchen carrying three bowls of popcorn. He handed one to Creed and another to Knox. He smiled down at me. "Nice pajamas."

I couldn't tell if he was teasing or not. Narrowing my eyes, I put my hands on my hips, ready to defend my cute PJs. He surprised me when he circled an arm around my waist and pulled me down into his lap. We were all the way on the end, which allowed my legs to stretch out to the side and my back to rest against the armrest. He placed the bowl of popcorn in my lap with an innocent smile before turning to look at his brothers.

Colt and Creed weren't happy. They'd become two glaring statues who appeared to be moments away from maiming Keelan.

Keelan smirked. "You get her all the time. Learn to share."

Knox rolled his eyes and pressed play on the remote to the TV. The show began to play and Colt and Creed still hadn't stopped glaring in our direction.

"I don't know how I feel about this," Colt grumbled and looked to Creed.

"He's not going to bite her. Let it go and watch the TV," Knox said.

I felt the strong urge to go over there and sit by them, but Keelan was my friend, too. I didn't want to hurt his feelings either. It wasn't until Colt and Creed eventually focused on the show that I could relax and finally dig into the popcorn.

About halfway through our second episode I was fighting to keep my eyes open. "Why don't you lie down?" Keelan whispered.

I shook my head to refuse, but I could already feel him lifting me up and laying me down on the couch. "Don't let me fall asleep," I mumbled. I felt fingers brush some hair away from my forehead before I gave up the fight and fell asleep.

"Shiiiii...lloooooohh! Come out, come out wherever you are!" Mr. X shouted from another room. My heart was racing, and my inner arm was bleeding where Mr. X had cut me. Blood dripped from my fingers as my arm dangled at my side limply, leaving a bloody trail in my wake as I quietly snuck through the house in the dark. Dashing into the kitchen, I scooped up one of the kitchen towels hanging in front of the oven. Biting my lip to keep myself from crying out, I wrapped the

towel around my arm. I made quick work of my makeshift bandage and moved on. I couldn't linger or he'd find me. I needed to get out of here and get help. I clung to a sliver of hope that I could still save Shayla.

Moving as quickly and silently as possible, I headed for the back door just off the dining room. Every window I had tried had been nailed shut. I couldn't give up. Reaching out for the gold door knob, I turned it. The door wouldn't budge. "No!" I whispered as I tried to slam my body against it. It wouldn't budge. I had no choice but to move on.

"Shiloh," a voice whispered from behind me.

My heart accelerated to a speed so fast, I was afraid it'd give out. Panting, I turned to find Mr. X right behind me. I screamed as loud as my lungs would allow, hoping the neighbors would hear, and fell backward to the floor.

The drop to the floor was short and I landed on carpet. We didn't have carpet in the dining room. I didn't have time to stop and think about that as I scrambled to my feet. I took off running the moment I was off the floor, but something strange happened. I wasn't even in the dining room anymore. I was in the living room on the other side of the house. The room where both of my parents had been murdered. My dad's corpse was still sprawled out on the couch and my mom was still dead on the floor where I had watched Mr. X stab her repeatedly. "How did I get here?"

"Shi?" a muffled voice called out to me. I turned to search for the voice. There wasn't anyone there. My family's living room blurred out for a second, revealing a different living room—one with a huge sectional couch facing a monstrously large entertainment center.

I knew that living room.

"Shiloh?" a different but just as muffled voice said. I turned my head again and saw Knox standing by the entertainment center. Then my family's living room returned. Knox and I were both standing in the darkness with my parents' bodies a handful of feet away. Knox regarded me with caution and worry in his eyes. I didn't understand why he was here, and I didn't have time to find out.

"I need to get help," I whispered as I stepped closer to him. "We need to get out of here before he finds us."

Knox's brows furrowed.

"I don't think she's fully awake," another muffled voice said. I had to ignore it because we didn't have time to just stand here. If we lingered here, Mr. X would find us.

I stepped toward Knox and grabbed his wrist. I tugged a little, trying to get him to move, but he wouldn't budge. "He's somewhere in the house. If we stay here, we will die. We have to get help," I said and tugged some more.

The result was the same. He didn't budge. "Who's in the house?" he asked.

"Who the hell cares?! We need to wake her up," a voice argued, and it was clear this time. Not that it mattered.

"Please," I begged. "Shayla is still upstairs. She's dying. If we don't get help right now, she won't make it."

Knox's expression changed from confusion to what looked like sadness.

I didn't understand why he wasn't moving, and I couldn't leave him behind. I couldn't let anyone else die. "Please, Knox. We have to go get help." I tugged on him again with all my strength. I got him to move one step before he yanked his wrist free and grabbed mine instead.

He then tried to pull me toward him. "Shiloh."

I resisted. "Please!" I pleaded loudly as tears pooled in my eyes. "If I don't get help in time, she will die. Please help me, Knox. Please! If she dies, I'll be all alone! I don't want to be alone! Please, don't make me be alone!" I cried as I screamed at him. Sobs ripped out of me and there was nothing I could do to stop them. His eyes were wide as I fell apart in front of him. My knees gave out and I crumpled to the floor. At that point I didn't care anymore. I wanted to give up. If Mr. X came in and killed me right now, so be it. I had no more fight left.

Knox knelt in front of me and pulled me into his arms. I climbed into his lap, wrapped my arms around his neck, and buried my face into *his shoulder. My whole body shook as I cried and that just made him tighten his arms around me.*

"Fuck," someone cursed.

~

The smell of coffee woke me. I had to blink a few times to see clearly. My eyes felt puffy. I was surprised to find myself waking up on the guys' couch. What shocked me the most was the heart beating steadily beneath my ear and the large body it belonged to that I was pretty much lying on top of.

I slowly lifted my head to see who it was. His size was my first clue. My eyes proved that it was indeed Knox beneath me. He was sleeping soundly. I sat up a little and his arm that was wrapped around my back tightened. It was then that I became very aware of everywhere we were touching. My leg was thrown over his. My upper thigh was touching a part of the male anatomy I had yet to be introduced to and it was currently hard enough to attach a flag to. His hipbone was also becoming well acquainted with the area between my legs.

Being very careful not to wake him, I pushed the blanket that was covering us down. I grabbed at the back of the couch, trying to pull myself up enough to gain leverage on my elbow. Once I was able to put my weight on my elbow, then my hand, I lifted my leg that was holding down his manhood to put it…*cheese and rice!* The only place I could put it was between his legs and that required me to shift my hip. Using what little upper body strength I had, with my leg hovering in the air, I shifted my hip and began falling off the couch.

I let out a yelp and braced myself for the ground. Knox's arm that was still at my back caught me and he yanked me back on top of him. Only this time I was completely on top of him—straddling him. I still had one hand locked onto the back of the couch and the other was flat on his chest. I gaped down at him, blushing like crazy because I could feel his flagpole through the thin—very thin fabric of my pajama shorts.

"Um…good morning," I said awkwardly.

Staring up at me, he threw an arm behind his head and sighed through his nose. "You need to work on your slipping-away skills."

"I was trying not to wake you to avoid this very awkward encounter."

"You woke me the moment you lifted your head off my chest," he said and yawned.

"Why didn't you say anything?"

He shrugged. "I wanted to see what you'd do."

"Why were we sleeping together?" I asked.

"Because we couldn't get you to let go of him," a voice said, startling the crap out of me. It was Keelan. He was just standing behind the couch with a mug of coffee in his hand, staring down at the two of us. "Am I interrupting?" he asked with a sly smirk, which he tried to hide with a sip of coffee.

I took that as my cue to climb off of Knox and they both chuckled. Once I was standing, what Keelan had said finally registered in my head. "What did you mean that you couldn't get me to let go of Knox?"

They exchanged a look and the mood in the room shifted.

Knox threw the blanket off his legs and sat up. "Do you remember having a nightmare last night?"

My back went ramrod straight and an uneasy feeling brewed in the pit of my stomach. Nervously, I twisted my fingers. "Did I wake everyone up screaming? I'm really sorry. I didn't mean to fall asleep here."

"I don't think she remembers," Keelan said to Knox.

Knox's eyes met mine. "Do you remember falling asleep?"

"Vaguely. Keelan laid me out on the couch," I answered.

"You were asleep for about a half hour when you started breathing heavily and talking in your sleep," Knox said.

"You said that you needed to stop the bleeding and that there was no way out," Keelan added.

As they spoke, my dream quickly came back to me and a sense of dread began to overwhelm me.

"Colt told us that you were having a nightmare and that we should wake you before it got bad," Knox continued. "Keelan was about to wake you when you screamed the most bloodcurdling scream I've ever heard and then you threw yourself off the couch. You were barely on the ground a second before you were on your feet and running across the room. I thought you were going to run straight into the TV, but you stopped and began looking around. You were frantic and looked terrified. You were acting like someone was chasing you."

I tried not to react, even though I was freaking out on the inside.

"We caught on pretty quickly that you weren't fully awake because we were all standing right in front of you, but it was like you couldn't see us," Keelan explained. "Colt and Creed wanted to shake you awake. I didn't think that was wise. Your guard was up, and I had a feeling that if any of us touched you, you'd attack. So we tried talking to you and calling out your name."

"It seemed like you heard Colt say your name and then you looked right at me," Knox said, watching me carefully. "You could see me. Do you remember any of that?"

I nodded a single nod. "I remember seeing you. I didn't think it was real."

"Do you remember what you said to me?" he asked.

"Not really," I lied.

"You said that there was someone in the house and that we needed to leave before he found us."

"That's really strange," I said, shifting my weight from one foot to the other. "But that's dreams for you."

Knox's eyes narrowed as he studied me. "You'd be a terrible poker player, Shiloh."

Alright, I was done with this conversation. "Where are Colt and Creed?"

"They should be home any moment. They went out to get fresh bagels for breakfast," Keelan replied.

Knox never took his eyes off me and it was making me want to squirm. I looked from him to Keelan. I knew they were waiting for me to elaborate and I could see the questions they were dying to ask. "You know what? I'm not really hungry," I said, stepping back. "I better get my run in before it gets too hot out. Don't you guys have to get ready for work?" I rambled before spinning on my heel and heading for the door.

"Who's Mr. X?" Knox asked.

I stumbled to a stop and slowly turned around. I didn't want to believe it. I begged the powers above that I was hearing things. "What did you just say?"

Knox's gaze was intense and unrelenting. "Who is Mr. X?"

24

THE WALLS FELT LIKE THEY WERE CLOSING IN ON ME AS THE PANIC rose and rose in my chest. "Where did you hear that?" I asked.

Knox stood in front of the couch and stepped toward me. I took a step back. He frowned at that, but didn't make another move closer. "After I got you to settle down and it was just the two of us out here, I asked you again, 'Who is in the house?' You said, 'Mr. X.'"

I rubbed at my breastbone as I tried to pull air into my lungs. What should I do? What could I say? "I have to go."

I bolted for the door again. Before I could get there, it opened. Colt and Creed walked in, carrying two brown bags from a bakery nearby. They took one look at me, then their brothers, and I could see that they knew what we were discussing.

Creed shut the door behind them and handed off his bag of bagels to Colt, who took off toward the kitchen with them. "You were supposed to wait until we got back to talk to her," Creed said, glaring at Knox and Keelan.

"Well, things didn't go as planned," Knox said, sounding irritated. "She's refusing to talk, anyways."

"Why don't we all sit down?" Keelan suggested as he rounded the couch. He and Knox took a seat next to each other.

Creed tried to reach for my hand, and I jerked out of his reach. I hated the look of hurt that flashed in his eyes. "Shiloh," he said. "You can't blame us for having questions after last night."

"I'm sorry you had to deal with that," I forced out.

"Stop doing that," Knox snapped. "Nothing about you is a burden. That's not what this is about."

Creed inched closer. "We've tried to not pry and wait for you to be ready to talk to us, but—"

"Please don't," I pleaded. This was it. This was the moment I'd known was coming.

"You don't trust us," Knox said.

The backs of my eyes began to burn. "I do trust you."

Knox shook his head. "Then what's the issue, Shiloh? We spend practically every day together. We share things with you, but you barely share anything with us and when things happen with you, like last night, you expect us to ignore it."

I understood his point. I really did. But my fear of telling them anything wasn't the only thing holding me back.

Colt returned with his hands stuffed in his pockets and had a dejected look on his face. "You scared the shit out of all of us last night, babe. But we're still here. I don't know what else we have to do to prove to you that you can talk to us and that you won't scare us away."

A single tear escaped my eye. "I can't tell you."

"Can't or won't?" Knox asked.

"I can't."

"Why?" he pushed.

"Because I can't," I snapped at him.

Knox opened his mouth to say something, but Keelan put his hand on Knox's shoulder. "Ease up, Knox. This isn't an inter-rogation."

"You owe me five answers to five questions," Colt said,

bringing up the bet I'd lost our first day of school. "You don't go back on your promises, right?"

Throwing my words back at me felt like a low blow. I hated this. "Fine. Ask away."

The intensity that filled Colt's eyes could have rivaled Knox's in that moment. "What was your dream about last night?"

"The night my family died," I answered. The terms of our bet were that I had to answer. Not be specific.

"Who is Mr. X?" he asked next.

My heart skipped a beat at that question. "He was my freshman English teacher."

"She's purposely being vague," Knox pointed out.

Colt didn't ask another question for moment. Instead, I watched as he thought about what he wanted to ask me next. "How did your family die?"

My forehead creased and my vision blurred. I had to blink to clear it. "I can't tell you."

"This is bullshit, Shiloh," Knox said as he got to his feet. "You refusing to tell us anything, that's what's going to push us away."

"I know!" I yelled. "You don't think I know that?"

"Then why are you doing it?" he roared back.

"Because I can't—" I started to say before Knox interrupted me.

"Stop saying you can't. You just don't want to."

"No, I can't!"

"Knox, calm down," Keelan said at the same time the twins said, "Knox, back off!"

Knox ignored them. "Why can't you?"

"Because I'm in witness protection!" I screamed at him as if the truth was a way to punish him. "My family was murdered! Is that sharing enough for you, Knox! Huh? I couldn't tell you because the monster who killed them is still out there," I wailed as I pointed at the door. "If anyone finds out who I really am, my life is at risk. Telling you puts my life at risk." My voice broke at the end.

The room fell silent.

As I took in their shocked faces, the reality of what I had just done hit me. I covered my wet face with my hands. "Oh, no."

I couldn't stand to be here any longer. I didn't want to stick around long enough for them to ask me to leave, either. I booked it for the door and this time nothing got in my way. I scooped up my keys and phone from the small table they kept by the front door. None of them tried to stop me and that was enough to tell me that everything was ruined between us.

Once I was inside my house, I had the urge to just collapse and cry. I stayed strong and walked to the kitchen. Under the sink, tucked behind the cleaning supplies, was the bottle of Jack I'd bought the day I had met Colt. It was unopened. I'd kept it to prove to myself that I didn't need it as a crutch anymore. Right now, I couldn't care less about proving anything.

I unscrewed the cap, tossed it in the trash because there was no doubt in my mind that I wouldn't need it again, and took a big swig from the bottle. The whiskey burned everything it touched as it went down. That was a far better feeling than my heart breaking.

~

The sound of knocking on the front door startled me awake. I couldn't remember when I'd passed out. It hadn't been long enough to sober me. A knock came again.

"Yeah. Yeah, I'm coming," I grumbled and stood from the couch. The world tilted to the left, then the right and I had to catch myself on the coffee table. *Yup, still drunk.* I blinked a couple of times, hoping that would stop the spinning. It helped enough for me to get to the door, which I unlocked and swung open.

Knox was standing on my porch. I had to squint at him to

keep from seeing two of him. His arms were crossed over his chest and his normal frowny face was in place.

"Can we talk?" he asked.

I smacked my forehead with my palm. "I forgot to look through the peephole. Logan's gonna to be so, so mad at me. Lemme do this again," I said, slurring a little, and slammed the door closed. I struggled to get my eye to line up with the peephole. "It's still Knox," I mumbled to myself and snorted. "I don't wanna talk to you. I'm not home," I yelled through the door before pushing off of it and heading toward the kitchen. I was hungry. I hadn't eaten today, and I was pretty sure I had left-over pasta salad in the fridge. Carbs sounded amazing right now.

I heard the front door open and close behind me. I spun around, stumbled, and had to catch myself on a piece of furniture again. This time it was my yellow armchair.

Knox was inside. He looked from me to the coffee table, eyeing the half-empty bottle of Jack. "You're drunk."

"Nope. I'm numb," I corrected and scooped the bottle off the coffee table. I zigged and zagged as I traveled to the kitchen. I opened my fridge. The cold air hitting my skin felt amazing. As I scanned the shelves, I took a big gulp from the bottle. The burning had long since passed and I couldn't taste it anymore. When I found the pasta salad, I sighed. "I want French fries and chicken nuggets."

"You don't like fast food. It's too fatty and greasy for you," Knox said from behind me.

"I don't care," I snapped. "I don't care about anything." I was starting to feel sad again. So I took another gulp, then another to make sure that feeling got washed away.

"I'll go get you all the chicken nuggets and French fries you want if you give me the bottle."

I turned to glare at him. He was watching me from the other side of the kitchen island. My gaze dropped to his tight white T-shirt that hugged all of his big muscles. Why did he have to be hot? "I'm mad at you."

"I know."

Really? Glad to know that he didn't care. "You're an asshole and your sexy muscles can go to hell." I turned back toward the fridge and pulled out the pasta salad. I slammed the door with my hip and dropped the container of pasta and bottle of Jack angrily on the counter.

"Shiloh."

I ignored him by pulling a plate from the cabinet and a spoon from the drawer. I slammed both the door and drawer shut because my anger needed an outlet.

"You think I'm sexy?" he asked.

I scoffed as I scooped some pasta onto my plate. *Someone is full of themselves.*

"You just said I was sexy."

"No, I didn't," I said and accidentally dropped a scoop of pasta on the counter. "Gah!" I threw the spoon down and ran my hands through my hair. Why couldn't anything go right today? Feeling sad again, I reached for the Jack.

My wrist was grabbed before I could touch the bottle and I was spun around. Knox stared down at me with that intense look he had down pat. It was a mixture of determined and searching, like he wouldn't give up until he was done seeing every inch of my soul. "Why are you here?" I asked.

He let go of my wrist to put his hand behind my neck. His fingers kneaded the base of my skull. "To apologize."

"I don't think you know how to apologize." What he was doing felt so good, I had to fight to keep my eyes from rolling back into my head. I bit my lip to stop from groaning. I didn't want to give him the satisfaction.

His eyes dropped to my mouth and he leaned closer until his mouth was almost touching mine. "I only apologize to people I care about." He was so close, I felt his words on my lips. It made my toes curl.

I wanted him to close the breadth of distance between us.

What did I have to lose?

Nothing.

All I did was lose and lose.

Right now, I wanted to take.

My hands went to his hips and I leaned forward. He pulled back a little, slightly stunned.

I pushed up onto my tiptoes. "Kiss me, Knox," I whispered against his lips.

I was pretty sure he stopped breathing. I thought I heard something clank behind me and I went to look. Knox's mouth captured mine before I could see. His hand at my neck pulled me even closer and he kissed the crap out of me. His lips were dominant and his tongue was controlling. Everything about the way he kissed represented him perfectly and because of that, I wanted to rebel. I enjoyed giving as good as I got with him way too much. I fisted the front of his shirt in my hands and kissed him back. My tongue caressed and danced with his in a passionate battle I knew he was enjoying just as much as I was.

He broke our kiss with a frustrated noise and pressed his forehead to mine. We both were breathing heavily. His hand at my neck squeezed a little as he stared down at me with a pained expression. His mouth moved back to mine and then pulled away.

Movement to my left caught my attention and I saw that he had my bottle of Jack.

"What are you doing?" I questioned and reached for it.

He lifted it out of my reach and backed away. I looked from the bottle to him. He actually looked remorseful as he walked over to the sink and tipped the bottle upside down, pouring it out.

I pressed my fingers to my lips. The betrayal was sobering enough that I felt humiliated and everything I was trying not to feel came rushing to the surface. The heartache. The fear. The anger. And he was dumping my way to escape it all down the drain.

I stormed out of the kitchen and went to my room. I ripped open my closet and flicked through my dresses angrily until I found a short, red summer dress with tie straps. I yanked it off the hanger.

Knox was standing by my bedroom door when I came out of the closet. "What are you doing?" he asked.

I ignored him as I tossed my dress on the bed and removed my top. I was still in my Hulk pajamas. I threw my shirt at him, which he caught. "Are you going to watch?" I snapped with my arms out.

The look he gave me said he was calling my bluff. Only I wasn't bluffing. I shrugged. "Fine." I pulled down my pajama shorts, then unhooked my bra and tossed that at him, too.

"Damnit, Shiloh," he cursed and looked toward the ceiling.

I slipped on my dress and stepped into a pair of black flats. I grabbed my purse, phone, and keys that were on my dresser next.

"Where are you going?" Knox questioned as I put the strap of my purse across my body.

"None of your business," I answered as I passed him to exit my room. "Lock up when you leave," I said over my shoulder before I walked out the front door. Once out on the porch, I pulled up a car service app on my phone. I was about to hit confirm after picking my destination, which was the nearest bar, when my phone was snatched out of my hand.

Knox read my phone before shoving it in his pocket. "You're not going to a bar. For one, you're not twenty-one. Two, you've had enough to drink today."

I wasn't going to argue with him. Fighting with him would only hurt me in the end because I was the only one of us who truly cared. I walked away instead.

"Where are you going?" he asked, sounding as frustrated as I felt.

I scoffed. "Like I'd tell you."

He let out a slew of curses, ran to catch up, and before I knew it, he threw me over his shoulder.

"Put me down!" I hit at his back and kicked my legs.

"No."

I didn't stop fighting as he walked past my house and went into his.

"You stupid, muscle-headed bastard!" I yelled, grabbing for the door frame as we went through it, but I couldn't get a good enough grip.

"What the hell is going on?" I heard Creed ask, just before Knox set me down in the middle of their living room.

Creed, Colt, and Keelan were all standing around the couch, staring at us wide-eyed.

I glared at Knox. "Why did you bring me here?"

"Because you're hellbent on self-destructing," he snapped.

"I was doing fine before you showed up," I snapped back and stomped my foot. "I feel so stupid for letting you kiss me!"

"What?" Keelan, Colt, and Creed said at the same time and looked at Knox.

Knox refused to look away from me. "You're drunk, Shiloh."

"So what?!" I yelled. The decision not to argue with him was thrown out the window. I wanted to fight now. I wanted to unleash everything on him. "You don't get to dictate how I deal with shit, especially when you were the one who hurt me. You pushed and pushed me to tell you something I wasn't ready to share, nor was allowed to tell you. You made me choose between the four of you and my safety. What did it get me? Nothing. Instead, it cost me everything, just as I knew it would."

The muscle in his jaw clenched. "Give me your purse," he said in a low voice.

"Stop caring, Knox. It would make your life so much easier

and it won't confuse the shit out of me," I said, raking my fingers through my hair angrily.

"I'm not letting you leave until you sober up. So you either give me your purse or I'll take it from you. It's your choice."

How dare he act calm now? I ripped my purse off my body and threw it at him. He caught it when it hit his chest. After that, I stormed past him, then Colt, Creed, and Keelan, heading for the twins' side of the house.

"Have you eaten anything today?" Knox asked me.

"Go to hell!" I shouted over my shoulder before disappearing down the hall.

"You said you were going to apologize to her, not make it worse," I heard Colt say, sounding pissed off. "And what did she mean when she said you kissed her?"

Knox grumbled something I couldn't hear.

I decided to hide out in Creed's room. I refused to sit out there for however long Knox was keeping me here. The last thing I wanted was to be around them. Not when it hurt so much. Tears dripped from my eyes as I kicked off my shoes and climbed onto Creed's bed. Lying on my side, I grabbed one of Creed's pillows and hugged it tight. I had no choice but to feel and it was awful.

25

I'd been crying nonstop for what felt like hours. I tried to sleep, but no matter how much I tried, I couldn't. Creed's pillow, which I'd been hugging, was soaked. The bed dipped on either side of me and said pillow was pulled from my arms. I slowly opened my puffy eyes to Colt scooting close, trying to take the pillow's place. A body that I knew belonged to Creed cuddled me from behind and he draped his arm around my waist.

Colt tucked my hair behind my ear before cupping my cheek and brushing away some tears with his thumb. "We're sorry," he said, laying his head next to mine so close that our noses were only a few inches apart. "We should have been more patient. It was wrong of us to push you like that."

Creed's arm tightened around my waist. "Tell us what we can do to fix this, Shi."

"Can you turn back time?" I whispered.

Colt's brow furrowed. "Nothing has changed, babe. I told you that whatever you were keeping from us wouldn't scare us away."

I saw sincerity in his eyes, but I was scared to believe him. "How can you not see me differently?"

"We don't, I promise," Creed insisted. "Things make a lot of sense to us now, but Colt's right. We should have waited until you were ready."

I sighed. "It wouldn't have mattered if I was ready to tell you or not. I wasn't supposed to tell you."

"You know we won't say anything to anyone, Shi," Creed said, nuzzling the back of my neck. "You're important to us and to Keelan. I know it's hard to believe right now, but you're important to Knox, too."

I scoffed at that.

Colt gave me a tight smile. "It's true. I think he cares for you so much, he doesn't know how to deal with it."

"He needs to pull his head out of his ass," Creed grumbled and nuzzled my neck again. He then inhaled deeply and exhaled a heavy sigh. "I've been wanting to do this all day."

A corner of my mouth twitched. "Smell me?"

Colt snorted.

"No." Creed's hand flattened on my stomach. "Hold you."

"Oh," I said. Hearing him say that made my heart ache more and I was desperate to soothe it. Even though I was sobering up, I was still in the *take what I want* state of mind. "Will you hold me tighter?"

Creed's arm moved up around my ribs and his hand rested just below my breast. Colt scooted even closer, bringing his nose right up to mine. I grabbed his hand that was cupping my cheek and hugged it under my chin. Having them so close lifted a crippling weight off me and my eyelids quickly began to feel heavy.

"Why don't you try and sleep for a little bit? We'll wake you for dinner," Colt suggested.

All I could do was nod before I drifted off.

"Shi," Creed whispered in my ear before my hair was pulled away from my neck. "Dinner's almost ready."

"Five more minutes," I mumbled sleepily.

His lips pressed where my neck curved into my shoulder. I let out a pleased sigh. His lips moved up to the middle of my neck and kissed me there. A shiver rippled through me, starting from where he'd kissed me down to my curling toes. He moved up again and pressed his lips below my ear. I gasped. The butterflies in my stomach fluttered to life and flew south.

He ran his nose along my ear. "Do you want me to keep going?"

I finally opened my eyes and turned my head, bringing us face to face. "Yes."

His eyes searched mine as if he didn't quite believe what I had said. Tired of waiting, I put my hand behind his head and pulled him to me. The moment our lips met, his hesitation vanished. I loved the thrill I got from taking charge. It was addictive and empowering. He tried to take over, but I wasn't ready to give him the reins just yet. I rolled my body to face his, threw my leg over his hip, pushed him onto his back, and climbed on top of him, never breaking our kiss as I did. He smiled against my lips and sat up, making me sit in his lap.

His hands went to my waist and I put mine behind his neck. I sucked his bottom lip between mine and lightly grazed my teeth over it. He let out a breathy groan and he grew hard beneath me. Feeling his arousal pressed against mine caused me to throb and my panties to become wet. I surprised us both when I rocked my hips, grinding myself against him, seeking relief.

He groaned louder before breaking our kiss. "Are you still drunk?"

"No." I moved my hands to his cheeks and pecked him on the lips. "Why?"

"Because," he started. "I thought you had a no kissing rule."

I dropped my hands from his face and bit my lip as my confidence quickly plummeted. "You don't want to kiss me?"

His hands moved to my butt, squeezing as he ground his

bulge against me. My breath hitched. "I want to do more than kiss you, Shi," he said in a deep, purely male voice.

I put my hands on his chest and brought my lips to his. "Then more than kiss me."

He wrapped his arms around me and flipped us so I was on my back and he was holding himself above me. His mouth went back to my neck. It became obvious he had been holding back before. This time his tongue came into play. When he found that spot below my ear again, I moaned.

He pulled at the ties of my straps, untying them as he kissed along my shoulder and down past my collarbone. Two of his fingers hooked into the top of my dress between my breasts. He paused and his gaze met mine, giving me the opportunity to protest. When I didn't, he slowly pulled down. My chest rose and fell as he revealed my heavy-feeling breasts.

I could feel his eyes on me, taking in my pale mounds and my peaked, pink nipples. My heart pounded in my chest so hard, I was sure he could hear it.

He cupped one breast and his mouth descended on the other. I whimpered when he sucked my nipple into his mouth, then tugged it gently between his teeth. I buried my fingers in his hair and arched beneath him, needing more.

I had never been touched like this—never gone this far with anyone. My whole body was trembling. The need pulsing through me made me feel like I was on fire. It wasn't a painful fire, but a maddening, addictive burn.

His hand dropped from my breast and moved down between my legs. The skirt of my dress had bunched up at my hips, displaying my underwear, which was red silk with black Spider-Man lace webbing. Creed touched me through my underwear, rubbing up and down over my clit. "Creed," I panted pleadingly and I wasn't entirely sure what for.

Releasing my breast, he chuckled and stared down at me as his fingers pulled my underwear to the side. "Is this what you want?" he asked, watching me as he touched me again without a barrier.

My forehead scrunched up and I put the back of my hand over my mouth to keep from moaning again.

"You're so wet." His voice had gone hoarse.

Heat scorched my cheeks. "I'm sorry."

"That's nothing to be sorry about, Shi." He moved my hand away from my mouth and kissed me. "It's fucking hot and makes me want to taste you."

Taste me? Oh, he means...

"I've never—I mean—if you want to you can," I said nervously.

"Are you sure?" he asked, his eyes reading mine.

I nodded. He kissed me one more time before moving down my body. He sat back on his haunches between my legs. His fingers hooked into my panties at my hips and began pulling them down. I helped him remove them by pulling my feet from them one at a time. He tossed my underwear to the floor and scooted back a little. My heart raced with anticipation and I couldn't help but bring my legs together.

He pressed his lips to my knee. "You say stop and we stop, Shi."

I knew that. I trusted him. I was ready and wanted to do this with him. But *oh-my-lanta*, I was nervous. It was a good nervous, though.

I slowly opened my legs. Just as slowly, he placed open-mouth kisses down my inner leg until he reached my center. He pushed my legs open wider and hooked them over his shoulders. I felt his warm breath on me before the lap of his tongue over my clit. I sucked in a breath and returned the back of my hand to my mouth.

Next came the intense flicking of his tongue that made my legs shake. I moaned behind my hand. I did my best to keep my legs open, but when he sucked my clit into his mouth, my thighs tried to snap closed around his head. His hands caught me and held me open for him. A pressure grew in my core, like a coil, twisting tighter and tighter the more he devoured me. My hand fisted the bedding, trying to anchor myself for what was quickly coming. My other hand did very little to muffle the sounds he was drawing from me.

"Creed," I moaned as I shook my head from side to side. That coil inside me was tightened to the max and when he did that flicking motion with his tongue again, it snapped, and I came. I cried out as I contracted with rippling pleasure.

The bedroom door burst open. "Is everything okay?" Colt asked as he and Keelan came storming in, looking worried. The worried looks quickly changed to surprise as they noticed I was practically naked, with my breasts out, my dress bunched around my stomach, and Creed's head between my legs. I let out a yelp and covered up my breasts.

"Was she having another nightmare?" I heard Knox ask just before he walked into the room next. Creed chose that moment to sit up from between my legs and wipe my essence off his mouth and chin. He glared at his brothers. "What the hell?!" he yelled.

For a moment all they did was stand there staring, all of them stunned speechless.

Knox snapped out of his shock and glared right back at Creed. "What the fuck were you thinking? She's drunk."

"I'm sober," I said.

Knox's glare shifted to me. "I highly doubt that."

I sighed tiredly. "I don't want to fight with you anymore, Knox." I wasn't admitting defeat. I just didn't want to look back at this moment as one that had ended with Knox and me lashing out at each other. I wanted what Creed and I had done to be a happy memory. I pulled the skirt of my dress down and sat up. I let go of my breasts to pull the top of my dress up and over them. "What time is it?"

Keelan stared at the ceiling. "Uh, a little after seven." Both him and Colt had been polite enough to avert their eyes when I'd sat up. Knox, on the other hand, hadn't removed his angry stare from me.

"Crap," I said and climbed off the bed. "I need my purse."

"Why?" Knox asked, his glare never easing up.

"Stop fucking staring at her like that," Creed snapped.

Knox looked to Creed, seeming ready to tear into him.

Before Knox could open his mouth, I stepped into his line of sight. "Don't fight," I said firmly. I did my best to stay calm. "Where is my purse? I haven't checked in with my uncle today."

"It's in the kitchen," Knox finally answered.

Holding my dress up by the front so that it wouldn't fall, I walked around the three of them, head held high. I wasn't ashamed of what Creed and I had done.

"We'll talk about this later," I heard Knox say in a hushed tone the moment I stepped into the hall.

I was able to get one of my straps retied by the time I made it to the kitchen. The dining room table was set and food looked ready to be served in the kitchen. I spotted my purse on the island. I quickly tied my other strap and put it back in place on my shoulder before opening my purse and pulling out my personal cell phone and burner. Sure enough, I had multiple texts and missed calls from Logan on both of my phones.

As I was looking over the messages, my burner started ringing. I immediately answered it. "I'm so sorry, Logan. I forgot to check in. I know I messed up."

"Damnit, Shi," he cursed with a sigh of relief. "I almost called the police to do a welfare check on you."

"I'm sorry I worried you." The sound of chairs sliding on the tile floor in the dining room caught my attention. I looked in that direction and saw the guys sitting down around the table.

"What have you been doing that you forgot to do your check-ins?" Logan asked.

"I—" I didn't want to tell him the truth. Not yet, at least. "I wasn't feeling well and spent most of the day sleeping."

"Are you alright?"

The concern in his voice gutted me. I closed my eyes and rubbed my forehead. "Yeah, I overdid it running again."

"You gotta stop doing that to yourself, Shi."

"I know," I said.

"Well, I'm glad you're okay. Don't miss your check-ins tomorrow," he said, and we said our goodbyes. I snapped the phone closed and tossed it on the counter. Frowning down at it, I chewed on my lip, feeling guilty.

"Why'd you lie to him?" Knox asked.

I glanced at the four of them sitting around the table watching me. "If I told him the truth, he'd have me relocated with a new identity by morning. I don't want to uproot my life again."

"I told you we won't say anything," Colt said.

I moved over to the table and sat in my chair between the twins. "My uncle won't care. To him, my safety is compromised, and he'll make it his top priority to get me somewhere safe. I wouldn't put it past him to put me in handcuffs and drag me all the way to the next location of his choosing if I tried to protest."

They went quiet and exchanged looks.

I sighed. "You might as well ask what you want to know. It's not like I can take back this morning."

"Why do you have a second phone?" Creed asked.

"It's a prepaid burner and harder to trace," I answered. "My uncle calls me on my personal phone from a secure line once a week so we can catch up."

"Why isn't he here with you?" Keelan asked.

"Because he was asked to help find Mr. X."

"That's who killed your family?" Knox asked bluntly.

I nodded, leaning back in my chair. I knew I was going to have to tell them everything or we'd be here all night and I really wanted to just get this over with. "Mr. X was my freshman

English teacher," I said. "At first he acted like a regular teacher. I couldn't tell you when things changed, but I started noticing him watching me, even when I wasn't in his class at the time. Then the staring turned into innocent or accidental touches, like putting his hand on my shoulder, rubbing my back, or bumping into me so that he could hold me close. In my gut, I knew it was intentional and something wasn't right. I tried talking to Shayla about it. She laughed it off and made me feel stupid. I started doubting myself after that and because of that doubt, I agreed to stay after class one day when Mr. X asked me to." I took a deep breath to steel my nerves. "He tried to rape me on his desk." I saw all of them go still and I thought I saw Knox's hand squeeze into a fist before he lifted it off the table and set it in his lap. "I begged him to stop and to let me go. He thought I was playing hard to get. He was convinced that I wanted him just as much as he wanted me. The school principal walked in as he was about to…"

Colt scooted closer and grabbed my hand.

I continued on. "She screamed at him to let me go. He refused. Instead, he went on and on about how we loved each other and what he was doing was consensual. The more he talked, it was obvious that he was crazy, and I was so grateful that she thought so, too.

"She tried to call the police on her cell phone. He let go of me to stop her. He hit her, knocking the phone out of her hand. I took that opportunity to get away. As soon as I was out of the classroom, I started screaming at the top of my lungs for help. Teachers came out of their classrooms to help us. But by that point, Mr. X had run. Police searched for him at his home and found a shrine of me in his bedroom, but no sign of Mr. X. He had disappeared and no one could find him.

"A few months later, I received a letter from him in the mail. It was a love letter and inside it was a picture of me sitting in a movie theater with my friends. It had been taken from a few rows away. After that, more letters and pictures consistently came every couple of weeks and in between those, I'd receive texts telling me how much he missed me and video messages of him touching himself. No matter how many times I changed my number, he'd find out what the new one was.

"I did my best to ignore it and continue living my life like normal. I held out for about a year until I couldn't take it anymore. I stopped hanging out with friends and leaving the house unless it was for school. I was terrified all the time. I could never shake the feeling of being watched or stop wondering each time I left the house if that was the day he was going to get me. It was like the world had become so small and there was nothing I could do, nowhere I could go to escape him. It was suffocating."

"You felt helpless," Keelan said.

"Yeah," I said. "Sometimes I would hide in my closet and I would tell myself that if he couldn't see me, he couldn't get me. That was somewhat true, and it pissed Mr. X off. When I stopped going out as much, he escalated things. He broke into our house while my sister and I were at school and my parents were at work. He stole all of my panties and a few other things, like my hairbrush and a teddy bear my dad had won for me at the fair when I was eight. He left rose petals all over my bed, along with some rope, a vibrator, and a letter with explicit instructions on what to do with the vibrator. The letter also explained that the rope was a sneak peek of what he was going to do to me when it was time for us to be together. I wish I could say that the upside was that I eventually got all my panties back." A disgusted shiver ripped through me. "He sent them back to me one at a time after he...pleasured himself with them."

They all reacted with disgust. Creed cursed. Keelan shook his head. Colt and Knox were glaring at the table.

"Did your family ever consider moving?" Keelan asked.

"Logan suggested we move to Texas to be closer to him after Mr. X broke in, but my parents didn't want to move. My mom had finally achieved her dream of owning her own restaurant.

My dad had just made partner at his law firm. They would have had to give up so much to move and if we did move, there was still a chance Mr. X might follow us and then it would have all been for nothing."

"This went on for years?" Creed asked.

"It stopped for a couple of months after our last family trip during spring break, my junior year. I had been so depressed. I was barely getting out of bed. Our parents woke Shayla and me up in the middle of the night and snuck us away to Texas to visit Logan. It was the best week I'd had in the longest time. We spent pretty much every day at the beach. It's where that picture I showed you of Shayla and me was taken."

They all nodded, remembering.

"After we returned from Texas, we didn't hear from Mr. X for a few months. Then one afternoon my dad found a DVD with a note taped to his car window outside his work. The DVD had a video of me changing my clothes in my bedroom on it and the note was a threat. If my dad ever took me away again, Mr. X would kill him and my mom. My dad came home stumbling drunk that night and my parents argued about what to do.

"Seeing how happy we'd been in Texas and receiving a threatening note from Mr. X seemed to change their perspective on things, or it was their breaking point. I'm not sure, but they were considering moving. Not to Texas, though. My parents and Logan figured that if we were going to move, we had to do it in a way that would make it hard for Mr. X to follow us. Logan came up with a plan to spirit us away, get us set up in a small town with different names. The only issue was that Shayla wasn't on board.

"Despite what had been going on with me, she had the perfect life. She was popular, had a bunch of friends, was on track to be the captain of the cheerleading squad. Moving was her worst nightmare. Little did I know at the time, she complained about it out in the open with her friends and that was how Mr. X found out. Which brings us to the night he killed them." I trailed off.

Staring at the empty plate on the table in front of me, my mind wandered back to that night. For over a year, I had done my best to evade the memories from that night. Now, I was about to take a stroll through them.

Colt squeezed my hand. I felt so much support with such a small gesture. "In the few months Mr. X had left us alone, I had reconnected with a friend. That day, I went over to her house right after school to hang out. I didn't get home until a little after nine. I knew something wasn't right the moment I walked through the door. All the lights were off and it was too quiet. I went into the living room when I saw that the TV was on but muted. I found my dad on the couch. With the light coming off the TV I could see all the blood on his…" With my free hand I gestured to my whole torso. "I tried to convince myself that it was dark and I was seeing things. So I flicked on the lamp." I squeezed my eyes shut as if to hide my eyes from seeing that image again. Panic was quickly growing in my chest. "I can't." Squeezing Colt's hand, I shook my head. "I'm sorry, but I can't."

Creed put his hand on my thigh. "It's okay, Shi, you don't have to."

"Creed's right," Keelan said. "You've shared enough. The rest you can share with us when you're ready."

I nodded.

Knox stood from the table and headed for the kitchen. "We should eat dinner, anyways."

Keelan followed him and the both of them pulled dishes out of the oven and brought them over to the table. Knox had made baked chicken, homemade French fries, and coleslaw.

"It's not the chicken nuggets and French fries you were wanting, but I figured once you sobered up you'd want a somewhat healthier version," Knox said, watching me.

I looked back at my food. "You did this for me?"

Knox shrugged and started putting food on his plate.

Creed went to grab the tongs to pick up some chicken and

Keelan smacked his hand away. "Since you've already eaten, you can go last."

Colt snorted and hid his mouth behind my hand that he was still holding. When he caught me staring, he cleared his throat. "Sorry."

Keelan took the tongs, picked up a piece of chicken, and put it on my plate.

"I was going to serve Shiloh," Creed deadpanned.

"Well, you've serviced her enough tonight," Keelan said in a put-off tone.

Everything Keelan had been saying to Creed registered in my head at that moment and I blushed. Colt kissed the back of my hand to comfort me.

Creed straightened in his chair. "Sounds like you're jealous."

The glare Keelan fixed on Creed surprised me. It wasn't a look I'd ever seen on his happy and carefree face. "What if I am?" he asked Creed.

"I didn't think pretty boys got jealous," Creed snapped.

Keelan smirked. "Sounds like I'm not the only one who's jealous."

I let go of Colt's hand and stood. "Maybe I should go."

Knox slammed his hand down on the table. "Enough!" he snapped at Keelan and Creed. Then he looked at me. "You don't get to leave this house until you've eaten something."

I arched a brow at him.

"Shiloh," he said in a strained voice. "I will feed you myself if I have to."

Pick your battles. Pick your battles. "I'd like to see you try and throw me over your shoulder now that I'm sober, you bench-pressing jerk face," I muttered to myself as I plopped back in my chair. I angrily scooped coleslaw onto my plate. "I'm pretty sure I could take your giant butt to the floor in three moves." I grabbed a large portion of fries next.

"I can hear everything you're saying," Knox grumbled.

I bit a fry in half. "You were supposed to."

Keelan snorted from across the table, followed by Creed. That caused Colt to erupt with laughter. Keelan and Creed burst out next and the room filled up with the three of them laughing.

"I would pay to see Shiloh kick your ass," Keelan wheezed at Knox in between laughs.

Knox rolled his eyes and dug into his food.

26

THE NEXT MORNING, I WAS STILL EMOTIONALLY DRAINED FROM THE day before. I was kind of physically worn out, too, but that was because I'd gotten a good run in this morning. I'd needed it. Instead of running to escape the things I didn't want to face, I'd tried to think through some stuff. Mainly about the guys. They all swore nothing had changed now that they knew. I was little reluctant to truly believe them.

I was still mad at Knox. I had forgiven Colt and Creed. Keelan really hadn't done anything wrong, but he'd still pulled me aside last night and apologized. Knox had yet to express any remorse. I couldn't look at him without replaying how I'd thrown myself at him and begged him to kiss me in my head.

Remembering it again, I cringed as I looked through my dresses in my closet. Because of the heat, I decided to wear another summer dress, this one white with short sleeves. I kept my makeup light and I straightened my hair. I was putting on white strappy sandals when I heard my front door open. Glancing down the hall from where I sat on my bed, I saw Colt.

"Hey," I greeted him as I picked up my phone from my nightstand. According to the time, I still had fifteen minutes before I had to leave. I was driving myself to school today because I had to go to the gym right after school and the twins had practice. Today was my first day helping Keelan teach women's jiu-jitsu for beginners.

Leaning against my door frame with his hands in his pockets, he let his gaze roam all over me. "You look beautiful."

I smiled, but it quickly dropped when I saw apprehension etched around his eyes. I stood and went over to him. I placed my hand on his upper arm. "What's wrong?"

"I wanted to talk about what happened with you and Creed."

My brows rose and I blushed. "Oh."

"Do you want to be with him?"

I looked down. "I have feelings for him." I shifted my weight from one foot to the other. "But I have feelings for you, too."

He pulled his hands from his pockets and reached for me. One arm hooked around the small of my back, pulling me close, and his other hand cupped the back of my neck, forcing me to look up at him. The moment our eyes met, he kissed me.

I wanted nothing more than to kiss him back. "Don't make me choose," I begged, pulling away a little.

Understanding what I was telling him—what I refused to do —his eyes bored into mine. "We won't."

Relieved, I kissed him. I poured everything I felt for him into that kiss. My trust. My desire. I may have even handed over a little bit of my heart.

He walked us further into my room. When we made it to my bed, he spun us and fell backward with me on top of him. The drop made me squeal. He laughed as we bounced on the mattress.

I sat up and straddled his hips. "We need to leave for school soon," I said, smiling down at him.

His hands went to my outer thighs and slid up under the skirt of my dress. My skin broke out in goosebumps under his soft touch. "Or we can be late," he suggested as each of his hands smoothed over my butt cheeks.

Surprising us, a voice said, "Knox and Keelan will kick your ass."

It was Creed.

Colt tilted his head to look past me and shrugged. "It'd be worth it."

I felt Creed behind me before my hair was pulled away from my neck. His lips pressed to that sensitive spot beneath my ear and my eyes became heavy-lidded. "I have to agree," Creed whispered in my ear as he put his hand flat on my stomach. "You're definitely worth it." His hand moved down between my legs and cupped me over my dress. "I can still taste you on my tongue."

His words made my core flood. It took a lot of willpower to form the words I needed to, but I did it. "No."

They froze.

"School," I forced out as I climbed off of Colt. "Responsibilities," I forced out next as I crawled away to the foot of the bed and got to my feet. I smoothed down my dress. "Must be good."

They both chuckled.

Creed gave me a sinful smirk. "I think we broke her."

I pointed to the door. "You gotta go."

"We'll leave together," Colt said.

I shook my head. "I need you to leave before me."

Creed frowned. "Why?"

I went over to my underwear drawer. "Because I need to change my panties now, thank you very much." I pulled out my only other pair of white undies.

Creed groaned. "It's not nice to tease, Shi."

I crossed my arms over my chest. "You started it."

Colt sighed and pushed Creed toward the door.

"I wasn't teasing. I had every intention of following through," Creed grumbled as they left my room.

At lunch, Isabelle and I sat next to each other. She was telling me that my hair was giving her courage to dye her long, dirty blonde hair a bold color. She was considering pink. Hearing that, I had to stop myself from cringing. I wouldn't let my hang-ups with the color affect Isabelle's choice. With her pale complexion and blue eyes, she'd rock the color pink, and I told her so. I gushed over her nails again. They were black with neon snakes on the ring fingers.

"I'm going back to the nail salon Friday after school if you want to go together," she asked.

I beamed. "I'd love to."

"Speaking of Friday," Ethan said, capturing everyone's attention, "I'm having a party at my house after the game. As my best friends, you're expected to be there."

"Keelan's party is Saturday, which you're expected to be at," Colt said.

Ethan smiled. "You guys rarely get the weekend off. I figured we might as well make the most of it."

Colt and Creed looked to me to see what I thought.

"I've never been to a party," I said.

"Do you want to go?" Creed asked.

Ethan gave me sad puppy eyes, which made Isabelle laugh and throw a chip at him. The two of them had been dating for almost a month now and they were adorable together.

"Sure, sounds like fun," I answered.

"It's decided, then." Ethan said, rubbing his hands together. "I hope your beer pong skills are still up to par."

"We can't get trashed. Knox will kill us if we're hung over the next day," Creed said to Colt.

Colt patted Creed's shoulder. "You don't have to worry about being hung over because it's your turn to be the DD."

"Fantastic," Creed grumbled.

"Want to go shopping for something to wear to the party after we get our nails done?" Isabelle asked me.

To have a girls' day…I hadn't had one in so long. The last time I'd had one had been with my mom and Shayla. It had been during our trip in Texas. We had seen a cute nail salon by the beach, and we'd gotten mani pedis. It had been heaven to spend that time together and pamper ourselves a little. "Sure."

Isabelle smiled and leaned close. "I'm really relieved you're going because this will be my first party, too," she whispered.

In gym class, the coaches sent us out to run the track. Ethan, Colt, Creed, and I were stretching.

"What are the stakes this time?" Creed asked.

I groaned. "Not this again."

"If I win, Shiloh has to play five drinking games at my party," Ethan said.

"No," Colt and Creed objected at the same time.

"We want her to have a good time," Colt said.

"Not be trashed within the first hour," Creed added.

Ethan shrugged. "Fine. Three games."

Before the twins could protest, I took over. "One game. If I win, you have to drink water all night."

Ethan grinned. "Deal." He looked at the twins. "If I beat you two, you host the Halloween party this year. Preferably at the cabin."

I looked at the twins. "Cabin?"

Colt grimaced. "We have a cabin up in the mountains. Every year for winter break the four of us go up there to unplug and have family time. We ski, go fishing, and celebrate the holidays together. We haven't told you because it hasn't come up."

"It's okay," I assured. "That sounds like a really wonderful way to spend time as a family."

"So do we have a deal?" Ethan pushed.

Colt and Creed exchanged a look.

"Will Knox and Keelan be okay with having a party at your cabin?" I asked.

"Yeah," Creed said. "As long as we clean up afterward and we keep people from having sex in their beds, they'll be cool with it."

Colt sighed and looked to Ethan. "It's a deal, but you'll have to beat both of us."

"I'll beat you," Ethan said confidently.

I faced the twins with an evil grin. "If I win, I get to pick what you go as to the Halloween party."

They thought about it for a moment, then agreed.

Colt looked to Creed. "If Shiloh is alright with it, whoever wins gets to take her on a date first."

My brows shot up. *A date?*

"Deal," Creed said and they both looked at me.

I nodded. "I expect ice cream on this date."

"Noted," they said at the same time.

"If I beat you, babe," Colt started. "I pick what you'll go as to the Halloween party."

"Same," Creed said.

I thought about it. "Deal."

We all lined up, counted down, and took off. Like I'd done before, I paced myself. By the twentieth lap, I was having déjà vu. Ethan zoomed right past everyone, followed by Colt, leaving Creed and I neck and neck. I knew I wasn't going to beat Creed or even tie with him this time. My energy was depleting fast. I didn't know if it had to do with the heat or the fact that I'd already run that day. Either way, I was beat. Creed took the lead and I slowed to a walk for the remaining ten feet. I had to bend over and put my hands on my knees to catch my breath.

"You okay, babe?" Colt said, running over to me.

I stood up straight. "Yeah. I'm a little worn out."

"Class is almost over. Do you want me to carry you back to the locker room?"

I smiled up at him and shook my head. "Don't spoil me. I might get used to it."

He grabbed my hand and pulled me close. He dipped his head until our lips were almost touching and said, "What if I like spoiling you?" He gave me a featherlike kiss before pulling away. Needing more, I threw my arms around his neck and made him give me a real kiss. His hands went to the backs of my thighs and he picked me up. I gasped and quickly locked my legs around his waist.

We received some catcalls as other students passed by. We broke apart, laughing, and Colt walked us over to where Creed and Ethan were drinking water off to the side of the track. Colt set me down as soon as we made it over to them and Creed handed me my water bottle. As I was taking a drink, a shoulder slammed into mine. I stumbled. Both Colt and Creed caught me.

"What the hell, Amber?!" Colt yelled. I turned and sure enough, Amber and Cassy were walking away.

Amber spun around, walking backward toward the locker rooms. She gave us this mean smirk. "I hope she doesn't give you syphilis."

Cassy laughed with a sinister look in her eyes and the two of them continued on toward the locker room.

"You need to kick their asses, Shiloh," Ethan grumbled.

I sighed. "I promised Mr. Morgan I wouldn't. I'm supposed to let them dig their own grave. His words, not mine."

"You know Cassy is encouraging Amber and the rest of her shitty friends to come after you for her," Creed said.

I nodded. "I've noticed. She likes to stand back and watch."

"She does it so that she doesn't get into trouble if they're ever caught. Her dad's a cop and everything is about appearances to him," Creed explained.

Colt shook his head at Creed. "I'll never understand why you went there."

Creed glared at his brother. "You have no room to talk. You *went there* with just as many girls after Emma."

Hearing Emma's name made my brows shoot to my hairline. It was the first time they had ever brought her up.

He glared back at Creed. "At least none of them are going after Shiloh."

"No, just the one you refused to fuck," Creed quipped.

"Enough." I grabbed both of their hands. "It's no one's fault but Cassy's, so knock it off. I don't like it when you fight."

Looking contrite, they both mumbled an apology.

Ethan whistled. "You're both whipped."

I fixed him with a disapproving look. "I have Isabelle's phone number."

He lifted his hands up in surrender. "I take it back."

Colt and Creed chuckled and the four of us headed in.

The air in the locker room was nice and cold when I walked in. I was debating whether I had enough time to take a fast shower at home before I had to head to the gym. The class started an hour and a half after school ended. *That's plenty of time*, I mused as I unlocked my locker and went to take off my shirt. Just as I pulled my head from my shirt, I was shoved forward and fell into the lockers. Hands grabbed my arms, holding me against them. I immediately tried to get free.

"Hold her still," I heard Amber order from behind me. Cold metal slid up my spine, scaring the crap out of me. For a moment, I thought it was a knife. When I heard the soft sound of a snip and the band of my bra was cut, I knew it was scissors.

"Pull her pants down," Amber said next. Another pair of hands yanked my gym shorts down, then the side of my underwear was cut next. "Should I cut the troll's hair, too?" Amber asked her friends.

My fear wore off and my need to fight took over. I stepped

out of my shorts and slammed my foot down on the person to my right's instep. She cried out and let me go. I pushed away from the lockers and easily yanked my left arm free from my other captor. I whirled around and came face to face with Amber, who was holding metal scissors. I threw my leg out and kicked her in the stomach, sending her flying into the lockers behind her.

"What's going on in here?" Coach Matthews, the girls' tennis coach, yelled from the other side of the locker room. Everyone surrounding us dispersed.

"This isn't over," Amber threatened as she stalked away, holding her stomach.

I glanced down. My panties had fallen down to my ankle and my boobs were about to slip out of the cups of my bra. I quickly grabbed my dress out of my locker, yanked off my bra, and put my dress on. I felt completely exposed not having any under-things on, especially in a white dress. I changed into my sandals, grabbed the rest of my stuff, and booked it out of there. I only slowed to toss my ruined bra and underwear in the trash on my way out of the locker room.

I rushed to the parking lot, anxious to leave and get home. I started to dig my keys out of my bag when I spotted the roof of my 4Runner. Once it was fully in sight, I unlocked it, but my quick walk slowed after I noticed that the back tires were completely flat. The closer I got, the more obvious it became that they were slashed, and it wasn't just the back tires, either. The front tires were slashed as well.

"Stay calm," I told myself. "Don't let them see you upset." I was positive Cassy and Amber were behind this and were probably watching. Speaking of Cassy, I hadn't seen her when Amber and her friends had attacked me in the locker room.

I pulled out my phone and was going to call the twins, but remembered that they were probably starting practice and wouldn't have their phones on them. I called Keelan instead.

He answered on the second ring. "Hey, are you on your way?"

"Keelan," I said with a shaky voice. "Amber and two of her friends attacked me in the locker room and someone slashed all my tires," I blurted quickly because if I'd said it any slower, I would have cried. I refused to cry. I wouldn't give Cassy and Amber the satisfaction.

"First off, are you alright?" he asked.

"Yeah. I'm a little shaken up."

"I know, baby girl," he said. "I'm going to come and get you, but until then, I want you to wait in the school's office or go watch Colt and Creed practice. I don't want you to be alone."

"Okay."

"I'll be there soon."

We hung up and I headed back in the direction I'd come. Just past the gym was the building that housed the school's pool. When I got inside, I noticed there were more students than normal watching the swim team practice. To my dismay, Cassy, Amber, and a bunch of their friends, including Gabe, Cassy's cousin and the guy who'd pushed me during a game of volleyball, were all sitting in the bleachers.

They snickered amongst themselves when they saw me walk in. I spotted Colt and Creed sitting on the bottom bench of the bleachers with some other swimmers, while the rest of the team was taking their turn practicing in the pool. I beelined for them, with the intent to sit close by.

They spotted me as I got closer and jumped to their feet. I tried to appear calm. Just by looking at them and the concerned look in their eyes, I was failing.

Before I could reach them, someone grabbed me from behind, squeezing my breast as they did, and then I was thrown toward the pool. I let out a scream as I hurtled toward the water. Plunging into the cold water, my dress rose up, reminding me that I had nothing underneath. I quickly pushed it down and tried to swim to the surface. My backpack weighed me down and it was hard to kick my feet in my sandals.

Colt speared into the water next to me. He grabbed the straps of my bag and yanked them down my arms. The bag sank to the bottom of the pool as he wrapped an arm around me and helped me swim up. Once I made it to the surface, I could hear yelling. By the side of the pool, where I'd been thrown, one of the swim coaches was pulling Creed off of Gabe.

Cassy ran to Gabe's side and helped him sit up. Blood leaked from Gabe's nose and busted lip. There was a cut along his cheekbone and one of his eyes was already swelling.

Creed was being pushed further and further away by the coach, but when Creed glanced in our direction and saw that we were swimming to the pool's edge, he jerked out of the coach's hold and ran toward us.

Creed grabbed my hand and pulled me out of the water. "Are you alright?" he asked, cupping my cheeks.

I nodded.

Gabe chuckled, drawing everyone's attention. "Nice tits, Shiloh."

I glanced down and saw that my dress was completely transparent now that it was wet. I had everything on display. I quickly covered myself with my arms, but dropped them to grab Creed, stopping him from going after Gabe again. "Don't. You'll just get into more trouble."

He listened and pulled me into his arms, shielding my body as much as he could. "Someone get me a towel, now!" he yelled.

"I got one," Colt said, appearing next to us with a towel in his hands. His face was hardened with rage as he covered me from the back. I wrapped the towel around me so that my front was covered as well.

"Creed and Gabe! Principal's office, now!" Coach Reed, the head swim coach, yelled.

"Here's her bag, Colt," one of the twins' teammates said from where he'd popped up in the water. He held my bag out to Colt.

"Thanks, man." Colt took it from him and the bag leaked water all over the pool deck.

"Call Knox and Keelan," Creed said as he walked away with Coach Reed.

"Keelan's already on his way," I told Colt and then went on to tell him what had happened, starting with the girls' locker room.

27

KEELAN AND KNOX SHOWED UP RIGHT BEFORE GABE'S PARENTS DID.
Mr. Morgan took Gabe and his parents into his office first. We
could hear Gabe's mother yelling from behind the closed door.
Colt was quietly explaining to Knox and Keelan what had
happened while I paced, unable to sit still. This was all my fault. I
should have gone to the office instead. I needed to find a way to
fix this somehow.

I still had a towel wrapped around my drenched dress. Colt
and Creed had been provided swim team shirts from their coach
to wear with their swim trunks.

"Shi, it's going to be alright. Just sit down, please," Creed
pleaded.

I paused my pacing to argue, but Mr. Morgan's office door
swung open and Gabe's mother came storming out with Gabe
and his father right behind her.

She stopped in front of where the guys were sitting and
sneered down at them. "We'll be pressing charges."

When she went to leave, I stepped in front of her. "If you're
going to be pressing charges, then so am I," I threatened, chan-
neling Shayla. "Your son grabbed me and threw me in the pool.

That's battery. I don't know what his motive was, but this isn't the first time he's tried to hurt me. He shoved me in the gym a month ago and there were many witnesses. I wonder what a judge will make of that. He also groped my breast when he grabbed me today. So I'll be going after him for sexual assault as well." I looked at Gabe. "Good luck getting into a decent college with that on your record."

"Whoa, now," Gabe's father said, stepping closer.

Knox got to his feet and came to stand behind me.

Gabe's father looked up at Knox, taking in his giant build before his gaze dropped back to me. "Let's talk about this," he said, sounding a little nervous. "I'm sure we can find a way to settle things amicably."

"Henry!" Gabe's mother hissed. "The little bitch is bluffing."

I took all of her in. Her hair was big, her makeup was heavy, and her clothes were too young for her. Her handbag told me all I needed to know. The label read Louis Vuitton, but it was a knockoff. I could tell from the stitching. This woman was trying to look like she had money.

"I come from money and a lot of it. I will get the best lawyer money can buy and I will take you to court for however long it takes. Lawyers charge a lot of money by the hour. I can afford it. Can you?" I asked.

Insinuating that she was poor only made her red in the face, but I was really talking to her husband. He seemed to be the reasonable one at the moment.

"What can we do to resolve this?" he asked.

"Henry!" his wife hissed again.

"Shut up, Connie!" Henry snapped. "Gabe admitted to throwing her in the pool and the principal said they caught it all on the school's security cameras. An assault charge could fuck up his future, especially a sexual assault charge."

"If you promise not to press any charges against Creed, I won't press charges either," I said.

"Shiloh, don't," Creed said, standing.

I refused to look away from Henry. "It's my deal to make."

Henry nodded. "We'll agree to that."

Connie huffed and stomped out of the office. Gabe walked past me next. "This isn't over, bitch," he threatened.

"Gabriel!" Henry barked.

Knox moved me behind him. "It better be, because we'll be getting a copy of today's footage of the pool. If you touch her again, it'll be the first thing she'll hand off to her lawyer to use against you."

Henry grabbed Gabe by the collar of his shirt and dragged him out of the office.

My shoulders slumped with relief.

"Now that's settled, Creed, can you and your guardians please come into my office?" Mr. Morgan asked from where he stood by his door watching us.

Keelan and Knox followed Creed into Mr. Morgan's office. I sat in the chair next to Colt. He took my hand in his and we waited.

About a half hour later, the guys came out. All of them looked a little defeated. "What happened?" I asked.

"I'm suspended for two weeks," Creed answered.

My mouth dropped open. "Wait here," I said and stormed past them into Mr. Morgan's office.

"Two weeks?" I said a little loudly.

Mr. Morgan looked up from his desk. "Miss Pierce, why don't you shut the door and take a seat?"

I didn't move. "Did Gabe get the same punishment?"

Mr. Morgan laced his fingers together and leaned back in his chair. "He was suspended."

I narrowed my eyes at the way he said that. "But not for two weeks?"

He didn't confirm or deny it. With all the yelling Gabe's mother had done in here, I wouldn't have been surprised if she'd threatened Mr. Morgan into giving Gabe a lesser punishment.

I shook my head. "That's unfair and you know it."

"We have a zero—"

"Tolerance for violence policy, I know," I finished for him. After I'd had to serve lunch detention for defending myself against Amber, I'd read up on the school's policies. "The policy states that you have to punish the student, but it doesn't state the severity of the punishment. It's at your discretion."

"That is true," he confirmed.

What would my parents do in this situation? Shayla had always gotten into trouble. She'd been caught smoking weed behind the bleachers. She'd keyed a student's car after they'd insinuated that I'd already been screwing Mr. X and when he'd been caught trying to rape me, I'd thrown Mr. X under the bus to save myself. She'd also smashed a girl's face into the basketball court after the girl had said Shayla looked fat in her cheerleading uniform. To be honest, Shayla had been a Cassy and my dad had made a lot of donations to our school to keep her from getting into any serious trouble.

"Lower his punishment to two weeks lunch detention and I'll make a generous donation to the school."

He huffed a laugh. "Are you bribing me, Miss Pierce?"

"I'll donate ten thousand dollars," I said. "I wasn't lying when I told Gabe's parents I came from money."

His eyes widened a little. "Miss Pierce—"

"Twenty thousand," I upped. "As I was looking at schools in this area to attend, I saw that you were trying to raise money to get new computers for the school's computer lab. Twenty thousand dollars could help you reach that goal a lot faster."

He was quiet for a minute and I could tell he was debating it.

"I could bring you a check first thing tomorrow morning," I added.

"Two weeks lunch detention, the donation, and he's also off

the swim team for the next two weeks," he countered.

"Deal."

He gestured to one of the chairs in front of his desk. "Will you please take a seat now? I want to get your statement of what happened today. I heard your tires were slashed?"

I sat and began telling him everything that had happened. As we were talking, he informed me that he would be investigating the locker room incident and see if they'd caught the person responsible for slashing my tires on camera.

"We don't have a lot of cameras on campus, but there is one pointed at the student parking lot," he told me.

After we were done talking, Mr. Morgan followed me out of his office. The guys were waiting where I'd left them.

"Mr. Stone," Mr. Morgan said, looking at Creed. "Your punishment has changed. You'll be serving two weeks lunch detention and you're suspended from the swim team for two weeks. If any of you have any questions, you know where to find me."

I scooped up my wet backpack from the floor next to where Colt was sitting. Knox shook Mr. Morgan's hand, and we left the school admin office. As soon as we were outside, Creed got in front of me. "What did you do, Shi?"

"Yeah, how did you get Mr. Morgan to lessen his punishment?" Colt asked.

I sighed. "I just reasoned with him."

They both frowned at me.

"Can we please just go home? I'm tired, wet, and I need to call a tow truck or something for my car. No, wait. I can't call because both of my cell phones are ruined from my trip into the pool. I don't have my car to go get replacements, either. Which means I don't have a way to check in with Logan tonight."

Keelan came forward, put his hands on my shoulders, and leveled his gaze with mine. "I already called a tow truck and they picked up your car while you were talking with the principal.

After we get home and you get dry, I'll take you to get however many new phones you need."

I sagged against his touch. "Thank you."

"Why don't you two go get your stuff and we'll meet you at home?" Knox said to the twins. Colt and Creed agreed and left for the boys' locker room.

Keelan took my bag from me and the three of us headed for the parking lot. Keelan's Jeep was parked in the spot next to where my 4Runner had been parked. Once we were on the road, heading home, I remembered the class I was supposed to help Keelan teach. From the back seat I read the time on Keelan's dash. The class should have started a half hour ago. "Keelan, I'm so sorry about today's class. Not only did I miss it, but it's my fault you missed it, too."

"It's okay, baby girl," he said as he pulled into our neighborhood. "I was able to get a couple of other instructors to cover today's class."

That was good. The car went quiet again, but as we were about to turn into their driveway, Knox spoke. "I know what you did, Shiloh."

"What?" I asked. He had been quietly staring out the side window the entire drive.

He turned in his seat to face me. "You paid to get Creed's suspension brought down to lunch detention."

I looked away. "I don't know what you're talking about."

"The door was open. I heard everything," Knox said.

Keelan shifted his Jeep into park and looked at Knox. "How much?"

"Twenty thousand," Knox answered.

"Holy fuck." Keelan gaped.

"Where are you getting that kind of money?" Knox asked me.

"I told you my family left me money," I said.

Knox shook his head. "You said you bought your house with your parents' life insurance money."

"I did. That's what I choose to live off of because I have to, not because I want to. I don't like to touch my family's money," I explained.

"Why?" Keelan asked.

I chewed on my lip as I debated how honest I wanted to be. "The only reason I have it is because they're dead and the reason they're dead is because of me."

Keelan reached out to touch my hand. "Shiloh, no—"

I moved out of his reach. "It's true. Today was my fault, too, and I did what I could to fix it."

Knox made a frustrated noise and climbed out of the car. Keelan and I watched him as he rounded the vehicle, coming to our side.

"I'm tempted to lock my door," I joked.

"Please don't. My car will suffer for it," Keelan said as my door was ripped open.

"You're a royal pain in the ass, you know that?" Knox raged at me. "You need to stop being so hard on yourself. Mr. X is a psychotic bastard who developed an obsession with a young girl he had no business even looking at. You are not responsible for what he did to you and your family. He is. You did nothing wrong then and you've done nothing wrong today."

He was quite literally chastising me for doing the same thing I had talked to the twins about earlier today regarding Cassy.

"Creed had accepted his suspension because at the end of the day it was his choice to pummel that little fucker. If I had been there, that punk would have gone home in a wheelchair because he should have never put his hands on you."

My mouth opened but I had no words.

"Did you only offer the money to Mr. Morgan because you felt guilty?" Knox asked. "If so, don't you dare pay it."

"No, that's not the only reason I did it," I said.

"Then why?"

"You know why," I shot back.

"Tell me anyway."

"Why must you be a pushy jerk?" I snapped.

"I'm only pushy when it comes to you," he snapped back.

"That makes me feel so special," I said caustically.

Keelan sighed and climbed out of the car. "I swear I'm going to lock the two of you in a room together until you hash out whatever is going on between you." He shut his door and went inside their house.

I looked up at Knox. "Can I get out now? I need to shower."

"Not until you tell me."

Cheese and rice. He infuriated me. "Fine." I slid across the bench seat and exited the car from the other side.

He slammed the Jeep's door. "Very clever, Shiloh."

I thought so.

He met me as I rounded the Jeep. "Why can't you just answer the damn question?"

"Why do I need to? You made your point. I offered that money to protect Creed—to protect his academic future. I know he doesn't know what he wants to do right now, but having a suspension on his academic record will limit his options when he does decide. I would have offered a lot more if I'd had to because he's important to me. You all are. But you already know that because I've told you that before."

"Then how come it's okay for you to protect us but it makes you feel guilty when we do the same?"

I walked around him. "I told you why I felt guilty today."

He followed me. "I'm not just talking about today. It's a battle anytime we want to do something for you."

"I don't know what you're talking about," I grumbled as I dug around my wet backpack for my keys.

"Keelan offered to train with you for free, but you couldn't just accept it, and he had to give you a job so that you'd be comfortable with it," he pointed out and picked up his pace so he could cut me off before I reached the steps leading up to my front door. "The twins had to argue to bring you home after Gabe hurt you the first time. And what about the swing that's been sitting on your back porch waiting to be built? You have yet to ask any of us for help. We don't even charge you a membership fee to our gym anymore and we haven't told you because you'd fight us about it."

"What?" I hadn't even noticed. "When did you stop charging me?"

"Of course that's all you heard," he muttered.

"What is your point, Knox?"

"I think it scares you."

His words knocked my soul on its butt. I walked around him again, trotted up the steps, and unlocked my front door.

"You have nothing to say because you know I'm right," he said from behind me.

"Yeah, well, I'm still mad that you kissed me," I shot over my shoulder and went inside.

He followed me. "We're not talking about that right now."

I whirled around to face him. "Why, because it's not something you want to talk about?"

He let out a frustrated sigh. "I want to know why it scares you to rely on us."

"Because it just does," I admitted, just as frustrated.

"Why?"

"Because I don't know how to French braid my hair," I blurted.

He blinked at me. "What?"

"My mom always used to French braid my hair. It's what she did if I was ever upset or stressed. She'd start off by running her fingers through my hair to help calm me and when she could tell I was feeling better, she'd braid my hair. I never learned to French braid my hair because I thought I'd always have my mom around to do it." My voice broke and I had to pause to find the strength to continue on. "I'm terrible at putting nail polish on my right hand. Shayla would always help me. And my dad…" My eyes began to burn, and I had to look up at the ceiling to regain my composure. "My dad was who went with me to see the newest Marvel or DC movie that had released and who I would yell for when there was a spider."

Knox was quiet as he listened.

"Every day I find something new that reminds me that I don't have them anymore and it's a living hell. So when the four of you try to do something for me or help me, it scares me sometimes. Not all the time but sometimes. And it's not the stuff that you do, but how I feel when you do it. I feel happy and not alone. I honestly love it, but I know how easy it is to have all that ripped away. That fear overwhelms me."

"We're not going anywhere, Shiloh," he said softly.

"There are other ways to lose people you care about," I pointed out. Not that I needed to. He knew. I saw the understanding in his eyes.

"After my dad died, I felt that way for a very long time," he admitted. "It scared me to death when the twins wanted to get their driver's licenses. But living in fear isn't living."

I nodded. "I know. I've been trying to get past it because I won't be able to move on if I don't. So please be patient with me."

His shoulders slumped. "You don't even have to ask."

"Are you sure about that?" I asked with an incredulous look. "You've been up my butt about all this since Keelan put the car in park."

His signature frown returned. "That's because I wanted to understand what was going on with you and instead of answering like a normal person, you had to be a pain in the ass about it."

I ground my teeth together to keep myself from exploding. "I'm going to go take a shower now." My tone was pleasant, yet I was hitting him repeatedly with a stick in my head. "Lock the door when you leave," I told him and headed for my bedroom.

28

WEDNESDAY AFTER SCHOOL, I SUCCESSFULLY MADE IT TO THE GYM for Keelan's class. I wore all black—black leggings and matching top—to match Keelan's black gi. Stephanie was sitting at the front desk when I entered. I said hello but got nothing in return. Instead, her eyes followed me as I rounded the desk and headed for the hall that led to Keelan's office.

"Where do you think you're going?" she asked as I was about to walk down the hall.

I stopped. "To see Keelan."

"Do you have an appointment?"

"I don't need an appointment," I said.

"Yes, you do, and if you try to go back there, I'll call security," she threatened.

Done being polite, I brought forth a smile I'd seen on Shayla a million times. I called it her *bless your heart* smile. "Go ahead."

I continued down the hall. I went to Keelan's office and found it empty. Then I went across the hall, to Knox's office. He was on the phone. I took a seat in one of the chairs in front of his desk and pulled out my new cell phone from my gym bag. I sent a quick text to Keelan, telling him I was in Knox's office.

As I waited for Knox to finish up with his call, I scrolled through my phone. I tried not to be rude and listen, but I did. He was talking to someone about a mud run.

When he hung up, I had many questions about it. "Desert Stone is sponsoring a mud run?"

He just looked at me.

"That's like a marathon in the mud, right?" I asked next.

He picked up a yellow flyer off his desk and held it out to me. "Yes, we're sponsoring it and it's an endurance run with muddy obstacles."

I took the flyer and looked it over. The mud run was being held in October just before Halloween. "This sounds like a lot of fun. Are sponsors allowed to participate?"

"If by sponsors you mean Colt, Creed, and Keelan, then yes."

I pouted a little. "You don't want to do it with us?"

"No," he said, completely unaffected. "Even if I did, I couldn't. I need to man our table at the event. We'll be advertising our gym and offering membership discounts to anyone who signs up at the run."

"Poor Knox. All work and no play."

"Ain't that the truth," Keelan said as he walked into Knox's office. He kissed the top of my head before taking a seat in the chair next to me. "What were you two talking about?"

I showed him the mud run flyer. "Want to do this with me?"

Keelan took the flyer. "The mud run, huh? You get really dirty doing one of these."

"So? Getting dirty sounds like a fun time to me," I said.

They both snorted.

"It usually is," Keelan said, making Knox chuckle.

Realizing that they were purposely misconstruing what I had said, I ripped the flyer out of Keelan's hand.

Grinning, Keelan stood from his chair. "I'm only teasing, Shiloh. Of course I'll do the mud run with you."

"Good," I said, standing. I set my gym bag on the floor in front of Knox's desk. "I'm leaving my bag in here, Knox."

"I'll leave my door open in case you need to get it and I'm not here," he said.

"Um…about that," I said apprehensively. "Can you introduce me to Stephanie? Because she's been acting like she doesn't know me and threatened to call security on me for coming back here."

They both just stared at me in disbelief. Then Knox stood and walked ahead of us out of his office. Once we were out of the hall and by the front desk, Knox said, "Hey, Stephanie?"

She spun around in her desk chair with a bright and friendly expression. "Yeah, boss?" The way she looked at him brewed some major jealousy within me. It didn't help that she had the appearance of a blonde, busty model. Her skin was flawless. Not a blemish in sight. I went to touch one of my scars on my wrists, then stopped myself. I shouldn't compare us. It was stupid and unfair to do that to myself. I tore myself down enough as it was. Comparing my beauty to someone else's was not something I wanted to add.

"Have you met Shiloh?" Knox asked.

"No, but I've seen her around," she replied. "Is she a friend of yours?"

"Something like that," Knox said. "Anytime Shiloh is here, she's allowed back in our offices, even if we're not back there."

She gave Knox a sugary-sweet smile. "You got it, boss."

Knox looked down at me and I gave him a tight smile. Keelan threw his arm over my shoulder and steered me away. As we walked through the gym, I battled not to frown. Stephanie had made me look like a lying idiot.

"What's wrong, baby girl?"

"Nothing," I lied.

He pulled me closer and I had to wrap my arm around him to keep myself from tripping. "Come on, out with it."

"My mom always said that if I had nothing nice to say, I shouldn't say anything at all."

He chuckled. "You don't have that kind of restraint when it comes to Knox."

"Knox is a special case." Saying that made him full-on laugh.

When we made it to the room for Keelan's class, there were already a bunch of women waiting inside. Keelan greeted them as we took off our shoes. Most of them said hello and a few of them whispered to each other and giggled. Keelan and I waited in front of the class for the rest of the students to show up. "I'm going to pull your hair today," he whispered suggestively in my ear. "A lot."

Smiling, I shook my head.

"Last week, I asked them what they were most worried about when it came to being attacked. The majority said their hair being grabbed," he whispered.

That made sense. Hair was an easy thing to grab. I guessed it was fate that my hair was in a ponytail.

When the last of the class showed up, Keelan stepped forward and I watched him shift into teaching mode. "Afternoon, class. I want to start off by introducing my new partner, who will be helping me teach this class." He gestured to me. "This is Shiloh."

I waved at them with a smile.

"Feel free to ask her any questions you have. She's here to help," Keelan said, then gestured for me to move to the center of the room. "Okay, everyone, circle around," Keelan instructed. I lay down on the padded floor with my knees bent, feet flat on the ground. Keelan knelt between my legs and began explaining what we were going to do to the class.

He wrapped his fingers around my ponytail and tugged a little. "If your attacker has you on the ground like this…" He went on to explain what I was to do. "Shiloh and I are going to demonstrate and then slow it down." His grip on my hair pulled and my need to act took over. I grabbed his arm connected to my hair, jerked my hips to the side out from under him, and threw one leg under his neck and the other across his chest. Still holding onto his arm, I pushed him up using my legs and hyperextended his arm. I stopped before I could hurt him. Had he been a real attacker, I would have continued to push him away with my legs until I'd broken his arm.

He tapped my thigh, signaling for me to release. I let him go and dropped my legs. He surprised me a little when he grabbed me by the thighs and slid me around on the floor, getting us back in position. I fought to not smile and remain professional. I thought he noticed because the corner of his mouth twitched.

"Okay, we're going to slow it down," he said and grabbed my hair again. I grabbed his arm and he had me pause. "See how she's grabbing my arm that's got her by the hair," he pointed out. "That's to keep me from pulling or letting go. It also helps Shiloh slide her hips out from under me so she can throw her outer leg up and get it under my neck." Moving slow, I did everything he was explaining. When I had my legs under his neck and across his chest, he had me pause again. "Next, Shiloh's going to push up with her legs and she isn't going to let go of my arm. She's going to extend it and if she pushes far enough, she could easily break it in this hold."

We repeated the scenario a few more times before Keelan asked the students to pair up and try. Keelan and I split up and moved around the room, helping those who were having trouble. After a little bit, Keelan asked the pairs to switch positions, so those who were playing the attackers had a chance to practice.

As I was walking around, I heard someone say, "Mina, it's okay. Look, I'm not touching you."

I turned around and saw a woman lying on the ground, staring up at the ceiling, panting. I recognized the fear in Mina's wide eyes. Her partner, playing the role of the attacker, was next to her, trying to console her.

I rushed over and knelt next to her. "Hey, you're okay," I said calmly. I grabbed both of her hands. She was young. She didn't appear to be much older than me. "Can you hear my voice, Mina?" I asked her.

By the terror in her eyes, I knew her mind had taken her away from the present. Then she began to cry out.

"It's not real, Mina. You're safe. Squeeze my hands and you'll see," I told her. She continued to cry but she squeezed a little. "Tighter, Mina. Feel that you're here with me and not there. You're safe." She squeezed my hands even tighter. "Keep squeezing. That's it," I encouraged. "You are safe, Mina," I reminded her over and over because I knew how important it was for me to be reminded of that.

Her cries eventually turned into deep breaths and she blinked her wide eyes. "I'm so sorry," she said, her voice cracking.

I helped her sit up. I would have hugged her, but I was worried touching her like that would trigger her again. I settled with squeezing her hands. "You have nothing to be sorry about." A bunch of voices agreed. I did a quick glance around and noticed that we were surrounded by the class. "Can someone get her some water?" I asked.

Her partner, who was paired with Mina, took off toward the cubbies where everyone left their shoes and water bottles. She quickly returned with a water bottle, which I assumed belonged to Mina.

A hand came down on my shoulder. I peered behind me and saw that it was Keelan. "Are you her friend?" he asked the partner. She nodded as she handed the bottle to Mina. "Why don't the two of you come sit off to the side here? We'll make sure that no one stands in the way so that you can still see the lessons. And if you feel comfortable enough to try again, jump back in at any time."

Mina nodded and her friend helped her move to the side of the room. I ran my fingers over the thick scar around one of my wrists as I watched them, my thoughts threatening to drift to my own trauma.

Hands went under my arms and I was lifted to my feet. I knew it was Keelan. I spun around to face him.

He stared down at me, eyes full of concern. "Are you okay?" he whispered.

I nodded. I would be. "What's next?"

"You're going to show them how to put me in a choke hold this time," he said.

I smiled. "Okay."

And I did just that. We demonstrated a few other situations of hair-grabbing and what they should do. Overall, it felt good to show someone else something that may help or save them one day. It was a really rewarding experience and I was looking forward to the next class. Mina never did rejoin, but she stayed until the end, watching everything we taught.

Keelan dismissed the class and I plopped down on the floor, feeling a little tired. After the last student left the room, he sat down next to me. "What'd you think?" he asked, lightly bumping his shoulder into mine.

"I liked it."

"You did good today. Especially how you helped Mina."

I hugged my legs to my chest. "I only did what I'd want someone to do for me."

"Hey," he said, moving so that he was kneeling in front of me. "You recognized what she was going through and knew exactly what to do. You didn't hesitate and you helped pull her from a dark place. That's something to be proud of."

It did make me happy that I'd been able to help her. "I hope she comes back."

"Me, too," he said, getting to his feet. He held his hand out to me and pulled me to mine.

"We'll be teaching something other than hair-grabbing next time, right?" I asked, walking ahead of him toward the shoe cubbies.

"I don't know. You seemed to enjoy it when I pulled your hair," he teased and before I could respond, my hair was grabbed.

I whirled around, grabbed a hold of his forearm with one hand, and grabbed the back of his neck with my other. Using all my weight, I pulled him to the ground. He tried to catch himself with his free hand so that he wouldn't crush me. We both landed with a grunt and I tried to shift out from under him. Recognizing what I was trying to do, he rolled us so that I was on top of him.

He still had a firm grip on my hair. "What are you going to do, baby girl?" he taunted.

"If you were anyone else, I would have hit your pretty face," I grumbled, making him chuckle.

I did something reckless and let go of his arm that was attached to my hair. Crossing my arms like an X, I grabbed a hold of the collar of his shirt and tried to choke him out. His free hand yanked one of my hands away easily and he pulled a little on my hair. My mind went blank as to what I should do, apart from doing an elbow jab to his face. I didn't want to hurt him, and I didn't want to admit defeat, so I kissed him. I could tell I'd caught him off guard, which was the whole purpose of the kiss, but things changed very quickly. He snapped out of the shock. Instead of shoving me off, he released my hair and cupped the back of my head. His tongue demanded entrance into my mouth. Temptation demanded that I open for him and I did.

Submitting to temptation was a slippery slope. It made it harder to be rational and I really, really didn't want to stop kissing him.

I felt him try to roll us. I quickly came to my senses and shoved his shoulder back to the ground. I ripped my mouth from his. "I shouldn't have done that." I scrambled off of him and got to my feet.

"Shiloh."

I couldn't look at him and headed to get my shoes.

He caught up to me at the cubbies. Grabbing me by my arm, he made me face him. "Talk to me. What just happened?"

"I crossed a line," I said and grabbed my shoes.

"I'm not upset, if that's what you think," he said. "I've been wanting to kiss you for the longest time."

My shoulders slumped. "That's not what I meant."

His brow furrowed.

"Colt and Creed…" I stumbled for the right thing to say. "I don't know what's going on between me and them. Kissing you… I'm scared it is going to hurt them."

He straightened. "Can I ask one thing?"

I nodded as I slipped my feet into my shoes.

"Pretend it wouldn't hurt Colt and Creed—is kissing me something you want?"

I met his eyes and debated whether or not the truth would damn me. "Yes."

He nodded and ran his fingers through his hair. "You better go because all I want to do right now is kiss you again."

My cheeks flushed and I slowly backed out of the room. My face was hot and my heart was still racing when I made it to Knox's office. As I walked in, my stomach dropped. Colt and Creed were both standing around Knox's desk talking to him.

"Hey, what are you two doing here?" I asked.

They both turned, with smiles on their faces. They looked like they were going to answer, but they paused once they saw me. I wouldn't have doubted if they'd told me that I had a red letter A stamped on my forehead.

"Why are you all flushed?" Colt asked.

"Shit," I cursed, closing my eyes for a moment. I opened them again, determined to do the right thing. "I need to talk to the two of you."

"It must be really serious because she just cursed," Creed said to Colt.

At that moment, Keelan walked in.

"Oh, fuck," I blurted.

"Really, really serious," Creed commented.

Keelan stared at me, probably seeing the sheer panic I was feeling. He shoved his hands into his pockets and looked at his brothers. "I kissed Shiloh."

"No," I said quickly. I wasn't going to let him take the fall. "I kissed Keelan."

The room went quiet.

Knox leaned back in his chair, shaking his head. "I knew this shit was going to happen."

Keelan looked at Knox. "I think it's time we have that conversation."

"What conversation?" I asked.

Colt's eyes flicked to me. "The conversation Knox has been avoiding since we all found out that he kissed you." I couldn't tell how he was feeling, but he didn't look hurt or angry.

"I told you that there was nothing to talk about," Knox said.

I couldn't help but feel hurt. "Glad to know that kissing me was nothing to you."

Knox's expression turned angry. "That's not what I said."

"That's exactly what you said," I snapped.

Colt came over and put his hands on my shoulders. "Babe," he said calmly. "The four of us need to have a talk. Can you please head home, and we'll meet you there when we're done?"

I stepped back, out of his reach, and his hands dropped from my shoulders. "Fine." I walked around him to grab my bag from where I'd left it on the floor. I avoided looking at any of them as I stormed out.

I was so angry and confused that all I could do was focus on getting to my car. I failed to pay attention to my surroundings. Approaching my 4Runner, which had gotten brand new tires yesterday, I saw the back left tire was flat. "You have got to be kidding me!" I assessed the tire, and it didn't look slashed this time. It actually just looked flat.

"Oh, flat tire. That sucks," someone said behind me. "Do you need some help changing that, Shiloh?"

When I heard the way the person said my name, I knew it was Jacob.

I turned to face him, and I found him right behind me. I took a step away. "No, thank you. I'll just go tell my boyfriend inside. He'll take care of it," I said and tried to walk past him.

He grabbed me by my arm. "Why can't I help you?" he asked tightly as he pulled me between the cars and I quickly realized that we were out of sight.

"Let me go," I told him.

"Listen—"

"I don't want to listen. Let me go," I snapped and yanked my arm from his grip.

As soon as I was free, he shoved me, and my back slammed into the side of my car. The wind knocked out of my lungs and I had to catch myself on the side mirror to keep myself from falling to the ground.

"I didn't want to have to do this," he said angrily and I saw a syringe with a needle in his hand. "But you stupid bitches won't spread your legs otherwise." He lunged at me, intending to stick me with the needle.

I caught his wrist and brought my leg up between his legs. He dropped to his knees with a grunt. I went to run away, but his hand locked around my ankle and I fell forward. I caught myself on my hands when I hit the ground. Gravel cut into my palms. I ignored the stinging and tried to get my feet free. He got a good hold on my leggings and pulled me toward him. I twisted onto my butt to face him because running was no longer an option. I felt a prick in my thigh as I jabbed my elbow into his face. He fell backward on his butt.

I quickly glanced down at my thigh and saw the syringe sticking out of me. I didn't know what he'd injected me with, but I had a feeling it was going to impair me so that he could rape me. Which meant I didn't have much time. If I ran, he would probably catch me before I could get help. That left me one option. I had to make sure he couldn't take me anywhere and I prayed that after this drug kicked in, a good person would stumble upon me and help me.

Jacob lunged for me, grabbing my wrists. I brought my knees to my chest as he pushed me to the ground. Using all of my strength, I pushed into his chest with my knees, until I could pull one of my legs out and sling it over his shoulder. I let him drop closer so I could hook that leg behind his neck. I threw my other leg out from between us and brought it up and hooked it around my ankle, putting him in a choke hold. I squeezed with everything I had. He let go of one of my wrists and started hitting and scratching at my thigh pressing into the side of his neck.

It took six seconds for someone to pass out. Those were the longest six seconds of my life. He eventually went limp, but I was scared to let go. What if he woke up?

That was when the drugs started to kick in. I felt weak all over and my vision was going blurry. I let go of Jacob and tried to crawl away. I saw my gym bag by my front tire, and I pulled it to me. I had difficulty working the zipper, but I got it open enough to stick my hand inside. My head began to feel heavy and I had to set it on the ground. My fingers felt around in my bag until I touched my phone. As I pulled it out, I dropped it on the ground. I was losing dexterity. All I could do was press the call button twice, which would dial the last person I had called. Creed's name appeared on the screen and I could hear it ringing.

"Hello?" I heard him answer.

"Creed…" That was all I could get out before the ability to form words left me and my eyes drifted closed.

To be continued…

WITSEC BOOK 2

Coming Soon!

ABOUT THE AUTHOR

Ashley N. Rostek is a wife and mother by day and a writer by night. She survives on coffee, loves collecting offensive coffee mugs, and is an unashamed bibliophile.

To Ashley, there isn't a better pastime than letting your mind escape in a good book. Her favorite genre is romance and has the overflowing bookshelf to prove it. She is a lover of love. Be it a sweet YA or a dark and lusty novel, she must read it!

Ashley's passion is writing. She picked up the pen at seventeen and hasn't put it down. Her debut novel is Embrace the Darkness, the first book in the Maura Quinn series.

You can find out more about Ashley and her upcoming works on social media!

Facebook Page
Facebook Group
Instagram

Made in the USA
Monee, IL
24 August 2023